"'Go I say!' cried the Leopard Woman. 'And hold up your head. If this is suspected of you, you will surely die'"

THE
LEOPARD WOMAN

BY

STEWART EDWARD WHITE

ILLUSTRATED BY

W. H. D. KOERNER

WILDSIDE PRESS

TABLE OF CONTENTS

CHAPTER I

THE MARCH

It was the close of the day. Over the baked veldt of equatorial Africa a safari marched. The men, in single file, were reduced to the unimportance of moving black dots by the tremendous sweep of the dry country stretching away to an horizon infinitely remote, beyond which lay single mountains, like ships becalmed hull-down at sea. The immensities filled the world—the simple immensities of sky and land. Only by an effort, a wrench of the mind, would a bystander on the advantage, say, of one of the little rocky, outcropping hills have been able to narrow his vision to details.

And yet details were interesting. The vast shallow cup to the horizon became a plain sparsely grown with flat-topped thorn trees. It was not a forest, yet neither was it open country. The eye penetrated the thin screen of tree trunks to the distance of half a mile or more, but was brought to a stop at last. Underfoot was hard-baked earth, covered by irregular patches of shale that tinkled when stepped on. Well-defined paths, innumerable, trodden deep and hard, cut into the iron soil. They nearly all ran

in a northwesterly direction. The few traversing paths
took a long slant. These paths, so exactly like those cross-
ing a village green, had in all probability never been trodden
by human foot. They had been made by the game animals,
the swarming multitudinous game of Central Africa.

The safari was using one of the game trails. It was a
compact little safari, comprising not over thirty men all
told. The single white man walked fifty yards or so ahead
of the main body. He was evidently tired, for his shoulders
drooped, and his shuffling, slow-swinging gait would anywhere have been recognized by children of the wilderness
as that which gets the greatest result from the least effort.
Dressed in the brown cork helmet, the brown flannel shirt
with spine-pad, the khaki trousers, and the light boots of
the African traveller little was to be made of either his face
or figure. The former was fully bearded, the latter powerful
across the shoulders. His belt was heavy with little leather
pockets; a pair of prismatic field-glasses, suspended from a
strap around his neck, swung across his chest; in the crook
of his left arm he carried a light rifle.

Immediately at his heels followed a native. This man's
face was in conformation that of the typical negro; but there
the resemblance ceased. Behind the features glowed a
proud, fierce spirit that transformed them. His head was
high but his eyes roved from right to left restlessly, never
still save when they paused for a flickering instant to examine some gazelle, some distant herd of zebra or wilde-

beeste standing in the vista of the flat-topped trees. His nostrils slowly expanded and contracted with his breathing, as do those of a spirited horse. In contrast to the gait of the white man he stepped vigorously and proudly as though the long day had not touched his strength. He wore a battered old felt hat, a tattered flannel shirt, a ragged pair of shorts, and the blue puttees issued by the British to their native troops. The straps of two canteens crossed on his breast; a full cartridge belt encircled his waist; he carried lightly and easily one of those twelve-pound double cordite rifles that constitute the only African life insurance.

Fifty yards in the rear marched the carriers. They were a straight, strong lot, dressed according to their fancy or opportunity in the cast-off garments of the coast; comical in the ensemble, perhaps, but worthy of respect in that all day each had carried a seventy-pound load under a tropical sun, and that they were coming in strong.

And finally, bringing up the rear, marched a small, lively, wizened little fellow, dressed as nearly as possible like the white man, and carrying as the badge of his office a bulging cotton umbrella and the *kiboko*—the slender, limber, stinging rhinoceros-hide whip.

It was the end of a long march. This could be guessed by the hour, by the wearied slouch of the white man, above all by the conduct of the safari. The men were walking one on the heels of the other. Their burdens, carried on their heads, held them erect. They stepped out freely. But against the wooden chop boxes, the bags of cornmeal *potio*, the bundles of canvas that made up some of the loads, the long safari sticks went *tap, tap, tap*, in rhythm. This tapping was a steady undertone to the volume of noise that arose from thirty throats. Every man was singing or shouting at the full strength of his lungs. A little file of Wakamba sung in unison one of the weird wavering minor chants peculiar to savage peoples everywhere; some Kavirondos simply howled in staccato barks like beasts. Between the extremes were many variations; but every man contributed to the uproar, and tapped his load rhythmically with his long stick. By this the experienced traveller would have known that the men were very tired, tired to the point of exhaustion; for the more wearied the Central African native, or the steeper the hill he, laden, must surmount, the louder he sings or yells.

"*Maji hapana m'bale, bwana*," observed the gun bearer to the white man. "Water is not far, master."

The white man merely nodded. These two had been together many years, and explanations were not necessary between them. He, as well as Simba, had noticed the gradual convergence of the game trails, the presence of small grass birds that flushed under their feet, the sing-sing buck behind the aloes, the increasing numbers of game animals that stared or fled at the sight and sound of the safari.

Nothing more was said. The way led to the top of one of those low transverse swells that conceal the middle distance without actually breaking the surface of the veldt. In the corresponding depression beyond now could be discerned a wandering slender line of green.

"*Maji huko!*" murmured Simba. "There is the water."

Suddenly he stooped low, uttering a peculiar hissing sound. The white man, too, dropped to the ground, throwing his rifle forward.

"*Nyama, bwana!*" he whispered fiercely, "*karibu sana!*"

He pointed cautiously over the white man's shoulder. The safari, at the sight of the two dropping to a crouch, had stopped as though petrified, and stood waiting in silence.

"We have no meat," Simba reminded his master in Swahili.

The white man eased himself back to a sitting posture, resting his elbows on his knees, as all sensible good rifle shots do when they have the chance. Simba, his eyes glowing fiercely, staring with almost hypnotic intensity over his master's shoulder, quivered like an eager dog.

"Hah!" he grunted as the loud spat of the bullet followed the rifle's crack. "*Na kamata*—he has it!" he added as the wildebeeste plunged into full view.

The hunter manipulated the bolt to throw in a new cartridge, but did not shift his position. In less remote countries the sportsman, unlimited in ammunition but restricted in chances, would probably have pumped in four or five shots until the quarry was down. The traveller and Simba watched closely, with expert eyes, to determine whether a precious second cartridge should be expended.

"Where?" asked the white man briefly.

"Low in the shoulder," replied Simba.

The wildebeeste plunged wildly here and there, kicking, bucking, menacing the unseen danger with his horns. For several seconds longer the two watched, then rose leisurely to their feet. Simba motioned to the waiting safari, who, correctly interpreting the situation, broke into a trot. Both Simba and his master knew that had the animal not received a mortal wound it would before this have whirled to look back. The fact that it still ran proved its extremity. Sure enough, within the hundred yards it suddenly plunged forward on its nose, rolled over, and lay still.

The fierce countenance of the gun bearer lit up in triumph. He shifted the heavy rifle and reached out to touch the lighter weapon resting again in the crook of his master's arm.

"*Nyama Yangu! Nyama Yangu!*" he murmured. That was Simba's name for the light rifle that did most of the shooting. The words meant simply "my meat." Simba had a name for everything from the sheath knife of his office to the white man himself. Indeed Culbertson in the Central countries was Culbertson to none. Should you inquire for news of him by that name news you could not obtain; but of Bwana Kingozi you might learn from many tribes and peoples.

But now the safari, topping the hill, swept down with a rapid fire of safari sticks against the loads and a chorus whose single word was "*n'yama!*"

Simba was already at the carcass, *Kisu M'kubwa*, his thin-bladed knife, in his hand. The men eased their loads to the ground, and stood about with eagerly gleaming eyes, as would well-trained dogs in like circumstances. Simba briefly indicated the three nearest to act as his assistants. The wildebeeste was rapidly skinned and as rapidly dismembered, the meat laid aside. Only once did the white man speak or manifest the slightest interest.

"*Sarrara indani yangu*—the tenderloin is mine."

The wizened little headman with the umbrella and the *kiboko*, who answered to the name of Cazi Moto, stepped forward and took charge of the indicated delicacy. Soon all was ready for a resumption of the march. Nothing was left of the wildebeeste save the head and the veriest offal. The stomach and intestines, even, had been emptied of their contents and packed away in the hide.

Already the carrion birds had gathered in incredible numbers. The sky was full of them circling; an encompassing ring of them sat a scant fifty yards distant, their wings held half out from their bodies, as though they felt overheated. And in the low bushes could be discerned the lurking, furtive, shadowy jackals.

The men were laughing, their weariness forgotten. Maulo, the camp humourist, declaimed loudly at the top of his lungs, mocking the marabouts, the buzzards, the vultures great and small, the kites and the eagles.

"Go to the lion," he cried, "he kills much, and leaves. Little meat will you get here. We keep what we get!"

And the men broke into meaningless but hearty laughter, as though at brilliant wit.

But Bwana Kingozi's low voice cut across the merriment. "*Bandika!*" he commanded.

And immediately Cazi Moto and Simba took up the cry. "*Bandika! bandika! bandika!*" they vociferated over and over. Cazi Moto moved here and there, lively as a cricket, his eyes alert for any indication of slackness, his *kiboko* held threateningly.

But there was no need for the latter. The men willingly enough swung aloft their loads, now augmented by the meat, and the little caravan moved on.

Scarcely had Cazi Moto, bringing up the rear, quitted the scene when the carrion birds swooped. They fell from the open sky like plummets, their wings half folded. When within ten feet of the ground they checked their fall with pinion and tail, and the sound of them was like the roar of a cataract. Those seated on the ground moved forward in a series of ungainly hops, trying for more haste by futile urgings of their wings. Where the wildebeeste had fallen was a writhing, flopping, struggling brown mass. In an incredibly brief number of seconds it was all over. The birds withdrew. Some sat disgruntled and humpbacked in the low trees; some merely hopped away a few yards to indulge in gloomy thoughts. A few of the more ambitious rose heavily and laboriously with strenuous beating of pinions, finally to soar grandly away into the infinities of the African sky. Of the wildebeeste remained only a trampled bloody space and bones picked clean. The jackals crept forward at last. So brief a time did all this occupy that Maulo, looking back, saw them.

"Ho, little dogs!" he cried with one of his great empty laughs; "your stomachs will go hollow but you can fill your noses!"

They tramped on steadily toward the low narrow line of green trees, and the sun sank toward the hills.

CHAPTER II

THE CAMP

The game trails converged at a point where the steep, eroded bank had been broken down into an approach to a pool. The dust was deep here, and arose in a cloud as a little band of zebra scrambled away. The borders of this pool were a fascinating palimpsest: the tracks of many sorts of beast had been impressed there in the mud. Both Kingozi and Simba examined them with an approach to interest, though to an observer the examination would have seemed but the most casual of glances. They saw the indications of zebra, wildebeeste, hartebeeste, gazelles of various sorts, the deep, round, well-like prints of the rhinoceros, and all the other usual inhabitants of the veldt. But over these their eyes passed lightly. Only three things could here interest these seasoned African travellers. Simba espied one of them, and pointed it out, just at the edge of the narrow border of softer mud.

"There is the lion," said he. "A big one. He was here this morning. But no buffalo, *bwana;* and no elephant."

The water in the pool was muddy and foul. Thousands of animals drank from it daily; and after drinking had stood or wallowed in it. The flavour would be rich of the barn-yard, which even a strong infusion of tea could not disguise. Kingozi had often been forced to worse; but here he hoped for better.

The safari had dumped down the loads at the top of the bank, and were resting in utter relaxation. The march was over, and they waited.

Bwana Kingozi threw off the carefully calculated listless slouch that had conserved his strength for an unknown goal. His work was not yet done.

"Simba," he directed, "go that way, down the river* and look for another pool—of good water. Take the big rifle."

"And I to go in the other direction?" asked Cazi Moto.

Bwana Kingozi considered, glancing at the setting sun, and again up the dry stream-bed where, as far as the eye could reach, were no more indications of water.

"No," he decided. "It is late. Soon the lions will be hunting. I will go."

The men sprawled in abandon. After an interval a shrill whistle sounded from the direction in which Bwana Kingozi had disappeared. The men stretched and began to rise to their feet slowly. The short rest had stiffened them and brought home the weariness to their bones. They grumbled and muttered, and only the omnipresence of Cazi Moto and the threat of his restless whip roused them to activity. Down the stream they limped sullenly.

---

* Every watercourse with any water at all, even in occasional pools, is *m'to*—a river—in Africa.

Kingozi stood waiting near the edge of the bank. The thicket here was very dense.

"Water there," he briefly indicated. "The big tent here; the opening in that direction. Cook fire over there. Loads here."

The men who had been standing, the burdens still on their heads, moved forward. The tent porter—who, by the way, was the strongest and most reliable of the men, so that always, even on a straggling march, the tent would arrive first—threw it down at the place selected and at once began to undo the cords. The bearers of the kitchen, who were also reliable travellers, set about the cook camp.

A big Monumwezi unstrapped a canvas chair, unfolded it, and placed it near his master. The other loads were arranged here, in a certain long-ordained order; the meat piled there. Several men then went to the assistance of Mali-ya-bwana, the tent bearer; and the others methodically took up various tasks. Some began with their *pangas* to hew a way to the water through the dense thicket that had kept it sweet; others sought firewood; still others began to pitch the tiny drill tents—each to accommodate six men—in a wide circle of which the pile of loads was the centre. As the men fell into the ordered and habitual routine their sullenness and weariness vanished.

Kingozi dropped into the canvas chair, fumbled for a pipe, filled and lighted it. With a sigh of relief he laid aside his cork helmet. The day had not only been a hard one, but an

anxious one, for this country was new to every member of
the little expedition, native guides had been impossible to
procure, and the chances of water had been those of an arid
region.

The removal of the helmet for the first time revealed
the man's features. A fine brow, upstanding thick and
wavy hair, and the clearest of gray eyes suddenly took
twenty years from the age at first made probable by the
heavy beard. With the helmet pulled low this was late
middle age; now bareheaded it was only bearded youth.
Nevertheless at the corners of the eyes were certain
wrinkles, and in the eyes themselves a direct competent
steadiness that was something apart from the usual
acquisition of youth, something the result of experience
not given to most.

He smoked quietly, his eye wandering from one point to
another of the new-born camp's activities. One after another the men came to report the completion of their tasks.

"*Pita ya maji tayiari*," said Sanguiki coming from the
new-made water trail.

"*I zuru*," approved Kingozi.

"*Hema tayiari*," reported Simba, reaching his hand for
the light rifle.

Kingozi glanced toward the tent and nodded. A licking
little fire flickered in the cook camp. The tiny porter's
tents had completed their circle, and in front of each new
smoke was beginning to rise. Cazi Moto glided up and

handed him the *kiboko*, the rhinoceros-hide whip, the symbol of authority.   Everything was in order.

The white man rose a little stiffly and walked over to the pile of meat.   For a moment he examined it contemplatively, aroused himself with an apparent effort, and began to separate it into four piles.   He did not handle the meat himself, but silently indicated each portion with his *kiboko*, and Simba or Cazi Moto swiftly laid it aside.

"This for the gun-bearer camp," commanded Kingozi, touching with his foot the heavy "backstraps" and the liver—the next choicest bits after tenderloin.   He raised his voice.

"Kavirondo!" he called.

Several tall, well-formed black savages of this tribe arose from one of the little fires and approached.   The white man indicated one of the piles of meat.

"Wakamba!" he summoned; then "Monumwezi"; and finally "Baganda!"

Thus the four tribes represented in his caravan were supplied.   The men returned to their fires, and began the preparation of their evening meal.

Kingozi turned to his own tent with a sigh of relief. Within it a cot had been erected, blankets spread.   An officer's tin box stood open at one end.   On the floor was a portable canvas bath.   While the white man was divesting himself of his accoutrements, Cazi Moto entered bearing a galvanized pail full of hot water which he poured into the tub. He disappeared only to return with a pail of cold water to temper the first.

"Bath is ready, *bwana*," said he, and retired, carefully tying the tent flaps behind him.

Fifteen minutes later Kingozi emerged. He wore now a suit of pajamas tucked into canvas "mosquito boots," with very thin soles. He looked scrubbed and clean, the sheen of water still glistening on his thick wavy hair.

The canvas camp chair had been placed before two chop boxes piled one atop the other to form a crude table on which were laid eating utensils. As soon as Cazi Moto saw that his master was ready, he brought the meal. It consisted simply of a platter of curry composed of rice and the fresh meat that had been so recently killed that it had not time to get tough. This was supplemented by bread and tea in a tall enamelware vessel known as a *balauri*. From the simplicity of this meal one experienced would have deduced—even had he not done so from a dozen other equally significant nothings—that this was no sporting excursion, but an expedition grimly in earnest about something.

The sun had set, and almost immediately the darkness descended, as though the light had been turned off at a switch. The earth shrunk to a pool of blackness, and the heavens expanded to a glory of tropical stars. All visible nature contracted to the light thrown by the flickering fires before the tiny white tents. The tatterdemalion crew

had, after the curious habit of Africans, cast aside its garments, and sat forth in a bronze and savage nakedness.
All day long under the blistering sun your safari man will
wear all that he hath, even unto the heavy overcoat dis-
carded by the latest arrival from England's winter; but
when the chill of evening descends, then he strips happily.
The men were fed now, and were content. A busy chatter,
the crooning of songs, laughter, an occasional shout testified
to this. A general relaxation took the camp.

The white man finished his meal and lighted his pipe. Even
yet his day's work was not quite done, and he was unwilling
to yield himself to rest until all tasks were cleared away.

"Cazi Moto!" he called.

Instantly, it seemed, the headman stood at his elbow.

"To-morrow," said Kingozi deliberately, and paused in
decision so long that Cazi Moto ventured a "Yes, *bwana*."

"To-morrow we rest here. It will be your *cazi* (duty) to
find news of the next water, or to find the water. See if
there are people in this country. Take one man with you.
Let the men rest and eat."

"Yes, *bwana*."

"Are there sick?"

"Two men."

"Let them come."

Cazi Moto raised his voice.

"*N'gonjwa!*" he summoned them.

Kingozi looked at them in silence for a moment.

"What is the matter with you?" he asked of the first, a hulking, stupid-looking Kavirondo with the muscles of a Hercules.

The man replied, addressing Cazi Moto, as is etiquette; and although Kingozi understood perfectly, he awaited his headman's repetition of the speech as though the Kavirondo had spoken a strange language.

"Fever, eh?" commented Kingozi aloud to himself, for the first time speaking his own tongue. "We'll soon see. Cazi Moto," he instructed in Swahili, "the medicine."

He thrust a clinical thermometer beneath the Kavirondo's tongue, glancing at a wrist watch as he did so.

"Cazi Moto," he said calmly after three minutes, "this man is a liar. He is not sick; he merely wants to get out of carrying a load."

The Kavirondo, his eyes rolling, shot forth a torrent of language.

"He says," Cazi Moto summarized all this, "that he was very sick, but that this medicine"—indicating the thermometer—"cured him."

"He lies again," said Kingozi. "This is not medicine, but magic that tells me when a man has uttered lies. This man must beware or he will get *kiboko*."

The Kavirondo scuttled away, and Kingozi gave his attention to the second patient. This man had an infected leg that required some minor surgery. When the job was over and Kingozi had washed his hands, he relighted his pipe and sat back in his chair with a sigh of content. The immediate foreground sank below his consciousness. He stared across the flickering fires at the velvet blackness; listened across the intimate, idle noise of the camp to the voice of the veldt.

For with the fall of darkness and the larger silence of darkness, the veldt awoke. Animals that had dozed through the hot hours and grazed through the cooler hours in somnolent content now quivered alert. There were runnings here and there, the stamp of hoofs, sharp snortings as taut nerves stretched. Zebras uttered the absurd small-dog barks peculiar to them; ostriches boomed; jackals yapped; unknown birds uttered hasty wild calls. Numerous hyenas, near and far away, moaned like lost souls. Kingozi listened as to the voice of an old acquaintance telling familiar things; the men chattered on, their whole attention within the globe of light from their fires.

But suddenly the noise stopped as though it had been cut by a knife. Total silence fell on the little encampment. The men, their various actions suspended, listened intently. From far away, apparently, a low, vibrating rumble stole out of the night's immensity. It rose and seemed to draw near, growing hollow and great, until the very ground seemed to tremble as though a heavy train were passing, or the lower notes of a great organ had been played in a little church. And then it died down, and receded to the great distance again, and was ended by three low, grunting coughs.

The veldt was silent. The zebra barkings were still; the night birds had hushed; the hyenas and jackals and all the other night creatures down—it almost seemed—to the very insects had ceased their calls and cries and chirpings. One might imagine every living creature rigid, alert, listening, as were these men about the little fires.

The tension relaxed. The men dropped more fuel on the fires, coaxing the flame brighter. A whispering comment rose from group to group.

"*Simba! simba! simba!*" they hissed one to the other.

A lion had roared!

CHAPTER III

THE RHINOCEROS

In the first gray dusk Simba and Cazi Moto slipped away on the errands appointed for them—to find people and to find water, if possible. The cook camp, too, was afoot, dark figures passing and repassing before a fire. But the rest of the men slept heavily, seizing the unwonted chance.

When the first rays of the sun struck the fly of the small green master's-tent Kingozi appeared, demanding water wherewith to wash. At the sound of his voice men stirred sleepily, sat up, poked the remains of their tiny fires. As though through an open tap the freshness of night-time drained away. The hot, searching, stifling African day took possession of the world.

After breakfast Kingozi looked about him for shelter. A gorgeous, red-flowering vine had smothered one of the flat-topped thorn trees in its luxuriance. The growths of successive years had overlaid each other. Kingozi called two men with *pangas* who speedily cut out the centre, leaving a little round green room in the heart of the shadow. Thither Kingozi caused to be conveyed his chop-box table, his canvas chair, and his tin box; and there he spent the entire morning writing in a blank book and carefully drawing from field notes in a pocketbook a sketch map of the country he had traversed. At noon he ate a light meal of bread, plain rice with sugar, and a *balauri* of tea. Then for a time he slept beneath the mosquito bar in his tent.

At this hour of fiercest sun the whole world slept with him. From the baked earth rose heat waves almost as tangible as gauze veils. Objects at a greater distance than a hundred yards took on strange distortions. The thorn trees shot up to great heights; animals stood on stilts; the tops of the hills were flattened, and from their summits often reached out into space long streamers. Sometimes these latter joined across wide intervals, creating an illusion of natural bridges or lofty flat-topped cliffs with holes clear through them to the open sky beyond. All these things shimmered and flickered and wavered in the mirage of noon. Only the sun itself stared clear and unchanging.

At about two o'clock Kingozi awoke and raised his voice. Mali-ya-bwana, next in command after Cazi Moto and Simba, answered.

"Get the big gun," he was told, "and the water bottles."

Mali-ya-bwana was not a professed gun bearer, but he could load, and Kingozi believed him staunch. Therefore, often, in absence of Simba, the big Baganda had been pressed into this service.

The blasting heat was fiercest at this hour. The air was saturated by it just as water may hold a chemical in solution. Every little while a wave would beat against the cheek as though a furnace door had been opened. Nevertheless Kingozi knew that this was also the hour when the sun's power begins to decline; when the vertical rays begin to give place. For it is not heat that kills, but the actinic power of rays unfiltered by a long slant through the earth's atmosphere.

The two men tramped methodically along, paying little attention to their surroundings. Game dozed everywhere beneath the scanty shade, sometimes singly, sometimes in twos or threes, sometimes in herds. Motionless they stood; and often, were it not for the switch of a tail, they would have remained unobserved. Even the sentinel hartebeestes, posted atop high ant hills on the outskirts of the herds, seemed half asleep. Nevertheless they were awake enough for the job, as was evidenced when the two human figures came too near. Then a snort brought every creature to its feet, staring.

The objective of the men seemed to be a rise of land which the lessening mirage now permitted to appear as a small kopje, a solitary hill with rocky outcrops. Toward this they plodded methodically: Kingozi slouching ahead, Mali-ya-bwana close at his heels, very proud of his temporary promotion from the ranks. Suddenly he snapped his fingers. At the signal Kingozi stopped and looked back inquiringly over his shoulder.

Mali-ya-bwana was pointing cautiously to a low red clay

ant hill immediately in their path and about thirty yards ahead. To the casual glance it looked no different from any of the hundreds of others of like size and colour everywhere to be seen. Kingozi's attention, however, now narrowed to a smaller circle than the casual. It did not need Mali-ya-bwana's whispered *"faru"* (rhinoceros) to identify the mound.

Cautiously the two men began to back away. When they had receded some twenty yards, however, the huge beast leaped to its feet. The rapidity of its movements was extraordinary. There intervened none of the slow and clumsy upheaval one would naturally expect from an animal of so massive a body and such short, thick legs. One moment it slumbered, the next it was afoot, warned by some slight sound or jar of the earth or—as some maintain—by a telepathic sense of danger. Certainly, as far as they knew, neither Kingozi nor Mali-ya-bwana had disturbed a pebble or broken a twig.

The rhinoceros faced them, snorting loudly. The sound was exactly that of steam roaring from a locomotive's safety valve. Strangely enough, in spite of the massive structure and the loose, thick skin of the beast, it conveyed an impression of taut, nervous muscles. Though it faced directly toward them, the men knew that they were as yet unseen. The rhinoceros' eyesight is very short, or very circumscribed, or both; and only objects in motion and comparatively close enter its range of vision. Kingozi and his man held themselves rigidly immovable, waiting for what would happen. The rhinoceros, too, held himself rigidly immovable, his nostrils dilating between snorts, his ears turning; for his senses of smell and hearing made up in their keenness for the defects of his eyes.

Suddenly, without the slightest warning, he stuck his tail perpendicular and plunged forward at a clumsy-looking but exceedingly swift gallop.

An inexperienced man would have considered himself the object of a deliberate "charge"; but an old African traveller, such as Kingozi, knew this for a blind rush in the direction toward which the animal happened to be headed. The rhinoceros, alarmed by the first intimation of danger, unable to get further news from its keener senses, had been seized by a panic. Were nothing to deflect him from the straight line, he would continue ahead on it until the panic had run out.

But the two men were exactly in that line!

Kingozi hitched his light rifle forward imperceptibly. Although this was at present only a blind rush, should the rhinoceros catch sight of them he would fight; and within twenty-five yards or so his eyesight would be quite good enough. As the beast did not slow up in the first ten yards, but rather settled into its stride, Kingozi took rapid aim and fired.

His intention was neither to kill nor to cripple his antagonist. If that had been the case, he would have used the heavy double rifle that Mali-ya-bwana held ready near his elbow.

The bullet inflicted a slight flesh wound in the outer surface of the beast's left shoulder. Kingozi instantly passed the light rifle back with his right hand, at the same motion seizing the double rifle with his left.

But at the *spat* of the bullet the rhino veered toward the direction from which it seemed to his stupid brain the hurt had come. Tail erect, he thundered away down the slope.

For a hundred yards he careered full speed, then slowed to a trot, finally stopped, whirled, and faced to a new direction. The sound of his blowing came clearly across the intervening distance.

A low bush grew near. The rhino attacked this savagely, horning it, trampling it down. The dust arose in clouds. Then the huge brute trotted slowly away, still snorting angrily, pausing to butt violently the larger trees, or to tear into shreds some bush or ant hill that loomed dangerously in the primeval fogs of his brain.

"Sorry, old chap," commented Kingozi in his own language, "but you're none the worse. Only I'm afraid your naturally sweet temper is spoiled for to-day, at least."

He turned to exchange guns with Mali-ya-bwana.

"*N'dio, bwana,*" assented the latter to a speech of which he understood not one word. Mali-ya-bwana was secretly a little proud of himself for having stuck like a gun bearer, instead of shinning up a thorn tree like a porter.

Kingozi slipped a cartridge into the rifle, and the two resumed their walk toward the kopje.

CHAPTER IV

THE STRANGER

By the time the two men had gained the top of the hill the worst heat of the day had passed. Kingozi seated himself on a flat rock and at once began to take sights through a prismatic compass, entering the observations in a pocketbook. Mali-ya-bwana, bolt upright, stared out over the thinly wooded plain below. He reported the result of his scouting in a low voice, to which the white man paid no attention whatever.

"*Twiga,** bwana*," he said, and then, as his eye caught the flash of many sing-sing horns, "*kuru, mingi.*" Thus he named over the different animals—the topi, the red hartebeeste, the eland, zebra, some warthogs, and many others. The beasts were anticipating the cool of the afternoon, and were grazing slowly out from beneath the trees, scattering abroad over the landscape.

From even this slight elevation the outlook extended. Isolated mountain ranges showed loftier; the tops of unguessed hills peeped above the curve of the earth; the clear line of the horizon had receded to the outer confines of

---

*Giraffe.

terrestrial space, but even then not far enough to touch the cup of the sky. Elsewhere the heavens meet the horizon: in Africa they lie beyond it, so that when the round, fleecy clouds of the Little Rains sail down the wind there is always a fleet of them beyond the earth disappearing into the immensities of the infinite. There is space in African skies beyond the experience of those who have dwelt only in other lands. They dwarf the earth; and the plains and mountains, lying in weeks' journeys spread before the eye, dwarf all living things, so that at the last the man of imagination here becomes a humble creature.

For an hour the two remained on top the kopje. The details of the unknown country ahead, toward which Kingozi gave his attention, were simple. From the green line of the watercourse, near which the camp showed white and tiny, the veldt swept away for miles almost unbroken. Here and there were tiny parklike openings of clear grass; here and there more kopjes standing isolated and alone, like fortresses. Far down over the edge of the world showed dim and blue the tops of a short range of mountains. Vainly did Kingozi sweep his glasses over the landscape in hope of another line of green. No watercourse was visible. On the other hand, the scattered growth of thorn trees showed no signs of thickening to the dense spiky jungle that is one of the terrors of African travel. There might be a watercourse hidden in the folds of the earth; there might be a rainwater "tank," or a spring, on any of the kopjes. Simba and Cazi Moto were both experienced, and capable of a long round trip. The problem of days' journeys was not pressing at this moment. Kingozi noted the compass bearings of all the kopjes; took back sights in the direction from which he had come; closed his compass; and began idly to sweep the country with his glasses. In an unwonted mood of expansion he turned to Mali-ya-bwana.

"We go there," he told the porter, indicating the blue mountain-tops.

"It is far," Mali-ya-bwana replied.

Kingozi continued to look through his glasses. Suddenly he stopped them on an open plain three or four miles back in the direction from which he had come the day before. Mali-ya-bwana followed his gaze.

"A safari, *bwana*," he observed, unmoved. "A very large safari," he amended, after a moment.

Through his prismatic glasses Kingozi could see every detail plainly. After his fashion of talking aloud, he reported what he saw, partly to the black man at his side, but mostly to himself.

"*Askaris*"* he said, "six of them. The man rides in a *machele*†—he is either a German or a Portuguese; only those people use *macheles*—unless he is sick! Many porters—four tin boxes—only one *machele*. I can see them all now: there

---

*Native troops, armed with Snider muskets.

†A hammock slung on a long pole, and carried by four men at each end.

are no more white men. More *askaris!*" He smiled a little contemptuously under his beard. "This is a great safari, Mali-ya-bwana. Four tin boxes and twelve *askaris* to guard them; and eighty or more porters; and sixteen men just to carry the *machele!* This must be a *Bwana M'Kubwa*."

"That is what Kavirondos might think," replied Mali-ya-bwana calmly.

Kingozi looked up at him with a new curiosity.

"But not yourself?"

"A man who is a *Bwana M'kubwa* does not have to be carried. He does not need *askaris* to guard him in this country. And where can he get *potio* for so many?"

"Hullo!" cried Kingozi, surprised. "This is not porter's talk; this is headman's talk!"

"In my own country I am headman of many people," replied Mali-ya-bwana with a flash of pride.

"Yet you carry my tent load."

But Mali-ya-bwana made no reply, fixing his fierce eyes on the distant crawling safari.

"It must be a sportsman's safari," said Kingozi, this time to himself, "though what a sportsman wants in this back-of-beyond is a fair conundrum. Probably one of these chappies with more money than sense: wants to go somewhere nobody else has been, and can't go there without his caviare and his changes of clothes, and about eight guns—not to speak of a Complete Sportsman's Outfit as advertised exclusively by some Cockney Tom Fool on Haymarket."

He contemplated a problem frowningly. "Whoever it is will be a nuisance—a *damn* nuisance!" he concluded.

"*N'dio, bwana,*" came Mali-ya-bwana's cheerful response to this speech in a language strange to him.

"You have asked a true question," Kingozi shifted to Swahili. "Where is *potio* to be had for so large a safari? Trouble—much trouble!" He arose from the flat stone. "We will go and talk with this safari."

At an angle calculated to intercept the caravan, Kingozi set off down the hill.

After twenty minutes' brisk walk it became evident that they were approaching the route of march. Animals fled past them in increasing numbers, some headlong, others at a dignified and leisurely gait, as though performing a duty. The confused noise of many people became audible and the tapping of safari sticks against the loads.

At the edge of a tiny opening Kingozi, concealed behind a bush, reviewed the new arrivals at close range, estimating each element on which a judgment could be based. As usual, he thought aloud, muttering his speculations sometimes in his own language, sometimes in the equally familiar Swahili.

"*Askaris* not *pukha** askaris of the government. Those are not Sniders they carry—don't know that kind of musket. Those boxes are not the usual type—wonder where they were bought!"

———
*Genuine—regular.

The hammock came into view, swinging on the long pole. It was borne by four men at each end—experienced *machele* carriers who would keep step with a gentle gliding. Eight more walked alongside as relay. They would change places so skilfully that the occupant of the hammock could not have told when the shift took place. Alongside walked a tall, bareheaded, very black man. Kingozi's experienced eye was caught by differences.

"Of what tribe is that man?" he asked.

But Mali-ya-bwana was also puzzled.

"I do not know, bwana. He is a *shenzi*." *

The unknown was very tall, very straight, most well formed. But his face was extraordinarily ugly. His flat, wide nose, thick lips, and small yellow eyes were set off by an upstanding mop of hair. His expression was of extraordinary fierceness. He walked with a free and independent stride, and carried a rifle.

"He is not of this country. He is from the west coast, or perhaps Nubia or the Sudan," was Kingozi's conclusion.

"Many of these people are *shenzis*," Mali-ya-bwana pursued his own thought.

"That is true," Kingozi acknowledged. "If this is a sportsman, from what part did he hail to have got together this lot! We will see."

As the swinging hammock came opposite his concealment, Kingozi stepped forward.

---

* Wild man.

Every one in sight looked in his direction, but none showed any astonishment at this apparition out of the wilderness. The sophisticated African has ceased to be surprised at anything a white man may do. If he can make fire by rubbing a tiny stick *once*, why should he not do anything under heaven he wants to? A locomotive, an automobile, a flying machine are miracles, but no less—and no greater—than ordinary matches. Once admit the ability to transcend natural laws, once admit the possibility of miracles, why be surprised at anything? If a white man chose to appear thus in an unknown country, why not? If he chose again to vanish into thin air, again why not? Only the fierce-looking savage carrying the rifle rolled his eyes uneasily.

But at this precise moment a diversion on the opposite side of the line attracted attention enough. A galvanic shiver ran down the string of porters, succeeded at once by a crashing of loads cast hastily to the ground. With unanimity the bearers swarmed across the little open space toward and to either side of Kingozi and his attendant. Reaching the fringe of flat-topped trees they sprang into the low branches, heedless of the long thorns, and scrambled aloft until at least partially concealed. A few of the bolder members lurked behind the trunks, but held themselves ready for an instant ascent. From a hundred throats arose a confused cry of "*Faru ! Faru !*"

Not joining this first flight remained only the *askaris*, the eight men bearing the hammock, and the tall Nubian. Of these the *askaris* were far ahead and to the rear; the hammock bearers were decidedly panicky; only the Nubian seemed cool and self-possessed. The occupant of the hammock thrust out a foot to descend.

But before this could be accomplished a rhinoceros burst fully into view across the open space. His tail was up, he was snorting loudly, and he headed straight for the hammock. That was large, moving, and directly in his line of vision. The sight was too much for the bearers. With a howl they dropped the pole and streaked it to join their brothers in the thorn trees. The pole and the canopy of the hammock tangled inextricably its occupant.

A ragged volley from the muskets of the *askaris* merely seemed to add to the confusion. With great coolness the Nubian discharged first one barrel then the other of the heavy rifle he carried. The recoil, catching him in a bad posture, knocked him backward. The bullets kicked up a tremendous dust part way between himself and the charging beast. He was now without defence. Nevertheless he stepped in front of the entangled struggling figure on the ground.

Before the appearance of the rhinoceros into the open Kingozi had exchanged rifles, and stood at the ready. He was a good hundred yards from the hammock. Even in the rush of events he, characteristically, found time for com-- ments, although they did not in the least interfere with his rapid movements.

"Hope they don't wing one another," he remarked of the *askaris'* volley. "Rotten shooting! rotten!" as the Nubian stood his ground. At the same time he pushed forward the safety catch and threw the heavy rifle to his shoulder.

A charging rhinoceros—or one rushing near enough a man's direction to be dangerous—is not a difficult problem. Given nerve enough, and barring accidents—which might happen in a London flat—a man is in no danger. If he opens fire too soon, indeed, he is likely to empty his weapon without inflicting a stopping wound, but if he will wait until the beast is within twenty yards or so, the affair is certain. For this reason: just before a rhinoceros closes, he drops his head low in order to bring his long horn into action. If the hunter fires then, over the horn, he will strike the beast's backbone. The shot can hardly be missed, for the range is very close and the outstanding flanges of the vertebræ make a large mark. The formidable animal goes down like a stone. In country open enough to preclude the deadly close-at-hand surprise rush, where one has no chance to use his weapon at all, the rhinoceros is not dangerous to one who knows his business.

But in this case Kingozi was nearer a hundred and twenty than twenty yards from the animal. The mark to be hit was now very small; and it was moving. In addition the heavy double rifle, while accurate enough at that range, was not, owing to its weight and terrific recoil, as certain as a lighter rifle. These things Kingozi knew perfectly. The muscles under his beard tightened; his gray eyes widened into a glare like that of Simba in sight of game.

Just before the rhinoceros dropped his head for the toss, the Nubian stepped directly into the line of fire.

"*Lala !*—lie down!" Kingozi shouted.

Somehow the whip-snap of authority in his voice reached the Nubian's consciousness. He dropped flat, and almost instantly the white man fired.

At the roar of the great gun the rhinoceros collapsed in mid career, going down, as an animal always does under a successful spine shot, completely, without a struggle or even a quiver.

"That was well shot, master," said Mali-ya-bwana.

Kingozi reloaded the rifle and started forward. At the same time the occupant of the hammock finally emerged from the tangle and came erect.

CHAPTER V

THE ENCOUNTER

Kingozi saw a tall figure without a coat, dressed in brown shirt, riding breeches, and puttees. The Nubian had retrieved a spilled sun helmet even before the stranger had scrambled erect, so the head and face were invisible. Kingozi's countenance did not change, but a faint contempt appeared in his eyes. The first impression conveyed by the numbers of the tin boxes and their bearers and escort had been deepened. Why? Because the riding breeches were of that exaggerated cut sometimes actually to be seen outside tailor's advertisements. They were gathered trimly around an effeminately slender waist, and then ballooned out to an absurd width, only to contract again skin tight around the knees

"*M'buzi!*" grunted Kingozi, applying to the stranger the superlative of Swahili contempt. He did not know he spoke aloud; for it is not well for one white man to criticise another to a native. But Mali-ya-bwana replied.

"*Bibi,*" he corrected.

Kingozi stared. "By Jove, you're right!" he exclaimed in English. "It *is* a woman!" He burst into an unexpected laugh. "It isn't balloon breeches; it's *hips!*" he cried. This correction seemed to him singularly humorous. He approached her, laughing.

It was evidently an angry woman, to judge by her gestures and the deprecating attitude of the Nubian. Kingozi surmised that she probably did not fancy being dumped down incontinently before an angry rhinoceros. After a moment, however, her attitude lost its rigidity, she gestured toward the dead monster, evidently commending the savage. He shook his head and motioned in Kingozi's direction. The woman turned, showing an astonished face.

Kingozi was now close up. He saw before him a personality. Physically she was beautiful or not, according as one accepted conventional standards. The dress she wore revealed fully the fact that she had a tall, well-knit figure of long, full curves; a thoroughly feminine figure in conformation, and yet one that looked competent to transcend the usual feminine incompetencies. So far she measured to a high but customary standard. But her face was as exotic as an orchid. It was long, narrow, and pale with three accents to redeem it from what that ordinarily implies—lips of a brilliant carmine, eyes of a deep sea-green, and eyebrows high, arched, clean cut, narrow as though drawn by a camel's-hair brush. Indeed, in civilization no one would have believed them to have been otherwise produced. In spite of the awkward sun helmet she carried her head imperiously.

"If you *will* ride in a hammock, you ought to teach your men to shoot," was Kingozi's greeting. "It's absurd to go barging through a rhino country like this. You look strong and healthy. Why don't you walk?"

Her crest reared and her nostrils expanded haughtily. For a half-minute she stared at him, her sea-green eyes darkening to greater depths. This did not disturb Kingozi in the least: indeed he did not see it. His eyes were taking in the surroundings.

The dead rhinoceros lay a scant fifteen paces distant; loads were scattered everywhere; the *askaris*, their ancient muskets reloaded, had drawn near in curiosity. From the thorn trees across the tiny grass opening porters were descending, very gingerly, and with lamentations. It is comparatively easy to ascend a thorn tree with the fear of death snapping at your heels: to descend in cold blood is another matter.

"Why don't you do your work!" he addressed the soldiers. "Do you want to catch *kiboko*?"

The startled *askaris* scuttled away about their business, which was, at this moment, to herd and hustle the reluctant porters back to their job. Kingozi, his head and jaw thrust forward, stared after them, his eyes—indeed, his whole personality—projecting aggressive force. The men hurried to their positions, their loud laughter stilled, glancing fearfully and furtively over their shoulders, whipped by the baleful glare with which Kingozi silently battered them.

" 'If you *will* ride in a hammock, you ought to teach your men
to shoot,' was Kingozi's greeting "

Only when the last man had picked up his load did Kingozi turn again to the woman. Although her bosom still heaved with emotion, it was a suppressed emotion. He met a face slightly and inscrutably smiling.

"You take it upon yourself to manage my safari?" she said. "You think I cannot manage my men? It is kind of you."

Her English was faultless, but some slight unusual spacing of the words, some ultra-clarity of pronunciation, rather than a recognizable accent, made evident that the language was not her own.

"Your *askaris* are slack," said Kingozi briefly.

"And how of these?" she demanded imperiously, sweeping with an almost theatrical gesture the miserable-looking group of hammock bearers.

"They are at fault," replied Kingozi indifferently, "but after all they are common porters. You can't expect gun-bearer service or *askari* service from common porters, now can you?"

He looked at her directly, his clear, steady eyes conveying nothing but a mild interest in the obvious. In contrast to his detached almost indifferent calm, the woman was an embodiment of emotions. Head erect, red lips compressed, breast heaving, she surveyed him through narrowed lids.

"So?" she contented herself with saying.

"It's the nature of the beast to run crazy," pursued Kingozi tranquilly. "You really can't blame them."

"Then am I to be thrown down, like a sack, when it pleases them to run?" she demanded tensely. "Really, you are incredible."

"I should expect it. The real point is that you have no business to ride in a hammock through a rhino country."

The woman's control slipped a very little.

"Who are you to teach me my business?"

For the first time Kingozi's careless, candid stare narrowed to a focus.

"You have not told me what your business is," he replied with an edge of intention in his tones. Their glances crossed like rapiers for the flash of an instant.

She turned to the hammock bearers.

"Lie down!" she commanded. Then to the impassive Nubian, "The *kiboko!* I suppose," she observed politely to Kingozi, "that you will admit these men should be punished, and that you will permit me to do so?"

"Surely they should be punished; that goes without saying."

"Give them thirty apiece," she ordered the Nubian.

"That is too many," interposed Kingozi. "Six is a great plenty for such people. It is their nature to run away."

"Thirty," she repeated to the Nubian, without a glance in the white man's direction.

The huge negro produced the rhinoceros-hide whip, and went to his task. To lay thirty lashes on sixteen backs and to do justice to the occasion is a great task. The Nubian's face streamed sweat when he had finished. The bearers, who had taken the punishment in silence, arose, saluted, and begun to skylark among themselves, which was their way of working off emotion.

"*Askaris!*" summoned the woman.

They came trotting.

"Lay down your guns! Lie down!"

A mild wonder appeared in Kingozi's gray eyes.

"Do you *kiboko* your *askaris?*" he asked.

She jerked her head in his direction.

"Do you presume to question my actions?"

"By no means; I am interested in methods."

She paid him no more attention. Kingozi waited patiently until this second bout of punishment was over. The *askaris* lay quietly face down until their mistress gave the word, then leaped to their feet, saluted smartly, seized their guns, and marched jauntily to their appointed positions. The woman watched them for a moment, and turned back to Kingozi.

Her mood had completely changed. The orgy of punishment had cleared away the nervous effects of the fright she had undergone.

"So; that is done," she said. "I have travelled much in Africa. I what you call know my way about. See how my men fall into line. It will be so at camp. *Presto!* Quick! The tents will be up, the fires made."

Her lips smiled at him, but her sea-green eyes remained steady and inscrutable.

"They seem smart enough," acknowledged Kingozi without interest. "Have you ever tried them out?"

"Tried them out?" she repeated. "I do not understand."

"You never know what hold you really have until you get in a tight place."

"And if I get in a 'tight place,'" she rejoined haughtily, "I shall get out again—without help from negroes—or anybody."

"Quite so," conceded Kingozi equably. His attitude and the tone of his voice were indifferent, but the merest flicker of the tail of his eye touched the dead rhino. His expression remained quite bland. She saw this. The pallor of her cheek did not warm, but her strangely expressive eyes changed.

"*Bandika!*" she cried sharply. The men began to take up their loads.

"I will wish you a good afternoon," observed Kingozi as though taking his leave from an afternoon tea. "By the way, do you happen to care for information about the next water, or do you know all that?"

"Thank you, I know all that," she replied curtly.

The *askaris* began to shout the order for the advance, "*Nenda! nenda!*" the men to swing forward. Kingozi stared after them, watching with a professional eye the way they walked, the make-up of their loads, the nature

of their equipment; marking the lame ones, or the weak
ones, or the ones recently sick. His eye fell on the figure
of the strange woman. She was striding along easily, the
hammock deserted, with a free swing of the hips, an easy
slouch of the relaxed knees that indicated the accustomed
walker. Kingozi smiled.

"'I know all that,'" he repeated. "Now I wonder if
you do, or if some idea of silly pride makes you say so."
He was talking aloud, in English. Mali-ya-bwana stood
attentive, waiting for something he could understand.
Kingozi's eye fell on the dead rhinoceros.

"There is good meat; tell the men they can come out to
get what they wish of it.   There will be lions here to-night."

"Yes, *bwana.*"

"If she 'knew all that,'" observed Kingozi, "she knew
more than I did. Small chance. Still, if she has information or guides, she may know the next water. But how?
Why?"

He shifted his rifle to the crook of his arm.

"That *bibi* is a great *memsahib*," he told Mali-ya-bwana.
"And this evening we will go to see her. Be you ready to go
also."

CHAPTER VI

THE LEOPARD WOMAN

In the early darkness of equatorial Africa Kingozi, accompanied by Mali-ya-bwana with a lantern, crossed over to the other camp. Simba and Cazi Moto had come in almost at dusk; but they were very tired, and Kingozi considered it advisable to let them rest. They had covered probably thirty-five miles. Cazi Moto had found no water, and no traces of water. Furthermore, the game had thinned and disappeared. Only old tracks, old trails, old signs indicated that after the Big Rains the country might be habitable for the beasts. But Simba had discovered a concealed "tank" in a kopje. He had worked his way to it by "lining" the straight swift flight of green pigeons, as a bee hunter on the plains used to line the flight of bees. The tank proved to be a deep, hidden recess far back under overhanging rocks, at once concealed and protected from the sun and animals. Its water was sweet and abundant.

"No one has used that water. It is an unknown water," concluded Simba.

"How far?"

"Four hours."

"*Vema*." Kingozi bestowed on him the word of highest praise.

The stranger woman's camp was not far away; in fact, but just across the little dry stream-bed. Her safari was using the same pool with Kingozi's.

At the edge of the camp he paused to take in its disposition. From one detail to another his eye wandered, and in it dawned a growing approval. Your native, left to his own devices, pitches his little tents haphazard here, there, and everywhere, according as his fancy turns to this or that bush, thicket, or clump of grass. Such a camp straggles abominably. But here was no such confusion. Back from the water-hole a hundred yards, atop a slight rise, and under the thickest of the trees, stood a large green tent with a projecting fly. A huge pile of firewood had been dumped down in front of it, and at that very moment one of the *askaris*, kneeling, was kindling a fire. Behind the big tent, and at some remove, gleamed the circle of porters' tents each with its little blaze. Loads were piled neatly, covered with a tarpaulin, and the pile guarded by an *askari*.

Kingozi strode across the intervening space.

Before the big tent a table had been placed, and beside the table a reclining canvas chair of the folding variety. On a spread of figured blue cloth stood a bottle of lime juice, a sparklets, and an enamelware bowl containing flowers. The strange woman was stretched luxuriously in the chair smoking a cigarette.

She wore a short-sleeved lilac tea gown of thin silk, lilac silk stockings, and high-heeled slippers. Her hair fell in two long braids over her shoulders and between her breasts, which the thin silk defined. Her figure in the long chair fell into sinuous, graceful, relaxed lines. As he approached she looked at him over the glowing cigarette; and her eyes seemed to flicker with a strange restlessness. This contrast —of the restless eyes and the relaxed, graceful body— reminded Kingozi of something. His mind groped for a moment; then he had it.

"*Bibi ya chui !*" he said, half to himself, half to his companion, "The Leopard Woman!"

And, parenthetically, from that moment *Bibi-ya-chui*— the Leopard Woman—was the name by which she was known among the children of the sun.

She did not greet him in any way, but turned her head to address commands.

"Bring a chair for the *bwana;* bring cigarettes; bring *balauri—limejuici*——"

Kingozi found himself established comfortably.

She moved her whole body slightly sidewise, the better to face him. The soft silk fell in new lines about her, defining new curves. Her red lips smiled softly, and her eyes were dark and inscrutable.

"I was what you call horrid to-day," she said. "It was not me: it was the frightenedness from the rhinoceros. I was very much frightened, so I had the porters beaten.

That was horrid, was it not? Do you understand it? I suppose not. Men have no nerves, like women. They are brave always. I have not said what I feel. I have heard of you—the most wonderful shot in Central Africa. I believe it—now."

Kingozi's eyes were lingering on her silk-clad form, the peep of ankles below her robe. She observed him with slanted eyes, and a little breath of satisfaction raised her bosom. Abruptly he spoke.

"Aren't you afraid of fever mosquitoes in that rig?" said he.

Her body stirred convulsively, and her finely pencilled eyebrows, with their perpetual air of surprise, moved with impatience; but her voice answered him equably:

"My friend, at the close of the hard day I must have my comfort. There can be no fever here, for there are no people here. When in the fever country I have my 'rig'"— subtly she shaded the word—"just the same. But I have a net—a big net—like a tent beneath which I sit. Does that satisfy you?"

She spoke with the obvious painstaking patience that one uses to instruct a child, but with a veiled irony meant for an older intelligence.

Kingozi laughed.

"I do appear to catechize you, don't I? But I am interested. It is difficult to realize that a woman alone can understand this kind of travel."

He had thrown off his guarded abstraction, and smiled across at her as frankly as a boy. The gravity of his face broke into wrinkles of laughter; his steady eyes twinkled; his smile showed strong white teeth. In spite of his bushy beard he looked a boy. The woman stared at him, her cigarette suspended.

"You have instructed me about my camp; you have instructed me about my men; you have instructed me about my marching; you have even instructed me about my clothes." She tallied the counts on her slender fingers. "Now I must instruct you."

"Guilty, I am afraid," he smiled; "but ready to take punishment."

"Very well." With a sinuous movement she turned on her elbow to face him. "Listen! It is this: you should not wear that beard."

She fell back, and raised the cigarette to her lips.

For a moment Kingozi stared at her speechless with surprise; but immediately recovered.

"I shall give to your advice the same respectful consideration you accord mine," he assured her gravely.

She laughed in genuine amusement.

"Only I have more excuse," continued Kingozi. "A woman—alone—so far away——"

"You said that before," she interrupted. "In other words, what in—what-you-call? Oh, yes! what in hell am I doing up here? Is that it?"

She turned on him a wide-eyed stare. Kingozi chuckled.
"That's it. What in—in hell *are* you doing up here?"

"Listen, my friend. In this world I do what I please—
always. And when I find that which people tell me cannot
be done, that I do—at once. My life is full of those things
which could not be done, but which I have done."

"I believe you," said Kingozi, but he said it to himself.

"I have done them at home—where I live. I have done
them in the cities and courts. Whatever the people tell me
is impossible—'Oh, it cannot be done!'—with the uplifted
hand and eye—you understand—that I do. Four years
ago I came to Africa, and in Africa I have done what they
tell me women have never done. I have travelled in the
Kameroons, in Nyassaland, in Somaliland, in Abyssinia.
Then they tell me—'yes, that is very well, but you follow a
track. It is a dim track; but it is there. You go alone—
yes; but you have us at your back.' And I ask them:
'What then? where is this place where there is no track?'
And they wave their hands, and say 'Over yonder'; so I
come!"

She recited all this dramatically, using her hands much
in gesticulation, her eyes flashing. In proportion as she
became animated Kingozi withdrew into his customary
stolid calm.

"Quite so," he commented, "spirit of adventure, and all
that sort of thing. Where did you get this lot?"

"What?"

He waved his hand.

"Your men."

She considered him a barely appreciable instant.

"Why—the usual way—from the coast."

"They are strange to me—I do not recognize their tribes," Kingozi replied blandly. "So you are pushing out into the Unknown. How far do you consider going?"

"Until it pleases me to stop."

Kingozi produced his pipe.

"If you do not mind?" he requested. He deliberately filled and lighted it. After a few strong puffs he resumed:

"The country, you say, is unknown to you."

"Of course."

"I imagined you told me this afternoon that you knew of this water. I must have been mistaken."

He blew a cloud, gazing straight ahead of him in obviously assumed innocence. She examined him with a narrow, sidelong glance.

"No," she said at last, "you were not mistaken. I did tell you so."

"Well?" Kingozi turned to her.

"I was very angry, so I lied," she replied naïvely. "Women always lie when they get very angry."

"Or tell the truth—uncomfortably," grinned Kingozi.

"Brava!" she applauded. "He does know something about women!" With one of her sudden smooth movements she again raised herself on her elbow. "How much?" she challenged.

"Enough," he replied enigmatically.

They both laughed.

Across the accustomed night noises came a long rumbling snarl ending sharply with a snoring gasp. It was succeeded by another on a different key. The two took up a kind of antiphony, one against the other, now rising in volume, now dying down to a low grumble, again suddenly bursting like an explosion.

"The lions have found that rhino," remarked Kingozi indifferently.

For a moment or so they listened to the distant thunders.

"I have not sufficiently thanked you even yet for this afternoon," she said. "You saved my life—you know that."

"Happened to be there; and let off a rifle."

"I know shooting. It was a wonderful shot at that distance and in those circumstances."

"Chancy shot. Had good luck," replied Kingozi shortly.

Undeterred by his tone, she persisted.

"But you are said by many to be the best shot in Africa."

He glanced at her.

"Indeed! I think that a mistake. For whom do you take me?"

"You are Culbertson," she told him. She pronounced the name slowly, syllable by syllable, as though English proper names were difficult to her.

He laughed.

"Whoever he may be. I am known as Kingozi here-abouts."

"You are not Cul-bert-son?"

"I am anything it pleases you to have me. And who are you?"

She had become the spoiled darling, pouting at him in half-pretended vexation.

"You are playing with me. For that I shall not tell you who I am."

"It does not matter; I know."

"You know! But how?"

"I know many things."

"What is it then? Tell me!"

He hesitated, smiling at her inscrutably. The flames from the fire were leaping high now, throwing the lantern-light into eclipse. An *askari*, wearing on his head an in-dividual fancy in marabout feathers, leaned on his musket, his strong bronze face cast into the wistful lines of the savage countenance in repose. The lions had evidently com-pounded their quarrel. Only an occasional rasping cough testified to their presence. But in the direction of the dead rhinoceros the air was hideous with the plaints of the wait-ing hyenas. Their peculiarly weird moans came in chorus; and every once in a while arose the shrill, prolonged titter that has earned them the name of "laughing hyena."

"*Bibi-ya-chui*," he told her at length.

She considered this, her red lower lip caught between her teeth.

"The Leopard Woman," she repeated, "and it is thus that I am known! You, Kingozi—the Bearded One; I, Bibi-ya-chui—the Leopard Woman!" She laughed. "I think I like it," she decided.

"Now we know all about each other," he mocked.

"But no: you have asked many questions, which is your habit, but I have asked few. What do you do in this strange land? Is it—what-you-call—'spirit of adventure' also?"

"Not I! I am an ivory hunter."

"You expect to find the elephant here?"

"Who knows—or ivory to trade."

"And then you get your ivory and make the magic pass, and presto! it is in Mombasa," she said, with a faint sarcasm.

"You mean I have not men enough to carry out ivory. Well, that is true. But you see my habit is to get my ivory first and then to get *shenzis* from the people roundabout to act as porters," he explained to her gravely.

Apparently she hesitated, in two minds as to what next to say. Kingozi perceived a dancing temptation sternly repressed, and smiled beneath his beard.

"I see," she said finally in a meek voice.

But Kingozi knew of what she was thinking. "She is a keen one," he reflected admiringly. "Caught the weak point in that yarn straight off!"

He arose to his feet, knocking the ashes from his pipe.

"You travel to-morrow?" he asked politely.

"That I have not decided."

"This is a dry country," Kingozi suggested blandly. "Of course you will not risk a blind push with so many men. You will probably send out scouts to find the next water."

"That is possible," she replied gravely; but Kingozi thought to catch a twinkle in her eye.

He raised his voice:

"Boy!"

Mali-ya-bwana glided from one of the small porters' tents.

"*Qua heri.*" Kingozi abruptly wished her farewell in Swahili.

"*Qua heri,*" she replied without moving.

He turned into the darkness. The tropical stars blazed above him like candles. Kingozi lapsed into half-forgotten slang.

"Downy bird!" he reflected, which was probably not exactly the impression the Leopard Woman either intended or thought she had made.

CHAPTER VII

THE WATER-HOLE

A seasoned African traveller in ordinary circumstances sleeps very soundly, his ear attuned only to certain things. So Kingozi hardly stirred on his cork mattress, although the lions roared full-voiced satisfaction when they left the rhinoceros, and the yells of the hyenas rose to a pandemonium when at last they were permitted to join the feast. Likewise the nearer familiar noises of men rising to their daily tasks at four o'clock—the yawning, stretching, cracking of firewood, crackling of fire, low-voiced chatter—did not disturb him. Yet, so strangely is the human mind organized, had during the night a soft whisper of padded feet, even the deep breathing of a beast, sounded within the precincts of the camp, he would instantly have been broad awake, the rifle that stood loaded nearby clasped in his hand. Thus he lay quietly through the noises of men working, but came awake at the sound of men marching. He arose on his elbow and drew aside the flap of his tent.

At the same instant Cazi Moto stopped outside. The usual formula ensued.

"*Hodie!*" called Cazi Moto.

"*Karibu*," replied Kingozi.

Thus Cazi Moto at once awakened and greeted his master, and Kingozi acknowledged.

Cazi Moto entered the tent and lighted the tiny lantern, for it was still an hour and a half until daylight.

"I hear men marching," said Kingozi.

Cazi Moto stopped.

"It is the safari of Bibi-ya-chui." Already Kingozi's nickname for her had been adopted.

Cazi Moto disappeared, and a moment later was heard outside pouring water into the canvas basin.

Instead of arising immediately, as was his ordinary custom, Kingozi lay still. The Leopard Woman was already travelling! What could that mean? She was certainly taking some chances hiking around thus in the dark. Perhaps some aged or weak lion had not been permitted a share of that rhinoceros. And again she was taking chances pushing out blindly with over a hundred men into the aridity of the desert. Kingozi contemplated this thought for some time. Then, making up his mind, he arose and began to dress.

As he was drying his face Simba came for the guns, and a half-dozen of the porters prepared to strike and furl the tent. Already the canvas washstand had disappeared.

"Simba," observed Kingozi in English, of which language Simba knew but three words, "she is no fool. She knows where there is water out yonder; but it is water at least

forty miles away. She's got to push and push hard to
make it, and that's why she's making so early a start. I
had a notion this 'country of the great Unknown' wasn't
quite so 'unknown' as it might be."

He finished this speech coincidentally with the drying of
his hands. The impatient Cazi Moto snatched the towel
deftly but respectfully and packed it away. Simba, who had
listened with deference until his *bwana* should finish this
jargon, grinned.

"Yes, suh!" he used two of his English words at a
bang.

Kingozi ate his breakfast by firelight. With the exception of his camp chair and the eating service, the camp was
by now all packed, and the men were squatting before their
fires waiting.

But there was a hitch. Kingozi called up Simba and
began to question him.

"You say the water is four hours' march?"

"Yes, *bwana*."

"Four hours for you, or four hours for laden men?"

"The safari can go in four hours, *bwana*."

"Is there game there?"

"No, *bwana*. It is a guarded water, and there is no game."
Kingozi considered.

"Very well. I want six men. Before the march we
must get meat."

Some time since the flames of the African sunrise had

spread to the zenith, glowing and terrible as a furnace. Although the sky was thus brilliantly illuminated, the earth, strangely enough, was still gray with twilight. Objects fifty yards distant were indeterminate. Objects farther away were lost. The light was daylight, but it was inadequate, as though charged with mist.

And then suddenly the daylight was clear.

It was like the turning on by a switch. The dim shapes defined clearly, becoming trees, rocks, distant hills. And almost immediately the rim of the sun showed above the horizon.

Kingozi had already decided on the best direction in which to hunt. Neither the direction taken by the Leopard Woman's safari nor the immediate surroundings of the night's orgy over the rhino carcass was desirable. The fact that the big water-hole below camp had not only remained unvisited, but apparently even desired, led him to deduce the existence of another, alternative, drinking place. He had yesterday explored some distance downstream; therefore he now turned up.

Simba with the big rifle followed close at his heels. The six porters stole along fifty yards in the rear. They were quite as anxious for meat—promptly—as anybody, and were as unobtrusive as shadows.

For upward of a mile the hunters encountered nothing but a few dik-dik and steinbuck—tiny grass antelope, too small for the purpose. Then a shift of wind brought to

them a medley of sound—a great persistent barking of
zebras supplying the main volume. At the same time they
saw, over a distant slight rise, a cloud of dust.

Simba's eyes were gleaming.

"Game! Much game there, *bwana !*" he cried.

"I see," replied Kingozi quietly.

The porters accompanied them to within a few rods of
the top of the rise. There they squatted, and the other
two crawled up alone.

Below them, probably three hundred yards away, was a
larger replica of the other water-hole. At its edge and in
its shallows stood a few beasts. But the sun was now well
above the horizon, the drinking time was practically over.

Three long strings of game animals were walking leisurely
away in three different directions. They were proceeding
soberly, in single file, nose to tail. The ranks ran with
scarcely a break, to disappear over the low swells of the
plain. Alongside the plodders skipped and ran, rushed
back and forth the younger, frivolous characters, kicking up
their heels, biting at one another, or lowering their horns in
short mimic charges—gay, animated flankers to the main
army. There were several sorts, each in its little companies
or bands, many times repeated, of from two or three to
several score; although occasionally strange assortments
and companionships were to be seen, as a black, shaggy-
looking wildebeeste with a troop of kongoni. Kingozi saw,
besides these two, also the bigger and smaller gazelles, many

zebra, topi, the lordly eland; and, apart, a dozen **giraffes**, two rhinoceros, and some warthogs. There were probably two thousand wild animals in sight.

The hunters lay flat, watching. This multiplicity afforded them a wonderful spectacle, but that was about all. If they should crawl three yards farther they would indubitably be espied by some one. It was impossible to single out a beast as the object of a stalk: all the others must be considered, too. There was no cover.

Kingozi was too old at the business to hurry. He considered the elements of his problem soberly before coming back to his first and most obvious conclusion. Then he raised himself slowly to his favourite sitting position and threw off the safety.

The distance was a fair three hundred yards, which is a long shot—when it *is* three hundred yards. The fireside and sporting magazine hunters of big game are constantly hitting 'em through the heart at even greater distances— estimated. It is actually a fact, proven many times, that those estimates should be divided by two in order to get near the measured truth! The "four hundred yards if it's an inch!" becomes two hundred—and even two hundred yards at living game in natural surroundings is a long and creditable shot.

In taking his aim Kingozi modified his usual custom because of the distance. When one can get his beast broadside on, the most immediately fatal shot is one high in the shoulder, about three-quarters of the way up. That drops an animal dead in his tracks. The next best is a bullet low in the shoulder. Third is a really accurate heart shot. This latter is always fatal, of course; but ordinarily the quarry will run at racing speed for some little distance before falling dead. In certain types of country this means considerable tracking, may even mean the loss of the animal. Next comes anywhere in the barrel forward of the short ribs—a chancy proceeding, and one leading to long chases. After that the likelihood of a cripple is too great.

Now it is evident that one must aim at what he can be sure of hitting. The high shoulder shot is all right if the distance is so short that one can be absolutely certain of placing his bullet within a six-inch circle. Otherwise the chance of over-shooting—always great—becomes prohibitive. The low shoulder shot increases the circle to from eight to twelve inches, with the chance outside that of merely breaking a foreleg, grazing brisket, or missing entirely under the neck. The heart shot—or rather an attempt at it—is safer for a longer range, not because the mark is larger, but because even if one misses the heart, he is apt to land either the shoulder or the ribs well forward. The only miss is beneath, and that is clear, as the heart is low in the body. And at extreme ranges, the forward one-third of the barrel is the point of aim. It should only rarely be attempted. Unless a man is certain he can hit that mark, *every time*, he is not justified in taking the shot.

This principle applies to every one: as well to the beginner as to the expert. The only difference between the two is the range at which this certainty exists. The tyro's limit of absolute certainty for the heart shot may be—and probably is—a hundred yards; for the high shoulder it may be as near as thirty. This takes into consideration his inexperience in the presence of game as well as his inaccuracy with the rifle, and it keeps in mind that he must hit that mark not merely nine times out of ten, but *every time*. If he cannot get within the hundred yards by stalking, then he should refuse the chance. As expertness rises in the scale the distances increase. Provided there were no such things as nerves, luck, faulty judgment, and the estimate of distances one man should be as mercifully deadly as another. Naturally the man who had to stalk to within a hundred yards would not get as many shots as the one who could take his chance at two hundred. This conduct of venery is an ideal that is only approximated. Hence misses.

But even if a man lives rigorously up to his principles and knowledge, there are other elements that bring in uncertainty. For one thing, he must be able to estimate distance with some degree of accuracy. It avails little to know that you can hit a given mark at two hundred and fifty yards, if you do not know what two hundred and fifty yards is. And here enter a thousand deceits: direction of light, slope of ground, nature of cover, temperature, mirage, time of day, and the like. An apparent hundred yards over water or across a cañon would—were, by some dissolving-view-change, bush-dotted plain to be substituted—become nearer three hundred in the latter circumstances. There is a limit to the best man's experience; a margin of error in the best man's judgment. Hence more misses.

There is only one method for any man to acquire even this proximate skill; and that requires long and patient practice. It is this: he should sight over his rifle at a wild animal, noting carefully the apparent relative size of the front sight-bead and the animal's body. He should then pace the distance between himself and that animal. After he has done this a hundred times, he will be able to make a pretty close guess by marking how large the beast shows up through the sights. That is, for that one species of game! In Central Africa, where in a well-stocked district there are from twenty to thirty species, the practice becomes more onerous. This same practice—of pacing the distances—however, has also trained a man's eye for country. He is able to supplement the front-sight method by the usual estimate by eye. Most men do not take this trouble. They practise at target range until they can hit the bull's-eye with fair regularity, miss with nearly equal regularity in the hunting field, and thenceforth talk vaguely of "missed him at five hundred yards." It must have been five hundred. The beast looked very small, there was an awful lot of country between him and it, and "I wasn't a bit rattled—cool as a cucumber—and I *know* I never miss an object of that size at any reasonable range." He was right: he shot as deliberately as he ever did at the butts. He missed, not because of the distance, but because he did not know the distance. It was exactly the range at which he had done the most of his practice—two hundred yards!

All these considerations have taken several pages to tell. Kingozi weighed each one of them. Yet so long had been his experience, so habitual had become his reactions, that his decision was made almost instantly. A glance at the intervening ground, another through his sights. The top of the bead covered half a zebra's shoulder. The distance was not far under or over three hundred. Kingozi knew that, barring sheer accident, he could hit his mark at that distance.

The animals meantime were moving forward slowly along the three diverging trails. The last of them had left the water-hole. Kingozi nodded to Simba. Simba, understanding from long association just what was required of him, rose slowly and evenly to his feet.

The apparition of this strange figure on the skyline brought a score of animals to a stand. They turned their heads, staring intently, making up their minds, their nostrils wide. Kingozi, who had already picked his beast and partially assured his aim, almost immediately squeezed the trigger.

Over a second after the flat crack of the rifle a hollow *plunk* indicated that the bullet had told. It was a strange sound, unmistakable to one who has once heard it, much as though one brought a drinking glass smartly, hollow down, into the surface of water.

"Hah!" ejaculated Simba.

"Where?" asked Kingozi, who knew by long experience that Simba's sharp eyes had noted the smallest particular of the beast's behaviour when the bullet landed, and thence had already deduced its location.

Without removing his eyes, Simba indicated with his fore-finger a shot about midway of the ribs.

At the sound the rear guard of the animals raced madly away for about seventy yards, whirled in a phalanx, and gazed back. Neither man moved. Simba continued to stare, and Kingozi had lifted his prism glasses. A tyro would have attempted to draw near for a finishing shot, and so would probably have been let in for a long chase. A freshly wounded animal, if kept moving, is capable of astonishing endurance. But these two knew better than that. In a very few minutes the zebra, without fright, with-out suffering—for a modern bullet benumbs—toppled over dead. Again Simba raised his voice exultantly to the wait-ing porters.

"*Nyama ! nyama !*" he shouted.

And they, racing eagerly forward, their faces illuminated with one of the strongest joys the native knows, shouted back:

"*Nyama ! nyama !*"

For another two days the provisioning was assured.

CHAPTER VIII

THE THIRST

The little safari made the distance to Simba's guarded water in a trifle over the four hours. Camp was made high up on the kopje whence the eye could carry to immense distances. The wall of mountains was now nearer. Through his glasses Kingozi could distinguish rounded foothills. He tried to make out whether certain dark patches were groves or patches of bush—they might have been either—but was unable to determine. Relative sizes did not exist. The mountains might be five thousand feet tall or only a fifth of that. And by exactly that proportion they might be a day's or a five days' journey distant!

Carefully Kingozi examined the length of the range. At length his attention was arrested. A thread of smoke, barely distinguishable against the gray of distance, rose within the shadow of the hills.

"Simba!" Kingozi summoned. Then, on the gun bearer's approach: "Look through the glasses and tell me whether that smoke is a house or a fire in the grass."

Simba accepted the glasses, but first took a good look with the naked eye. He caught the location of the smoke almost at once. Then for a full two minutes he stared through the lenses.

"It is a house, *bwana*," he decided.

As though the words had been a magic spell the mountains seemed in Kingozi's imagination to diminish in size and to move forward. They had assured a definite proportion, a definite position. Their distance could be estimated.

"And how far?" he asked.

"Very far, *bwana*," replied Simba gravely, "eleven hours; twelve hours."

Kingozi reflected. The safari of the Leopard Woman had passed the kopje not over a mile away; indeed Kingozi had left her trail only a short distance back. On the supposition that she was well informed, it seemed unlikely that she could expect to make the whole distance from the last camp to the mountains in one march. Therefore there must be another water between. In that case, if Kingozi followed her tracks, he would arrive at that water. On the other supposition—that she was striking recklessly into the unknown—well, all the more reason for following her tracks!

They commenced their journey before daylight the following morning. Each man was instructed to fill his water bottle; and the instructions were rigidly enforced. In the darkness they stumbled down the gentle slopes of the kopjes, each steering by the man ahead, and Kingozi steering by the stars.　The veldt was still, as though all the silences, driven from those portions inhabited by the beasts, had here made their refuge.　The earth lay like a black pool becalmed.　Overhead the stars blazed clearly, slowly faded, and gave way to the dawn.　The men spoke rarely, and then in low voices.

Kingozi led the way steadily, without hurrying, but without loitering.　Daylight came: the sun blazed.　The country remained the same in character.　Behind them the kopje dwindled in importance until it took its place with insignificant landmarks.　The mountains ahead seemed no nearer.

At the end of three hours, by the watch Kingozi carried on his wrist, he called the first halt.　The men laid down their loads, and sprawled about in abandon.　Kingozi produced a pipe.

The rest lasted a full half hour.　Then two hours more of marching, and another rest.　By now a normal day's march would be about over.　But this was different.　Kingozi rigidly adhered to the plan for all forced marches of this kind: three hours, a half-hour's rest; then two hours, a half-hour's rest; and after that march and rest as the men can stand it, according to their strength and condition.

This latter is the cruel period.　At first the ranks hold together.　Then, in spite of the efforts of the headman to bring up the rear, the weaker begin to fall back.　They must rest oftener, they go on with ever-increasing difficulty.

The strong men ahead become impatient and push on.   The
safari is no longer a coherent organization, but an aggregate
of units, each with his own problem of weariness, of thirst,
finally of suffering.   More and more stretches the distance
between the *bwana* and his headman.

No native of the porter intelligence has the slightest
forethought for the morrow, and very little for the day.   If
it is hot and he has started early, his water bottle is empty
by noon.

This wise program Kingozi entered upon carefully.   The
three hours' march went well; the two hours followed with
every one strong and cheerful; then two hours more without
trouble.   Kingozi's men were picked, and hard as nails.
By now it was one o'clock; coming the hottest part of the
day.   The power of the vertical sun attained its maximum.
Kingozi felt as though a heavy hand had been laid upon his
head and was pressing him down.   The mirage danced
and changed, its illusions succeeding one another mo-
mently as the successive veils of heat waves shimmered upward.   Reflected heat scorched his face.   His spirit retired far into its fastness, taking with it all his energies.
From that withdrawn inner remoteness he doled out the
necessary vitality parsimoniously, drop by drop.   Deliberately he withdrew his attention from the unessentials.   Not
a glance did he vouchsafe to the prospect far or near; not a
thought did he permit himself of speculation or of wandering interest.   His sole job now was to plod on at an even

gait, to keep track of time, to follow the spoor of the Leopard Woman's safari, to save himself for later. If he had spared any thought at all, it would have been self-congratulation that Simba and Cazi Moto were old and tried. For Simba relieved him of the necessity of watching for dangerous beasts, and Cazi Moto of the responsibility of keeping account of the men.

At the rest periods Kingozi sat down on the ground. Then in the relaxation his intelligence emerged. He took stock of the situation.

Mali-ya-bwana and nine others were always directly at his heels. They dropped their loads and grinned cheerfully at their *bwana*, their bronze faces gleaming as though polished. If only they were all like this! Then perhaps five minutes later a smaller group came in, strongly enough. The first squad shouted ridiculing little jokes at them; and they shrieked back spirited repartee, whacking their loads vigorously with their safari sticks. These, too, would cause no anxiety. But then Kingozi sat up and began to take notice. The men drifted in by twos and threes. Kingozi scrutinized them closely, trying to determine the state of their strength and the state of their spirit. And after twenty minutes, or even the full half hour allotted to the rest period, Cazi Moto came in driving before him seven men.

The wizened little headman was as cheerful and lively and vigorous as ever. He, too, grinned, but his eyes held a faint anxiety, and he had shifted his closed umbrella to his left hand and held the *kiboko* in his right. At the fifth rest period five of the seven men stumbled wearily in; but Cazi Moto and the other two did not appear before Kingozi ordered a resumption of the march.

But the mountains had moved near. When this had happened Kingozi could not have told. It was between two rest periods. From an immense discouraging distance, they towered imminent. It seemed that a half-hour's easy walk should take them to the foothills. Yet not a man there but knew that this nearness was exactly as deceitful as the distance had been before.

The afternoon wore on. Kingozi's canteen was all but empty, though he had drunk sparingly, a swallow at a time. His tongue was slightly swollen. The sun had him to a certain extent; so that, although he could rouse himself at will, nevertheless, he moved mechanically in a sort of daze.

He heard Simba's voice; and brought himself into focus.

The gun bearer was staring at something on the ground. Kingozi followed the direction of his gaze. Before him lay a dead man.

It was one of the common porters—a tall, too slender savage, with armlets of polished iron, long, ropy hair—a typical *shenzi*. His load was missing: evidently one of the *askaris* had taken it up.

Kingozi's safari filed by, each man gazing in turn without expression at the huddled heap. Only Maulo, the camp jester, hurled a facetious comment at the corpse. There-

upon all the rest laughed after the strange, heartless custom
of the African native.   Or is it heartless?   We do not know.

The day's march had passed through the phase of co-
ordinated action.   It was now the duty of each man to get
in if he could.   It was Kingozi's duty to arrive first, and
to arrange succour for Cazi Moto and those whom he
drove.

Twenty minutes beyond the dead man they came upon
three porters sitting by the wayside.   They were men in the
last extremity of thirst and exhaustion, their eyes wide and
vacant, their tongues so swollen that their teeth were held
apart.   Nothing was to be done here, so Kingozi marched
by.

Then he came upon a half-dozen bags of *potio*.   They
were thrown down pellmell, anyhow; so that Kingozi concluded they had been surreptitiously thrown away, and not
temporarily abandoned with intent to return for them.

After that the trail resembled the traces of a rout.   Every
few yards now were the evidences of desperation: loads of
potio, garments, water bottles emptied and cast aside in a
gust of passion at their emptiness.   At intervals also they
passed more men, gaunt, incredibly cadaverous, considering
that only the day before they had been strong and well.
They sat or lay inert, watching the safari pass, their eyes
apathetic.   Kingozi paid no attention to them, nor to the
loads of *potio*, nor to the garments and accoutrements; but
he caused Simba to gather the water bottles.   After a time

Simba was hung about on all sides, and resembled at a short distance some queer conical monster.

Then they topped the bank of a wide shallow dry streambed and saw the remnants of other safari below them.

The Leopard Woman sat on a tent load. Even at this distance her erect figure expressed determination and defiance. The Nubian squatted beside her. Men lay scattered all about in attitudes of abandon and exhaustion; yet every face was turned in her direction.

Kingozi descended the bank and approached, his experienced eye registering every significant detail.

She turned to him a face lowering like a thundercloud, her eyes flashing the lightnings, her lips scarlet and bitten. Kingozi noted the bloodied *kiboko*.

"They won't go on!" she cried at him harshly. "I can't make them! It is death for them here, but all they will do is to sit down! It is maddening! If they must die——"

She leaped to her feet and drew an automatic pistol.

"*Bandika!*" she cried. "Take your loads! Quickly!"

She threatened the man nearest her. He merely stared, his expression dull with the infinite remoteness of savage people. Without further parley she fired. Although the distance was short, she missed, the bullet throwing up a spurt of sand beneath the man's armpit. He did not stir, nor did his face change.

Kingozi's bent form had straightened. An authority, heretofore latent, flashed from his whole personality.

"Stop!" he commanded.

She turned toward him a look of convulsed rage. Then suddenly her resistance to circumstances broke. She hurled the automatic pistol at the porter, and flopped down on the tent load, hiding her face in her hands.

Kingozi paid her no further attention.

"Simba!" he called.

"Yes, suh!"

"Take one man. Collect all water bottles. Take a lantern. Go as rapidly as you can to find water. Fill all the bottles and bring them back. There are people in the hills. There will be people near the water. Get them to help you carry back the water bottles."

Simba selected Mali-ya-bwana to accompany him, but this did not meet Kingozi's ideas.

"I want that man," said he.

Simba and one of the other leading porters started away. Kingozi gave his attention to the members of the other safari.

They sat and sprawled in all attitudes. But one thing was common to all: a dead sullenness.

"Why do you not obey the *memsahib?*" Kingozi asked in a reasonable tone.

No one answered for some time. Finally the man who had been shot at replied.

"There is no water. We are very tired. We cannot go on without water."

"How can you get water if you do not go on?"

"*Hapana shauri yangu*," replied the man indifferently, uttering the fatalistic phrase that rises to the lips of the savage African almost automatically, unless his personal loyalty has been won—"that is not my affair." He brooded on the ground for a space then looked up. "It is the business of porters to carry loads; it is the business of the white man to take care of the porters." And in that he voiced the philosophy of this human relation. The porters had done their job: not one inch beyond it would they go. The white woman had brought them here: it was now her *shauri* to get them out.

"You see!" cried the Leopard Woman bitterly. "What can you do with such idiots!"

Kingozi directed toward her his slow smile.

"Yes, I see. Do you remember I asked you once when you were boasting your efficiency, whether you had ever tried your men? Your work was done smartly and well— better than my work was done. But my men will help me in a fix, and yours will not."

"You are quite a preacher," she rejoined. "And you are exasperating. Why don't you do something?"

"I am going to," replied Kingozi calmly.

He called Mali-ya-bwana to him.

"Talk to these *shenzis*," said he.

Mali-ya-bwana talked. His speech was not eloquent, nor did it flatter the Leopard Woman, but it was to the point.

"My *bwana* is a great lord," said he. "He is master of all things. He fights the lion, he fights the elephant. Nothing causes him to be afraid. He is not foolish, like a woman. He knows the water, the sun, the wind. When he speaks it is wisdom. Those who do what he says follow wisdom. *Bassi!*"

Immediately this admonition was finished Kingozi issued his first command:

"Bring all loads to this place."

Nobody stirred at first.

"My loads, the loads of Bibi-ya-chui—all to this place."

Mali-ya-bwana and the other fourteen of Kingozi's safari who were now present brought their loads up and began to pile them under Kingozi's direction.

"Quickly!" called Kingozi in brisk, cheerful tones. "The water is not far, but the day is nearly gone. We must march quickly, even without loads."

The import of the command began to reach the other porters. This white man did not intend to camp here then —where there was no water! He did not mean to make them march with loads! He knew! He was a great lord, and wise, as Mali-ya-bwana had said! One or two arose wearily and stiffly, and dragged their loads to the pile. Others followed. Kingozi's men helped the weakest. Kingozi himself worked hard, arranging the loads, covering them with tarpaulins, weighting the edges.

His intention reached also the Leopard Woman. She

watched proceedings without comment for some time. Then she saw something that raised her objection.

"I shall want that box," she announced. "Leave that one out. And that is my tent being brought up now."

Apparently Kingozi did not hear her. He bestowed the box in a space left for it, and piled the two tent loads atop. The Leopard Woman arose and glided to his side.

"That box——" she began.

"I heard you," replied Kingozi politely, "but it will really be impossible to carry anything at all."

"That box is indispensable to me," she insisted haughtily.

"You have no men strong enough to carry a load: and mine will need all the strength they have left before they get in."

He went on arranging the loads under the tarpaulins.

"Those loads are my tent," she said, as Kingozi turned away.

"We cannot take them."

Her eyes flashed. She whirled with the evident intention of issuing her commands direct. Kingozi's weary, slow indifference fell from him. In one bound he faced her, his chin thrust forward. His blue eyes had focussed into a cold, level stare.

"Don't dare interfere!" he ordered. "If you attempt it, I shall order you restrained—physically. Understand? I do not know how far you intend to travel—or where; but if you value your future authority and prestige with your own men, do not make yourself a spectacle before them."

"You would not dare!" she panted.

The tenseness relaxed. Kingozi became again the slow-moving, slouching, indifferent figure of his everyday habit.

"Oh, I can dare almost anything—when I have to. You do not seem to understand. You have come a cropper—a bad one. Left to yourselves you are all going to die here. If I am to help you to your feet, I must do it without interference. I think we shall get through: but I am not at all certain. Go and sit down and save your strength."

"I hate you!" she flashed. "I'd rather die here than accept your help! I command you to leave me!"

"Bless you!" said Kingozi, as though this were a new thought. "I wasn't thinking especially of *you;* I am sorry for your boys."

Mali-ya-bwana, under his directions, had undone the loads containing the lanterns. Everything seemed now ready for the start. All of Kingozi's safari had arrived except Cazi Moto and five men.

"Have you any water left?" Kingozi asked the Leopard Woman.

She stared straight ahead of her, refusing to answer. Unperturbed, Kingozi turned to the Nubian.

"Which is *memsahib's* canteen?"

The Nubian silently indicated two of the three hung on his person. Kingozi shook them, and found them empty.

His own contained still about a pint, and this he poured into one of hers. She appeared not to notice the act.

The march was resumed. Mali-ya-bwana was instructed to lead the way following the scraped places on the earth, the twigs bent over, and the broken branches by which Simba had marked his route for them. Kingozi himself brought up the rear. Reluctantly, apathetically, the Leopard Woman's men got to their feet. Kingozi was everywhere, urging, encouraging, shaming, joking, threatening, occasionally using the *kiboko* he had taken from one of the *askaris*. At last all were under way. The Leopard Woman sat still on the load, the Nubian crouched at her back. The long, straggling, staggering file of men crawled up the dry bank and disappeared one by one over the top. Each figure for a moment was silhouetted against the sky, for the sun was low. Kingozi toiled up the steep, his head bent forward. In his turn he, too, stood black and massive on the brink, the outline of his powerful stooped shoulders gold-rimmed in light. She watched him feverishly, awaiting from him some sign that he realized her existence, that he cared whether or not she was left behind. He did not look back. In a moment he had disappeared. The prospect was empty of human life.

She arose. For an instant her face was convulsed with a fairly demoniac fury. Then a mask of blankness obliterated all expression. She followed.

CHAPTER IX

ON THE PLATEAU

Two hours into the night Kingozi, following in the rear, saw a cluster of lights, and shortly came to a compact group of those who had gone before him. They were drinking eagerly from water bottles. Simba, lantern in hand, stood nearby. A number of savages carrying crude torches hovered around the outskirts. Kingozi could not make out the details of their appearance: only their eyeballs shining. He drew Simba to one side.

"There are many *shenzis* ?"

"Many, like the leaves of the grass, *bwana*."

"The huts are far?"

"One hour, *bwana*, in the hills."

"These *shenzis* are good?"—meaning friendly.

"*Bwana*, the *sultani* of these people is a great lord. He has many people, and much riches. He has told his people to come with me. He prepares the guest house for you."

"Tired, Simba?"

"It has been a long path since sunup, *bwana*. But I had water, and the people gave me *potio* and meat. I am strong."

"Cazi Moto is back there—in the Thirst," suggested Kingozi, "and many others. And there is no water."

"I will go, *bwana*, and take the *shenzis* with me."

He set about gathering the water bottles and gourds that had not been emptied. Mali-ya-bwana and, unexpectedly, a big Kavirondo of Kingozi's safari, volunteered. The rest prepared to continue the journey.

But another delay occurred. The Leopard Woman, who had walked indomitably, now collapsed. Her eyes were sunken in her head, her lips had paled; only the long white oval of her face recalled her former splendid and exotic beauty. When the signal to proceed was given, she stepped forward as firmly as ever for perhaps a dozen paces, then her knees crumpled under her.

"I'm afraid I'm done," she muttered to Kingozi.

In the latter's eyes, for the first time, shone a real and ungrudging admiration. He knelt at her side and felt her pulse. Without hesitation, and in the most matter-of-fact way, he unbuttoned her blouse to the waist and tore apart the thin chemise beneath.

"Water," he commanded.

With the wetted end of his neck scarf he beat her vigorously below the left breast. After a little she opened her eyes.

"That's better," said Kingozi, and began clumsily to rebutton her blouse.

A slow colour rose to her face as she realized in what manner she had been exposed, and she snatched her gar-

ments together. Kingozi, watching her closely, seemed to
see in this only a satisfactory symptom.

"That's right; now you're about again. Blood going
once more."

They proceeded. A man on either side supported the
Leopard Woman's steps.

Shortly the hills closed around them. The dark velvet
masses compassed them about, and the starry sky seemed
suddenly to have been thrust upward a million miles. The
open plain narrowed to a track along which they groped
single file. They caught the sound of running water to their
left; but far below. There seemed no end to it.

But then, unexpectedly, they found themselves on a
plateau, with the mass of the mountains on one side and the
sea of night on the other, as though it might be the spacious
deck of a ship. A multitude of people swarmed about
them, shining naked people, who stared; and there seemed
to be huts with conical roofs, and a number of little winking
fires that shifted position. The people led the way to a circular hut of good size, with a conical thatched roof and
wattle walls. Kingozi stooped his head, thrusting the
lantern inside. The interior had been swept. A huge
earthen tub full of water stood by the door. The place
contained no other furnishings.

"Bring the *memsahib* here," he commanded.

She was half dragged forward. Kingozi took her in his
arms to prevent her falling.

"Bring grass," he ordered.

The request was repeated outside in Swahili, and turned into a strange tongue. Kingozi heard many feet hurrying away.

He stood supporting the half-fainting form of the Leopard Woman. Her head rested against his shoulder. Her eyes were closed, her muscles had all gone slack, so that her body felt soft and warm. Kingozi, waiting, remembered her as she had looked the evening of his call—silk-clad, lithe, proud, with blood-red lips, and haughty, fathomless eyes, and the single jewel that hung in the middle of her forehead. Somehow at this moment she seemed smaller, in her safari costume, and helpless, and pathetic. He felt the curve of her breast against him, and the picture of her as he had seen her out there in the Thirst arose before his eyes. At that time it had not registered: he was too busy about serious things. But now, while he waited, the incident claimed, belated, his senses. His antagonism, or distrust, or coldness, or suspicion, or indifference, or whatever had hardened him, disappeared. He stared straight before him at the lantern, allowing these thoughts and sensations to drift through him. Subconsciously he noted that the lamp flame showed a halo, or rather two halos, one red and one green. By experience he knew that this portended one of his stabbing headaches through the eyes. But the thought did not hold him. He contemplated unwaveringly the spectacle of this soft, warm, helpless but indomitable piece of feminity fronting the African wilderness unafraid. Unconsciously his arms tightened around her, drawing her to him. She gave no sign. Her form was limp. Apparently she was either half asleep or in a stupor. But had Kingozi looked down when he tightened his arms, instead of staring at the halo-encircled lantern, he would have seen her glance sidewise upward into his face, he would have discerned a fleeting smile upon her lips.

Almost immediately the people were back with armfuls of the long grass that grows on the edge of mountainous country. Under Kingozi's directions they heaped it at one side. He assisted the Leopard Woman to this improvised couch and laid her upon it. She seemed to drop instantly asleep.

They brought more grass and piled it in another place. Mali-ya-bwana superintended these activities zealously. He had drunk his fill, had bolted a chunk of goat's flesh one of the savages had handed him, now he was ready to fulfil his *bwana's* commands.

"You will eat?" he asked.

But Kingozi was not hungry. His strong desire was for a tall *balauri* of hot tea, but this could not be. He knew it was unsafe to drink the water unboiled—it is unsafe to drink any African water unboiled—but this time it could not be helped. He was not even very tired, though his eyes burned. There was nothing more to do. Kingozi knew that Simba and Cazi Moto would not attempt to come in.

They now had both food and water, and would camp somewhere out on the plain.

"I will sleep," he decided.

Mali-ya-bwana at once thrust the savages outside, without ceremony, peremptorily. When the *bwana* of an African belonging to the safari class wants anything, the latter gets it for him. The headman of the author of these lines went single handed and stopped in its very inception a royal *n'goma*, or dance, to which men had come a day's journey, merely because his *bwana* wanted to sleep! Kingozi was here alone, in a strange country, for the moment helpless; but Mali-ya-bwana hustled the tribesmen out as brusquely as though a regiment were at his back. Which undoubtedly had its effect.

Kingozi sat down on the straw and blew out his lantern. The wattle walls were not chinked; so the sweet night wind blew through freely; and elusively he saw stars against the night. The Leopard Woman breathed heavily in little sighs. He was not sleepy. Then everything went black——

When Kingozi awakened it was full daylight. A varied murmur came happily from outside, what the Africans call a *kalele*—a compound of chatter, the noise of occupation, of movement, the inarticulate voice of human existence. He glanced across the hut. The Leopard Woman was gone.

"Boy!" he shouted.

At the sound of his voice the *kalele* ceased. Almost

immediately Cazi Moto stooped to enter the doorway.
Cazi Moto was dressed in clean khaki, and bore in his hand
a *balauri* of steaming tea. Kingozi seized this and drained
it to the bottom.

"That is good," he commented gratefully. "I did not
expect to see you, Cazi Moto.   Did all the men get in?"

"Yes, *bwana*."

"*Vema !* And the men of the Leopard Woman?"

"Many died, *bwana;* but many are here."

Kingozi arose to his feet.

"I must have food.   These *shenzis* eat what?"

"Food is ready, *bwana*."

"I will eat.   Then we must make *shauri* with these people
to get our loads.   My men must rest to-day."

"Come, *bwana*," said Cazi Moto.

Kingozi stooped to pass through the door.   When he
straightened outside, he paused in amazement.   Before
him stood his camp, intact.   The green tent with the fly
faced him, the flaps thrown back to show within his cot
and tin box.   White porters' tents had been pitched in the
usual circle, and before each squatted men cooking over
little fires.   The loads, covered by the tarpaulin, had been
arranged in the centre of the circle.   At a short distance
to the rear the cook camp steamed.

Cazi Moto stood at his elbow grinning.

"Hot water ready, *bwana*," said he; and for the first time
Kingozi noticed that he carried a towel over his arm.

"This is good, very good, Cazi Moto!" said he. "*Back-sheeshi m'kubwa* for this; both for you and for Simba."

"Thank you, *bwana*," said Cazi Moto. "Simba brought the water, and it saved us; and I thought that my *bwana* should not sleep on grass a second time before these *shenzis*."

"Who carried in the loads? Not our porters?"

"No, *bwana*, the *shenzis*."

Kingozi glanced at his wrist watch. It was only ten o'clock.

"When?"

"Last night."

"They went back last night?"

"Yes, *bwana*. Mali-ya-bwana considered that it was bad to leave the loads. There might be hyenas—or the *shenzis*——"

Kingozi slapped his thigh with satisfaction. This was a man after his own heart.

"Call Mali-ya-bwana," he ordered.

The tall Baganda approached.

"Mali-ya-bwana," said Kingozi. "You have done well. For this you shall have *backsheeshi*. But more. You need not again carry a load. You will be——" he hesitated, trying to invent an office, but reluctant to infringe upon the prerogatives of either Simba or Cazi Moto. "You will be headman of the porters; and you, Cazi Moto, will be headman of all the safari, and my own man besides."

The Baganda drew himself erect, his face shining. Placing his bare heels together, he raised his hand in a military salute. Kingozi was about to dismiss him, but this arrested his intention.

"Where did you learn to do that?" he asked sharply.

"I was once in the King's African Rifles."*

"You can shoot, then?"

"Yes, *bwana*."

"Good!" commented Kingozi thoughtfully. Then after a moment: *"Bassi."*

Mali-ya-bwana saluted once more and departed. Kingozi turned toward his tent.

It had been pitched under a huge tree, with low, massive limbs and a shade that covered a diameter of fully sixty yards. Before it the usual table had been made of piled-up chop boxes, and to this Cazi Moto was bearing steaming dishes. The threatened headache had not materialized, and Kingozi was feeling quite fit. He was ravenously hungry, for now his system was rested enough to assimilate food. His last meal had been breakfast before sunup of the day before. Without paying even casual attention to his surroundings he seated himself on a third chop box and began to eat.

Kingozi's methods of eating had in them little of the epicure. He simply ate all he wanted of the first things set before him. After this he drank all he wanted from the

_____

*Only, of course, Mali-ya-bwana gave the native name for these troops.

tall *balauri*. Second courses did not exist for Kingozi.
Then with a sigh of satisfaction he fumbled for his pipe
and tobacco, and looked about him.

The guest house had been built, as was the custom, a
little apart from the main village. The latter was evidently
around the bend of the hill, for only three or four huts were
to be seen, perched among the huge outcropping boulders
that were, apparently, characteristic of these hills. The
mountains rose rather abruptly, just beyond the plateau;
which, in turn, fell away almost as abruptly to the sweep
of the plains. The bench was of considerable width—
probably a mile at this point. It was not entirely level;
but on the other hand not particularly broken. A number
of fine, symmetrical trees of unknown species grew at wide
intervals, overtopping a tangle of hedges, rank bushes,
vines, and shrubs that appeared to constitute a rough sort
of boundary between irregular fields. A tiny swift stream
of water hurried by between the straight banks of an obviously artificial ditch.

But though the village was hidden from view, its inhabitants were not. They had invaded the camp. Kingozi
examined them keenly, with curiosity. Naked little boys
and girls wandered gravely about; women clung together
in groups; men squatted on their heels before anything
that struck their attention, and stared.

These people, Kingozi noted, were above middle size, of
a red bronze, of the Semitic rather than the Hamitic type,

well developed but not obviously muscular, of a bright and lively expression. The women shaved their heads quite bare; the men left a sort of skull cap of hair atop the head. Earlobes were pierced and stretched to hold ivory ornaments running up to the size of a jampot. There were some, but not many, armlets, leglets, and necklets of iron wire polished to the appearance of silver. The women wore brief skirts of softened skins: the men carried a short shoulder cape, or simply nothing at all. Each man bore a long-bladed heavy spear. Before squatting down in front of whatever engaged his attention for the moment, the savage thrust this upright in the ground. Kingozi, behind his pipe, considered them well: and received a favourable impression.

An immovable, unblinking semicircle crouched at a respectful distance taking in every detail of the white man's appearance and belongings, watching his every move. Nobody spoke; apparently nobody even winked.

Now appeared across the prospect two men walking. One was an elderly savage, with a wrinkled, shrewd countenance. He was almost completely enveloped in a robe of softened skins. Followed him a younger man, dangling at the end of a thong a small three-legged stool cut entire from a single block of wood. The old man swept forward with considerable dignity; the younger, one hand held high in the most affected fashion, teetered gracefully along as mincingly as any dandy.

The visitor came superbly up to where Kingozi sat, and uttered a greeting in Swahili. He proved to possess a grand, deep, thunderous voice.

"*Jambo!*" he rolled.

Kingozi stared up at him coolly for a moment; then, without removing his pipe from his teeth, he remarked:

"*Jambo!*"

The old man, smiling, extended his hand.*

Kingozi, nursing the bowl of his pipe, continued to stare up at him.

"Are you the *sultani?*" he demanded abruptly.

The old man waved his hand in courtly fashion.

"I am not the *sultani*," he answered in very bad Swahili; "I am the headman of the *sultani.*"

Kingozi continued to stare at him in the most uncompromising manner.   In the meantime the younger man had loosed the thong from his wrist and had placed the stool on a level spot.   The prime minister to the *sultani* arranged his robe preparatory to sitting down.

Kingozi removed his pipe from his lips, and sat erect.

"Stand up!" he commanded sharply.   "If you are not the *sultani* how dare you sit down before me!"

The youth whisked the stool away: the old man covered his discomfiture in a flow of talk. Kingozi listened to him in silence. The visitor concluded his remarks which—as far as they could be understood—were entirely general:

---

*Many African tribes shake hands in one way or another.

and, with a final courtly wave of the hand, turned away. Then Kingozi spoke, abruptly, curtly.

"Have your people bring me eggs," he said, "milk, *m'wembe.*"*

The old man, somewhat abashed, made the most dignified retreat possible through the keenly attentive audience of his own people.

Kingozi gazed after him, his blue eyes wide with their peculiar aggressive blank stare. A low hum of conversation swept through the squatting warriors. Those who understood Swahili murmured eagerly to those who did not. These uttered politely the long drawn "$\bar{\text{A}}$-$\bar{\text{a}}$-$\bar{\text{a}}$-$\bar{\text{a}}$!" of savage interest.

"Cazi Moto, where is my chair?" Kingozi demanded, abruptly conscious that the chop box was not very comfortable.

"Bibi-ya-chui has it."

"Where is she?"

"Right behind you," came that young woman's voice in amused tones. "You have been so busy that you have not seen me."

Kingozi turned. The chair had been placed in a bare spot close to the trunk of the great tree. He grinned cheerfully.

"I was pretty hungry," he confessed, "and I don't believe I saw a single thing but that curry!"

*A sort of flour ground from rape seeds.

"Naturally. It is not to be wondered at. Are you all rested?"

"I'm quite fit, thanks. And you?"

She was still in her marching costume; but her hair had been smoothed, her face washed. The colour had come back to her lips, the light to her expression. Only a faint dark encircling of the eyes, and a certain graceful languor of attitude recalled the collapse of yesterday.

"Oh, I am all right; but perishing for a cigarette. Have you one?"

"Sorry, but I don't use them. Are not all your loads up yet?"

"None of them."

"Well, they should be in shortly. Cazi Moto has given you breakfast, of course."

"Yes. But nobody has yet gone for my loads."

"What!" exclaimed Kingozi sharply. "Why did you not start men for them when you first awakened?'

She smiled at him ruefully.

"I tried. But they said they were very tired from yesterday. They would not go."

"Simba!" called Kingozi.

"Suh!"

"Bring the headman of Bibi-ya-chui. Is he that mop-headed blighter?" he asked her.

"Who? Oh, the Nubian, Chaké. No; he is just a faithful creature near myself. I have no headman."

"Who takes your orders, then?"

"The *askaris*."

"Which one?"

"Any of them." She made a mouth. "Don't look at me in that fashion. Is that so very dreadful?"

"It's impossible. You can never run a safari in that way. Simba, bring all the *askaris*."

Simba departed on his errand. Kingozi turned to her gravely.

"Dear lady," said he gravely, "I am going to offend you again. But this won't do. You are a wonderful woman; but you do not know this game well enough. I acknowledge you will handle this show ordinarily in tiptop style; but in a new country, in contact with new peoples—it's a specialist's job, that's all."

"I'm beginning to think so," she replied with unexpected humility.

"Already you've lost control of your organization: you nearly died from lack of water—— By the way, why didn't you push ahead with your Nubian, and find the water?"

"I had to get my men on."

He looked on her with more approval.

"Well, you're safe out of it. And now, I beg of you, don't do it any more."

"Is my little scolding all done?" she asked after a pause.

"Forgive me. I did not mean it as a scolding."

She sat upright and rested her elbows on her knees, her chin in her hands. Her long sea-green eyes softened.

"Listen: I deserve that what you say. I thought I knew, because always I have travelled in a good country. But never the hell of a dry country. I want you to know that you are quite right, and I want to tell you that I know you saved me and my men: and I would not know what to do now if you were not here to help me. There!" she made a pretty outward-flinging gesture. "Is that enough?"

Kingozi, like most men whose natural efficiency has been hardened by wide experience, while impervious to either open or wily antagonism, melted at the first hint of surrender. A wave of kindly feeling overwhelmed the last suspicions—absurd suspicions—his analysis had made. He was prevented from replying by the approach of Simba at the head of eight of the *askaris*. They slouched along at his heels, sullen and careless, but when they felt the impact of Kingozi's cold glare, they straightened to attention. Kingozi ran his eye over them.

"Where are the other four?" he demanded.

"Three are in the *shenzis*' village. One says he is very tired."

"Take Mali-ya-bwana and Cazi Moto. Take the leg chains. Bring that one man before me with the chains on him. Have him bring also his gun; and his cartridges."

Ignoring the waiting eight, Kingozi resumed his conversation with the Leopard Woman.

"They are out of hand," said he. "We must impress them."

"*Kiboko?*" she inquired.

"Perhaps—but you have rather overdone that. We shall see."

"I heard you talk with that old man a few moments ago," she said. "And I heard also much talk of our men about it. He is a very powerful chief—next to the *sultani.* Are not you afraid that your treatment of him will make trouble? You were not polite."

"What else have you heard?"

"This *sultani* has apparently several hundred villages. They keep goats, fat-tailed sheep, and some few cattle. They raise *m'wembe*, beans, peanuts, and bananas. They have a war caste of young men."

Kingozi listened to her attentively.

"Good girl!" said he. "You use your intelligence. These are all good points to know."

"But this old man——"

"No; I have not insulted him. I know the native mind. I have merely convinced him that I am every bit as important a person as his *sultani.*"

"What do you do next? Call on the *sultani.*"

"By no means. Wait until he comes. If he does not come by, say to-morrow, send for him."

Simba appeared leading a downcast *askari* in irons. Kingozi waved his hand toward those waiting in the sun; and the new captive made the ninth.

"Now, Simba, go to the village of these *shenzis*. Tell the other three *askaris* to come; and at once. Do not return without them."

Simba, whose fierce soul all this delighted beyond expression, started off joyfully, trailed by a posse of his own choosing.

"What are you going to do?" asked the Leopard Woman curiously.

"Get them in line a bit," replied Kingozi carelessly. "I feel rather lazy and done up to-day; don't you?"

"That is so natural. And I am keeping your chair——"

"I've been many trips without one. This tree is good to lean against——"

They chatted about trivial matters. A certain ease had crept into their relations: a guard had been lowered. To a small extent they ventured to question each other, to indulge in those tentative explorations of personality so fascinating in the early stages of acquaintanceship. To her inquiries Kingozi repeated that he was an ivory hunter and trader; he came into this country because new country alone offered profits in ivory these days; he had been in Africa for fifteen years. At this last she looked him over closely.

"You came out very young," she surmised.

"When my father took me out of the medical school to put me into the ministry. I had a knack for doctoring. I ran away."

"Why did you come to Africa?"

"Didn't particularly. Started for Iceland on a whaling ship. Sailed the seven seas after the brutes. Landed on the Gold Coast—and got left behind."

She looked at him hard, and he laughed.

"'Left' with my kit and about sixty pounds I had hung on to since I left home—my own money, mind you! *And a harpoon gun!* Lord!" he laughed again, "think of it—a harpoon gun! You loaded it with about a peck of black powder. Normally, of course, it shot a harpoon, but you could very near cram a nigger baby down it! And kick! If you were the least bit off balance it knocked you flat. It was the most extraordinary cannon ever seen in Africa, and it inspired more respect, acquired me more *kudos* than even my beard."

"So *that's* why you wear it!" she murmured.

"What?"

"Nothing; go on."

"Just the sight of that awe-inspiring piece of ordnance took me the length of the Congo without the least difficulty."

"Tell me about the Congo."

Apparently, at this direct and comprehensive question, there was nothing to tell about the Congo. But adroitly she drew him on. He told of the great river and its people, and the white men who administered it. The subject of cannibals seemed especially to fascinate her. He had seen living human beings issued as a sort of ration on the hoof to native cannibal troops.

Simba returned with the other three *askaris*.

Kingozi arose from the ground and stretched himself.

"I'm sorry," said he, "I'm afraid I shall have to ask you for the chair now."

She arose, wondering a little. He placed the chair before the waiting line of *askaris*, and planted himself squarely in it as in a judgment seat. He ran his eye over the men deliberately.

"You!" said he suddenly, pointing his forefinger at the man in irons. "You have disobeyed my orders. You are no longer an *askari*. You are a common porter, and from now on will carry a load. It is not my custom to use *kiboko* on *askaris;* but a common porter can eat *kiboko*, and Mali-ya-bwana, my headman of safari, will give you twenty-five lashes. *Bassi !*"

Mali-ya-bwana, well pleased thus early to exercise the authority of his new office, led the man away.

Kingozi dropped his chin in his hand, a movement that pushed out his beard in a terrifying manner. One after another of the eleven men felt the weight of his stare. At last he spoke.

"I have heard tales of you," said he, "but I who speak

know nothing about you. You are *askaris*, soldiers with guns, and next to gun bearers are the greatest men in the safari. Some have told me that you are not *askaris*, that you are common porters—and not good ones—who carry guns. I do not know. That we shall see. This is what must be done now, and done quickly: the loads of your *memsahib* must be brought here, and camp made properly, according to the custom. Perhaps your men are no longer tired: perhaps you will get the *shenzis*. That is not my affair. You understand?"

The answer came in an eager chorus.

He ran his eye over them again.

"You," he indicated, "stand forward. Of what tribe are you?"

"Monumwezi, *bwana*."

"Your name?"

The man uttered a mouthful of gutturals.

"Again.'

He repeated.

"That is not a good name for me. From now on you are—Jack."

"Yes, *bwana*."

"Do you know the customs of *askaris* ?"

"Yes, *bwana*."

"H'm," Kingozi commented in English, "nobody would guess it. Then understand this: You are headman of *askaris*. You take the orders: you report to me—or the *memsahib*," he added, almost as an afterthought. "To-morrow morning *fall in*, and I will look at your guns. *Bassi !*"

They filed away. Kingozi arose and returned the chair.

"Is that all you will do to them?" she demanded. "I tell you they have insulted me; they have refused to move; they should be punished."

"That's all. They understand now what will happen. You will see: they will not refuse again."

She appeared to struggle against a flare of her old rebellious spirit.

"I will leave it to you," she managed at last.

The squatting savages had not moved a muscle, but their shining black eyes had not missed a single detail.

CHAPTER X

THE SULTANI

Six hours later the Leopard Woman's camp had arrived, had been pitched, and everything was running again as usual. The new *askari* headman, Jack, had reported pridefully to Kingozi. The latter had nodded a careless acknowledgment; and had referred the man to his mistress. She had disappeared for a time, but now emerged again, bathed, freshened, dainty in her silken tea gown, the braids of hair down her back, the band of woven gold encircling her brow, the single strange jewel hanging in the middle of her forehead. For a time she sat alone under her own tree; but, as Kingozi showed no symptoms of coming to her, and as she was bored and growing impatient, she trailed over to him, the Nubian following with her chair. Kingozi was absorbed in establishing points on his map. He looked up at her and nodded pleasantly, then moved his protractor a few inches.

"Just a moment," he murmured absorbedly.

She lit a cigarette and yawned. The immediate prospect was dull. Savages continued to drift in, to squat and stare, then to move on to the porters' camps. There a lively bartering was going on. From some unsuspected store each porter had drawn forth a few beads, some snuff, a length of wire, or similar treasure; and with them was making the best bargain he could for the delicacies of the country. The process was noisy. Four *askaris*, with their guns, stood on guard. The shadows were lengthening in the hills, and the heat waves had ceased to shimmer like veils.

"That's done," said Kingozi at last.

"Thank the Lord!" she ejaculated. "This bores me. Why do we not do something? I should like some milk, some eggs—many things. Let us summon this king."

But Kingozi shook his head.

"That's all very well where the white man's influence reaches. But not here. I doubt if there are three men in this people who have ever even seen a white man. Of course they have all heard of us, and know a good deal about us. We must stand on our dignity here. Let the *sultani* come to us, all in his own time. Without his goodwill we cannot move a step farther, we cannot get a pound of *potio*."

"How long will it take? I want to get on. This does not interest me. I have seen many natives."

Kingozi smiled.

"Two days of visit. Then perhaps a week to get *potio* and guides."

"Impossible! I could not endure it!"

"I am afraid you will have to. I know the untamed savage. He is inclined to be friendly, always. If you hurry the process, you must fight. That's the trouble with a big mob like yours. It is difficult to feed so many peacefully. Even in a rich country they bring in *potio* slowly— a cupful at a time. With the best intentions in the world you may have to use coercion to keep from starving. And coercion means trouble. Look at Stanley—he left hostilities everywhere, that have lasted up to now. The people were well enough disposed when he came among them with his six or eight hundred men. But he had to have food and he had to have it quickly. He could not wait for slow, diplomatic methods. He had to *take* it. Even when you pay for a thing, that doesn't work. The news travelled ahead of him, and the result was he had to fight. And everybody else has had to fight ever since."

"That is interesting. I did not know that."

"A small party can negotiate. That's why I say you have too many men."

"But the time wasted!" she cried aghast.

"Time is nothing in Africa." He went on to tell her of the two travellers in Rhodesia who came upon a river so wide that they could but just see from one bank to the other; and so swift that rafts were of little avail. So one man went back for a folding boat while the other camped by the stream. Four months later the first man returned with the boat. The "river" had dried up completely!

"They didn't mind," said Kingozi, "they thought it a huge joke."

An hour before sundown signs of activity manifested themselves from the direction of the invisible village. A thin, high, wailing chant in female voices came fitfully to their ears. A compact little group of men rounded the bend and approached. Their gait was slow and stately.

"Well," remarked Kingozi, feeling for his pipe, "we are going to be honoured by that visit from his majesty."

The Leopard Woman leaned forward and surveyed the approaching men with some interest. They were four in number. Three were naked, their bodies oiled until they glistened with a high polish. One of them carried a battered old canvas steamer chair; one a fan of ostrich plumes; and one a long gourd heavily decorated with cowrie shells. The fourth was an impressive individual in middle life, hawkfaced, tall and spare, carrying himself with great dignity. He wore a number of anklets and armlets of polished wire, a broad beaded collar, heavy earrings, and a sumptuous robe of softened goatskins embroidered with beads and cowrie shells. As he strode his anklets clashed softly. His girt was free, and he walked with authority. Altogether an impressive figure.

"The *sultani* is a fine-looking man," observed Bibi-ya-chui. "I suppose the others are slaves."

Kingozi threw a careless glance in the direction of the approaching group.

"Not the *sultani*—some understrapper. Chief Heredi-
tary Guardian of the Royal Chair, or something of that
sort, I dare say."

The tall man approached, smiling graciously. Kingozi
vouchsafed him no attention. Visibly impressed, the new-
comer rather fussily superintended the unfolding and placing of the chair. The slaves with the plumed fan and the
gourd stationed themselves at either side. The other two
men fell back.

Now the shrill chanting became more clearly audible.
Shortly appeared a procession. Women bearing burdens
walked two by two. Armed men with spears and shields
flanked them. As they approached, it could be seen that
they were very gorgeous indeed; the women hung with
strings of cowries, bound with glittering brass and iron, bedecked with strings of beads. To one familiar with savage
peoples there could be no doubt that these were close to the
purple. Each bead, each shell, each bangle of wire had
been passed through many, many hands before it reached
this remote fastness of barbarity; and in each hand, you
may be sure, profits had remained. But the men were
more impressive still. Stark naked of every stitch of cloth
or of tanned skins, oiled with an unguent carrying a dull red
stain, their heads shaved bare save for a small crown patch
from which single feathers floated, they symbolized well the
warrior stripped for the fray. A beaded broad belt supported a short sword and the *runga*, or war club; an oval

shield of buffalo hide, brilliantly painted, hung on the left arm; a polished long-bladed spear was carried in the right hand. And surrounding the face, as a frame, was a queer headdress of black ostrich plumes. Every man of them wore about his ankles hollow bangles of considerable size; and these he clashed loudly one against the other as he walked.

It made a great uproar this—the clang of the iron, the wild wailing of the women's voices.

Kingozi moved his chair four or five paces to the front.

"I'm sorry," he told her, "but I must ask you to stay where you are. This is an important occasion."

He surveyed the oncoming procession with interest.

"Swagger old beggar," he observed. "His guard are well turned out. You know those markings on the shields are a true heraldry—the patterns mean families, and all that sort of thing."

The chanting grew louder as the procession neared. The warriors stared fiercely straight ahead. Before Kingozi they parted to right and left, forming an aisle leading to his chair. Down this the women came, one by one, still singing, and deposited their burdens at the white man's feet. There were baskets of *m'wembe*, earthen bowls of eggs, fowls, gourds of milk, bundles of faggots and firewood, woven bags of *n'jugu* nuts, vegetables, and two small sheep. Kingozi stared indifferently into the distance; but as each gift was added to the others he reached forward to touch it as a sign of acceptance. Their burdens deposited, they took their places in front of the ranks of the warriors.

"Am I supposed to speak?" asked the Leopard Woman.

"Surely."

"Shouldn't we order out our *askaris* with their guns to make the parade?"

"No. We could not hope to equal this show, possibly. Our lay is to do the supercilious indifferent." He turned to his attentive satellite. "Cazi Moto," he ordered, "tell our people, quietly, to go back to their camps. They must not stand and stare at these *shenzis*. And tell M'pishi to make large *balauris* of coffee, and put in plenty of sugar."

Cazi Moto grinned understandingly, and glided away. Shortly the safari men could be seen sauntering unconcernedly back to their little fires.

Suddenly the warriors cried out in a loud voice, and raised their right arms and spears rigidly above their heads. A tall, heavily built man appeared around the bend. He was followed by two young women, who flanked him by a pace or so to the rear. They were so laden with savage riches as to be almost concealed beneath the strings of cowrie shells and bands of beads. In contrast the man wore only a long black cotton blanket draped to leave one shoulder and arm bare. Not an earring, not a bangle, not even a finger ring or a bead strap relieved the sombre simplicity of the black robe and the dark skin.

"But this man is an artist!" murmured Bibi-ya-chui. "He understands effect! This is stage managed!"

The *sultani* approached without haste. He stopped squarely before Kingozi's chair. The latter did not rise. The two men stared into each other's eyes for a full minute, without embarrassment, without contest, without defiance. Then the black man spoke.

"*Jambo, bwana,*" he rumbled in a deep voice.

"*Jambo, sultani,*" replied Kingozi calmly.

They shook hands.

With regal deliberation the visitor arranged his robes and sat down in the battered old canvas chair. A silence that lasted nearly five minutes ensued.

"I thank you, *sultani*, for the help your men have given. I thank you for the houses. I thank you for these gifts."

The *sultani* waved his hand magnificently.

"It is not the custom of white men to give gifts until their departure," continued Kingozi, "but this knife is yours to make friendship."

He handed over a knife, of Swedish manufacture, the blade of which disappeared into the handle in a most curious fashion. The *sultani's* eyes lit up with an almost childish delight, but his countenance showed no emotion. He passed the knife on to the dignitary who stood behind his chair.

"This," said Kingozi, taking one of the steaming *balauris* from Cazi Moto, "is the white man's *tembo*."

The *sultani* tasted doubtfully. He was pleased. He gave
back the *balauri* at last with a final smack of the lips.

"Good!" said he.

Another full five minutes of silence ensued. Then the
sultani arose. He cast a glance about him, his eye, avid
with curiosity, held rigidly in restraint. It rested on the
Leopard Woman.

"I see you have one of your women with you," he remarked.

He turned, without further ceremony, and stalked off,
followed at a few paces by the two richly ornamented girls.
The warriors again raised their spears aloft, holding them
thus until their lord had rounded the cliff. Then, the
women in precedence, they marched away. Kingozi puffed
his pipe indifferently.

The Leopard Woman was visibly impatient, visibly
roused.

"Are you letting him go?" she demanded. "Do not
you inquire the country? Do not you ask for *potio*, for
guides?"

"Not to-day," replied Kingozi. He turned deliberately
to face her, his eyes serious. "Please realize once for all
that we live here only by force of *prestige*. My only chance
of getting on, our only chance of safety rests on my ability
to impress this man with the idea that I am a bigger lord
than he. And, remember, I have lived in savage Africa
for fifteen years, and I know what I am doing. This is

very serious. You must not interfere; and you must not suggest."

The Leopard Woman's eyes glittered dangerously, but she controlled herself.

"You talk like a sultan yourself," she protested at length. "You should not use that tone to me."

Kingozi brushed the point aside with a large gesture.

"I will play the game of courtesy with you, yes," said he, "but only when it does not interfere with serious things. In this matter there must be no indefiniteness, no chance for misunderstanding. Politeness, between the sexes, means both. I will repeat: in this you must leave me free hand —no interference, no suggestion."

"And if I disobey your commands?" she challenged, with an emphasis on the last word.

He surveyed her sombrely.

"I should take measures," he replied finally.

"You are not my master: you are not the master of my men!"

Kingozi permitted himself a slight smile.

"If you believe that last statement, just try to give an order to your men counter to an order of mine. You would see. And of course in case of a real crisis I should have to make myself master of you, if you seemed likely to be troublesome."

"I would kill you! I warn you; I go always armed!"

From the folds of her silken robe she produced a small

automatic pistol which she displayed. Kingozi glanced at it indifferently.

"In that case you would have to kill yourself, too; and then it would not matter to either of us."

"I find you insufferable!" she cried, getting to her feet.

She moved away in the direction of her camp. The faithful Nubian folded her chair and followed. At the doorway of her tent she looked back. Kingozi, his black pipe in his mouth, was bending absorbedly over his map.

CHAPTER XI

THE IVORY STOCKADE

The Leopard Woman, emerging from her tent shortly after sunup the next morning, saw across the opening her own *askaris* being drilled by Kingozi, Simba, and Cazi Moto. Evidently the instruction was in rifle fire. Two were getting individual treatment: Simba and Cazi Moto were putting them through a careful course in aiming and pulling the trigger on empty guns. Kingozi sat on a chop box in the shade, gripping his eternal pipe, and issuing curt orders and criticisms to the baker's dozen before him. When he saw the Leopard Woman he arose and strolled in her direction.

"That's the worst lot of so-called *askaris* I ever saw," he remarked. "Where did you pick them up?"

His manner was entirely unconscious of any discussions or dissentions. He looked into her eyes and smiled genially.

"I took them from the recruiting man, as they came," she replied. As always the deeps of her eyes were enigmatical; but the surfaces, at least, of her mood answered his.

"They know how to load a gun, and that is about all. I don't believe one of them ever fired a weapon before this

trip. They haven't the most rudimentary ideas of aiming. Don't even know what sights are for. My boys
will soon whip them into some sort of shape. I came over
to see how much ammunition you have for their muskets.
They really ought to fire a few rounds—after a week of
aiming and snapping. Then they'll be of some use. Not
much, though."

"I really don't know," she answered his question.
"Chaké will look and see."

"Send him over to report when he finds out," requested
Kingozi, preparing to return.

"What move does your wisdom contemplate to-day?"
she called after him.

"Oh, return his majesty's visit this afternoon. Like
to go?"

"Certainly."

"Well, I'll let you know when. And if you go, you must
be content to stand two or three yards behind me, and
to say nothing."

She flushed, but answered steadily enough:

"I'll remember."

It was nearing sundown when Kingozi emerged from
his tent and gave the signal to move. He had for the
first time strapped on a heavy revolver; his glasses hung
from his neck; his sleeve was turned back to show his wrist
watch; and, again for the first time, he had assumed a
military-looking tunic. He carried his double rifle.

"Got on everything I own," he grinned.

Simba and Cazi Moto waited near.   From the mysterious sources every native African seems to possess they had produced new hats and various trinkets.   Their khakis had been fresh washed; so they looked neat and trim.

The Leopard Woman wore still one of her silken negligées, and the jewel on her forehead; but her hair had been piled high on her head.   Kingozi surveyed her with some particularity.   She noted the fact.   Her satisfaction would have diminished could she have read his mind.   He was thinking that her appearance was sufficiently barbaric to impress a barbaric king.

They rounded the point of cliffs, and the village lay before them.   It rambled up the side of the mountain, hundreds of beehive houses perched and clinging, with paths from one to the other.   The approach was through a narrow straight lane of thorn and aloes, so thick and so spiky that no living thing bigger than a mouse could have forced its way through the walls.   The end of this vista was a heavy palisade of timbers through which a door led into a circular enclosure ten feet in diameter, on the other side of which another door opened into the village.   Above each of these doors massive timbers were suspended ready to fall at the cut of a sword.   Within the little enclosure, or double gate, squatted a man before a great drum.

"They're pretty well fixed here," observed Kingozi

critically. "Nobody can get at them except down that lane. The mountains are impassable because of the thorn. They must use arrows."

"Why?" asked the Leopard Woman.

"The form of their defence. They shoot between the logs of the palisade down the narrow lane. If they fought only with spears, the lane would be shorter, and it would be defended on the flank."

"Why don't they defend it on the flank also, even with arrows?" asked the Leopard Woman shrewdly.

"'It is not the custom,'" wearily quoted Kingozi in the vernacular. "Don't ask me *why* a savage does things. I only know he does."

Their conversation was drowned by the sound of the drum.

The guardian did not beat it, but rubbed the head rapidly with the stick, modifying the pressure scientifically until the vibrations had well started. It roared hollowly, like some great bull.

The visitors passed through the defensive anteroom and entered the village enclosure.

On the flat below the hills, heretofore invisible, stood a half-dozen large houses. At the end, where the cañon began to narrow, a fence gleamed dazzlingly white. From this distance the four-foot posts, planted in proximity like a stockade, looked to have been whitewashed.

People were appearing everywhere. The crags **and**

points of the hills were filling with bold black figures silhouetted against the sky. Men, women, children, dogs
sprang up, from the soil apparently. As though by magic
the flat open space became animated. Plumed heads appeared above the white fence in the distance, where, undoubtedly, their owners had been loafing in the shade. Another drum began to roar somewhere, and with it the echoes
began to arouse themselves in the hills.

Paying no attention to any of this interesting confusion
Kingozi sauntered straight ahead. At his command the
Leopard Woman had dropped a pace to the rear.

"The royal palace is behind the white fence," he volunteered over his shoulder.

They approached the sacred precincts. But while yet
fifty yards distant, Kingozi stopped with an exclamation.
He turned to the Leopard Woman, and for the first time
she saw on his face and in his eyes a genuine and uncon-
cealed excitement.

"My Lord!" he cried to her, "saw ever any man the likes
of that!"

The white posts of which the fence was made were elephants' tusks!

"Kingdom coming, what a sight!" murmured Kingozi.
"Why, there are hundreds and hundreds of them—and the
smallest worth not less than fifty pounds!"

Her eyes answered him whole-heartedly, for her imagination was afire.

"What magnificence!" she replied. "The thought is great—a palace of ivory! This is kingly!"

But the light had died in Kingozi's eyes. "Won't do!" he muttered to her. "Compose your face. Come."

Without another glance at the magnificent tusks he marched on through the open gate.

Other drums, many drums, were roaring all about. The cliff of the cañon was filled with sound that buffeted back and forth until it seemed that it must rise above the hills and overflow the world. A chattering and hurrying of people could be heard as an undertone.

The small enclosure was occupied by a dozen of the plumed warriors who had now snatched up emblazoned shield and polished spear; and stood rigidly at attention. Women of all ages crouched and squatted against the fence and the sides of a large wattle and thatch building.

Kingozi walked deliberately about, looking with detached interest at the various people and objects the corral contained. He had very much the air of a man sauntering idly about a museum, with all the time in the world on his hands, and nowhere much to go. Simba and Cazi Moto remained near the gate. The Leopard Woman, not knowing what else to do, trailed after him.

This continued for some time. At last her impatience overcame her.

"I suppose I may talk," said she resentfully. "How

much longer must this go on? Why do not you make your
call and have it over?"

Kingozi laughed.

"You do not know this game. Inside old Stick-in-the
mud is waiting in all his grandeur. He expects me to go
in to him. I am going to wait until he comes out to me.
Prestige again."

Apparently without a care in the world, he continued his
stroll. Small naked children ventured from hiding-places
and stared. To some of these Kingozi spoke pleasantly
with the immediate effect of causing them to scuttle back
to cover. He examined minutely the tusks comprising
the stockade. They had been arranged somewhat according to size, with the curve outward. Kingozi spent some
time estimating them.

"Fortune here for some one," he observed.

At the end of an hour the *sultani* gave up the contest and
appeared, smiling, unconcerned. The men greeted each
other, exchanged a few words. Women emerged from the
house carrying *tembo* in gourd bottles, and smaller half-
gourds from which to drink it. Their eyes were large with
curiosity as to this man and woman of a new species.
Kingozi touched his lips to the *tembo*. They exchanged a
few words, and shook hands again. Then Kingozi turned
away, and, followed by the Leopard Woman and his two
men, walked out through the ivory gateway, down through
the open flat, under the fortified portal, and so down the

lane of spiky walls.   The drums roared louder and louder.
Warriors in spear, shield, and plumed headdress stood rigid
as they passed.   People by the hundreds gazed at them
openly, peered at them from behind doors, or looked down
on them from the crags above.   They rounded the corner
of the cliff.   Before them lay their own quiet peaceful camp.
Only the voice of the drums bellowed as though behind
them in the cleft of the hills some great and savage beast
lay hid.

"That seemed to be all right," suggested the Leopard
Woman, ranging alongside again.

"They didn't spear us, if that's what you mean.   We
can tell more about it to-morrow."

"What will happen to-morrow?"

"Yesterday and to-day finished the 'side' and ceremony.
If to-morrow old Stick-in-the-mud drifts around quite on
his own, like any other *shenzi*, and if the women come into
camp freely, why then we're all right."

"And otherwise?"

"Well, if the *sultani* stays away, and if you don't see any
women at all, and if the men are painted and carry their
shields—they will always carry their spears—that won't be
so favourable."

"In which case we fight?"

"No: I'll alter my diplomacy.   There's a vast difference
between mere unfriendliness and hostility.   I think I can
handle the former all right.   I wish I knew a little more of

" Their eyes were large with curiosity as to this man and woman of a new species. . . .
Kingozi touched his lips to the *tembo*"

their language. Swahili hardly fills the bill. I'll see what I can do with it in the next few days."

"You cannot learn a language in a few days!" she objected incredulously.

"Of course not. But I seem to know the general root idea of this patter. It isn't unlike the N'gruimi—same root likely—a bastard combination of Bantu-Masai stock."

She looked at him.

"You know," she told him slowly, "I am beginning to believe you *savant*. You make not much of it, but your knowledge of natives is extraordinary. You better than any other man know these people—their minds—how to influence them."

"I have a little knowledge of how to go at them, that's true. That's about the only claim I have to being *savant*, as you call it. My book knowledge and fact knowledge is equalled by many and exceeded by a great many more. But mere knowledge of facts doesn't get far in practice," he laughed. "Lord, these scientists! Helpless as children!" He sobered again. "There's one man has the science and the psychology both. He's a wonderful person. He knows the native objectively as I never will; and subjectively as well if not better. It is a rare combination. He's 'way over west of us somewhere now—in the Congo headwaters—a Bavarian, name Winkleman."

Had Kingozi been looking at her he would have seen the

Leopard Woman's frame stiffen at the mention of this name. For a moment she said nothing.

"I know the name—he is great scientist," she managed to say.

"He is more than a scientist; he is a great humanist. No man has more insight, more sympathetic insight into the native mind. A man of vast influence."

They had reached Kingozi's camp under the great tree. He began to unbuckle his equipment.

"I'll just lay all this gorgeousness aside," said he apologetically.

But the Leopard Woman did not proceed to her own camp.

"I am interested," said she. "This Winkleman—he has vast influence? More than yourself?"

"That is hard to say," laughed Kingozi. "I should suppose so."

She caught at a hint of reluctant pride in his voice.

"Let us suppose," said she. "Let us suppose that you wanted one thing of natives, and Winkleman wanted another thing. Which would succeed?"

"Neither. We'd both be speared," replied Kingozi promptly. "Positive and negative poles, and all that sort of thing."

She puzzled over this a moment, trying to cast her question in a new form.

"But suppose this: suppose Winkleman had obtained his

wish. Could you overcome his influence and what-you-call substitute your own?"

"No more than he could substitute his were the cases reversed. I've confidence enough in myself and knowledge enough of Winkleman to guarantee that."

"So it would depend on who got there first?" she persisted; "that is your opinion?"

"Why, yes. But what does it matter?"

"It amuses me to get knowledge. I admire your handle of these people. You must be patient and explain. It is all new to me, although I thought I had much experience."

She arose.

"I am tired now. I go to the *siesta*."

Kingozi stared after her retreating figure. The direct form of her questions had stirred again suspicions that had become vague.

"What's she driving at?" he asked the uncomprehending Simba in English. He considered the question for some moments. "Don't even know her name or nationality," he confessed to himself after a while. "She's a queer one. I suppose I'll have to give her a man or so to help her back across the Thirst." He pondered again, "I might take her *askaris*. Country will feed them now. I'll have a business talk with her."

As the tone of voice sounded final to Simba he ventured his usual reply.

"Yes, suh!" said Simba.

CHAPTER XII

THE PILOCARPIN

The *sultani* duly appeared the next morning; women brought in firewood and products of the country to trade; all was well. The entire day, and the succeeding days for over a week, Kingozi sat under his big tree, smoking his black pipe. The *sultani* sat beside him. For long periods at a time nothing at all was said. Then for equally long periods a lively conversation went on, through an interpreter mostly, though occasionally the *sultani* launched into his bastard Swahili or Kingozi ventured a few words in the new tongue. Once in a while some intimate would saunter into view, and would be summoned by his king. Then Kingozi patiently did the following things:

(a) He performed disappearing tricks with a rupee or other small object; causing it to vanish, and then plucking it from unexpected places.

(b) With a pair of scissors—which were magic aplenty in themselves—he cut a folded paper in such a manner that when unfolded a row of paper dolls was disclosed. This was a very successful trick. The pleased warriors dandled them up and down delightedly in an *n'goma.*

(c) He opened and shut an opera hat. The ordinary "plug hat" was known to these people, but not an opera hat.

(d) He allowed them to look through his prism glasses.

(e) On rare occasions he lit a match.

This vaudeville entertainment was always a huge success. The newcomers squatted around the two chairs, and the conversation continued.

Bibi-ya-chui occasionally stood near and listened. The subjects were trivial in themselves, and repeated endlessly.

Ten minutes of this bored her to the point of extinction. She could not understand how Kingozi managed to survive ten hours day after day. Only once was he absent from his post, and then for only a few hours. He went out accompanied by Simba and a dozen *shenzis*, and shot a wildebeeste. The tail of this—an object much prized as a fly whisk—he presented to his majesty. All the rest of the time he talked and listened.

"It is such childish nonsense!" the Leopard Woman expostulated. "How can you do it?"

"Goes with the job. It's a thing you must learn to do if you would get on in this business."

And once more she seemed to catch a glimpse of the infinity of savage Africa, which has been the same for uncounted ages, impersonal, without history, without the values of time!

But had she known it, Kingozi was getting what he required. Information came to him a word now, a word then; promises came to him in single phrases lost in empty gossip. He collected what he wanted grain by grain from bushels of chaff. The whole sum of his new knowledge could have been expressed in a paragraph, took him a week to get, but was just what he wanted. If he had asked categorical questions, he would have received lies. If he had attempted to hurry matters, he would have got nothing at all.

About sundown the *sultani* would depart, followed shortly by the last straggler of his people. The succeeding hours were clear of *shenzis*, for either the custom of the country or the presence of strangers seemed to demand an *n'goma* every evening. In the night stillness sounds carried readily. The drums, no longer rubbed but beaten in rhythm; the shrill wailing chants of women; the stamp and shuffle of feet; the cadenced clapping of hands rose and fell according to the fervour of the dance. The throb of these sounds was as a background to the evening—fierce, passionate, barbaric.

After the departure of the *sultani* Kingozi took a bath and changed his clothes. The necessity for this was more mental than physical. Then he relaxed luxuriously. It was then that he resumed his relations with the Leopard Woman, and that they discussed matters of more or less importance to both.

The first evening they talked of the wonder of the ivory

stockade. Kingozi had not yet had an opportunity to find
out whence the tusks had come, whether the elephants had
been killed in this vicinity, or whether the ivory had been
traded from the Congo.

"It is very valuable," he said. "I must find out whether
old Stick-in-the-mud knows what they are worth, or whether
he can be traded out of them on any reasonable basis."

"You will not be going farther," she suggested one
evening, apropos of nothing.

"Farther? Why not?" he asked rather blankly.

"You told me you were an ivory hunter," she pointed
out.

"Ah—yes. But I have hardly the goods to trade—come
back later," he stumbled, for once caught off his guard.
"I'm really looking for new hunting grounds."

She did not pursue the subject; but the enigmatic smile
lurked for a moment in the depths of her eyes.

Every night after supper Kingozi caused his medicine
chest to be brought out and opened, and for a half-hour
he doctored the sick. On this subject he manifested an
approach to enthusiasm.

"I know I can't doctor them all," he answered her objection, "and that it's foolish to pick out one here and there;
but it interests me. I told you I was a medical student by
training." He fingered over the square bottles, each in its
socket. "This is not the usual safari drug list," he said.
"I like to take these queer cases and see what I can do with

them.   I may learn something; at any rate, it interests me.
McCloud at Nairobi fitted me out; and told me what it
would be valuable to observe."

She appeared interested, and shortly he became enough
convinced of this to show and explain each drug separately.
The quinine he carried in the hydrochlorate instead of the
sulphate, and he waxed eloquent telling her why.   Crystals
of iodine as opposed to permanganate of potash for anti-
septic he discussed.   From that he branched into antisepsis
as opposed to asepsis as a practical method in the field.

"Theory has nothing to do with it," said he.   "It's a
matter of which will *work !*"

It was all technical; but it interested her for the simple
reason that Kingozi was really enthusiastic.   True enthusiasm, without pose or self-consciousness, invariably
arouses interest.

"Now here's something you'll never see in another safari
kit," said he, holding up one of the square bottles filled
with small white crystals, "and that wouldn't be found
in this one except for an accident.   It's pilocarpin."

"What is pilocarpin?" she asked, making a difficulty of
the word.

"It is really a sort of eye dope," he explained.   "You
know atropin—the stuff an oculist uses in your eyes when
he wants to examine them—leaves your vision blurred
for a day or so."

"Yes, I know that."

"The effect of atropin is to expand the pupil. Pilo-carpin is just the opposite—it contracts the pupil."

"What need could you possibly have of that?"

"There's the joke: I haven't. But when I was out-fitting I could not get near enough phenacetin. I suppose you know that we use phenacetin to induce sweating as first treatment of fever."

"I am not entirely ignorant. I can treat fevers, of course."

"Well, I took all they could spare. Then McCloud suggested pilocarpin. Though it is really an eye drug, to be used externally, it also has an effect internally to induce sweating. So that's why I have it."

She was examining the bottles.

"But you have atropin also. Why is that?"

"There's a good deal of ophthalmia or trachoma float-ing around some native districts. I thought I might ex-periment."

"And this"—she picked up a third bottle—"ah, yes, morphia. But how much alike they all are."

"In appearance, yes; in effect most radically and fatally different—like people," smiled Kingozi.

But though Kingozi's scientific interest was keen in certain directions—as ethnology, drugs, and zoölogy—it had totally blind spots. Thus the Leopard Woman kept invariably on her table the bowl of fresh flowers; and she manifested an unfailing liking to investigate such strange shrubs, trees, flowers, or nondescript growths as flourished thereabouts.

"Do you know how one names these?" she asked him concerning certain strange blooms.

"I know nothing whatever about vegetables," he replied with indifferent scorn.

Several times after that, forgetting, she proffered the same question and received exactly the same reply. Finally it became a joke to her. Slyly, at sufficient intervals so that he should not become conscious of the repetition, she took delight in eliciting this response, always the same, always delivered with the same detached scorn:

"I know nothing whatever about vegetables."

In the meantime Simba, with great enthusiasm, continued his drill of the *askaris*. Kingozi gave them an hour early in the day. They developed rapidly from wild trigger yanking. An allowance of two cartridges apiece proved them no great marksmen, but at least steady on discharge.

The "business conversation" Kingozi projected with the Leopard Woman did not take place until late in the week. By that time he had pieced together considerable information, as follows:

The mountain ranges at their backs possessed three practicable routes. Beyond the ranges were grass plains with much game. Water could be had in certain known places. No people dwell on these plains. This was because of the tsetse fly that made it impossible to keep domestic cattle. Far—very far—perhaps a month, who knows, is the country of the *sultani* M'tela. This is a very great *sultani*—very great indeed—a *sultani* whose spears are like the leaves of grass. His people are fierce, like the Masai, like the people of Lobengula, and make war their trade. His people are known as the Kabilagani. The way through the mountains is known; guides can be had. The way across the plains is known; but for guides one must find representatives of a little scattered plains tribe. That can be done. *Potio* for two weeks can be had—and so on.

Kingozi was particularly interested in these Kabilaganis: and pressed for as much information as he could. Strangely enough he did not mentain the ivory stockade, nor did he attempt either to trade or to determine whether or not the *sultani* knew its value.

At the end of eight days he knew what he wished to know.

"I shall leave in two days," he told the Leopard Woman. "I should suggest that you go to-morrow. I will send Simba with you to show you the water-hole in the kopje. After that you know the country for yourself."

"But I am not going back!" she cried. "I am going on."

"That is impossible." He went on to explain to her what he had learned of the country ahead: omitting, however, all reference to M'tela and his warrior nation. "More plains: more game. That's all. You have more of that than you can use back where we came from. And with every step you are farther away. I am going on—very far. I may not come back at all."

She listened to all his arguments, but shook her head obstinately at their end.

"Your plan does not please me," said she. "I will go and see these plains for myself."

This was final, and Kingozi at last came to see it so.

"I was going to suggest that I relieve you of your *askaris*," said he, "but if you persist in this foolish and aimless plan, you will need them for yourself."

"Cannot we go together, at least for a distance?'

But to this he was much opposed.

"I shall be travelling faster than your cumbersome safari," he objected. "I could not delay."

And in this decision he seemed as firm as had she in her intention to proceed. After a light reconnaissance, so to speak, of argument, appeal, and charm, she gave over trying to persuade him, and fell back on her usual lazily indifferent attitude. Kingozi went ahead with his preparations, laying in *potio*, examining kits, preparing in every way his compact little caravan for the long journey before it. Then something happened. He changed his mind and decided to combine safaris with the Leopard Woman.

CHAPTER XIII

THE TROPIC MOON

For several nights the plain below the plateau had been a sea of moonlight, white, ethereal, fragile as spun glass. Each evening the shadow of the mountains had shortened, drawing close under the skirts of the hills. In stately orderly progression the quality of the night world was changing. The heavy brooding darkness was being transformed to a fairy delicacy of light.

And the life of the world seemed to feel this change, to be stirring, at first feebly, then with growing strength. The ebb was passed; the tides were rising to the brim. Each night the throb of the drums seemed to beat more passionately, the rhythm to become quicker, wilder: the wailing chants of the women rose in sudden gusts of frenzy. Dark figures stole about in shadows; so that Kingozi, becoming anxious, gave especial instructions, and delegated trusty men to see that they were obeyed.

"If our men get to fooling with their women, they'll spear the lot of us!" he explained.

And at last, like a queen whose coming has been prepared, a queen in whose anticipation life had quickened, the moon herself rose serenely above the ranges.

Immediately the familiar objects changed; the familiar shadows vanished. The world became a different world, full of enchantment, of soft-singing birds, of chirping insects, of romance and recollections of past years, of longings and the spells of barbaric Africa.

Kingozi sat with the Leopard Woman "talking business" when this miracle took place. When the great rim of the moon materialized at the mountain's rim, he abruptly fell silent. The spell had him, as indeed it had all living things. From the village the drums pulsed more wildly, shoutings of men commenced to mingle with the voices of the women; a confused clashing sound began to be heard. In camp the fires appeared suddenly to pale. A vague uneasiness swept the squatting men. Their voices fell: they exchanged whispered monosyllables, dropping their voices, they knew not why.

The Leopard Woman arose and glided to the edge of the tree's shadow, where she stood gazing upward at the moon. Kingozi watched her. He, old and seasoned traveller as he was, had indeed fallen under the spell. He did not consider it extraordinary, nor did it either embarrass or stir his senses, that standing as she did before the moon and the little fires her body showed in clear silhouette through her silken robe. Apparently this was her only garment. It made a pale nimbus about her. She seemed to the vague remnant of Kingozi's thinking perceptions like a priestess— her slim, beautiful form erect, her small head bound with the golden fillet from which, he knew, hung the jewel on her forehead. As though meeting this thought she raised both arms toward the moon, standing thus for a moment in the conventional attitude of invocation. Then she dropped her arms, and came back to Kingozi's side.

Again it was like magic, the sudden blotting out of the slim human figure, the substitution of the draped form as she moved from the light into the shadow. But on Kingozi's retina remained the vision of her as she was. He shifted, caught his breath.

As she came near him his hand closed over hers, bringing her to a halt. She did not resist, but stood looking down at him waiting. He struggled for an appearance of calm.

"Who are you?" he asked unsteadily. "You have never told me."

"You have named me—Bibi-ya-chui—the Woman of the Leopards."

She was smiling faintly, looking down at him through half-closed eyes.

"But who are you? You are not English."

"My name: you have given it. Let that suffice. Me— I am Hungarian." She stooped ever so slightly and touched the upstanding mop of his wavy hair. "What does it matter else?" she asked softly.

She was leaning: the moonlight came through the branches where she leaned; the little fires—again the silken robes became a nimbus—and the drums of the *n'goma*, the drums seemed to be throbbing in his veins——

He leaped to his feet and seized her savagely by the shoulders. The soft silk slipped under his fingers. She threw back her head, looking at him steadily. Her eyes glowed deep, and the jewel on her forehead. Kingozi was panting.

"You are wonderful—maddening!" he muttered. This sudden unexpected emotion swept him away, as a pond, quiet behind the dam, becomes a flood.

"I knew we could be such friends!" she said.

And then one of those tiny incidents happened that so often change the course of greater events. In the darkness that still lingered the other side of the camp an *askari* challenged sharply some lurking wanderer. According to his recent teaching he used the official word.

"*Samama !*" said he.

The metallic rattle of his musket and the brief official challenge awakened Kingozi as would a dash of cold water. His instinct to crush to his breast this alluring, fascinating, willing goddess of the moon was as strong as ever. But across that instinct lay the shadow of a former day. A clear picture flashed before his mind. He saw a man in the uniform of a high office, and heard that man's words of instruction to himself. The words had concluded with a few informal phrases of trust and confidence. While these were being spoken, outside a sentry had challenged: "*Samama !*"

and as he moved, the metal of his accoutrements had clicked.

With a wrench Kingozi turned, dropping her shoulders. He deliberately ran away. At the edge of his own camp he looked back. She was still standing as he had left her. The moonlight, striking through the opening in the branches, fell across her. At this distance she was merely a white figure; but Kingozi saw her again as she had stood in invocation to the moon. As though she had only awaited his turning, she raised her hand in grave salutation and disappeared.

Kingozi was too restless, too stirred, to sit still. After a vain attempt to smoke a quiet and ruminative pipe he arose and began to wander about. The men looked up at him furtively from their little fires where perpetually meat roasted. He strode on through the camp. His feet bore him to the narrow lane leading to the village. Down the vista he saw flames leaping, and figures leaping wildly, too, and the drums beat against his temples. He turned back seeking quiet, and so on through camp again, and past the Leopard Woman's tent. His mind was in a turmoil. No perception reached him of outside things—once the disturbance of human creatures was past. His feet led him unconsciously.

It was the old struggle. He desired this woman mightily. That he had been totally indifferent to her before argued nothing. He had been suddenly awakened: and he was in the prime of life. But the very strength of his desire warned him. If he had really been on a hunt for ivory—well—he wrenched his mind savagely from even a contemplation of possibilities. Still, it would be a very sweet relation in a lonely life—a women of this quality, this desirability, this understanding, able to travel the wilderness of Africa, eager for the life, young, beautiful, tingling with vitality. In spite of himself Kingozi played with the thought. The fever was in his brain, the magic of the tropic moon was flooding his soul.

Some warning instinct brought him back to the world about him. His steps had taken him down the cañon trail. He stood at the edge of the open plain.

Facing him and not twenty yards distant stood a lion.

The sight cleared Kingozi's brain of all its vapours. For the first time he realized clearly what he had done. He, a man whose continued existence in this dangerous country had depended on his unfailing readiness, his ever-present alertness and presence of mind, had committed two of the cardinal sins. In savage Africa no man must at any time stir a foot into the veldt or jungle unarmed; in savage Africa no man must go at night fifty feet from a fire without a torch or lantern.

By day a lion is usually harmless unless annoyed. Game herds manifest no alarm at his presence, merely opening through their ranks a lane for his indifferent passing. But at night he asserts his dominion.

Kingozi realized his deadly peril. The beast bulked huge and black—a wild lion is a third larger than his menagerie relative—looking as big as a zebra against the moonlight. His eyes glowed steadily as he contemplated this interloper in his domain. After a moment he sank prone, extending his head. The next move, Kingozi knew, would be the flail-like thrash of the long tail, followed immediately by the rush.

Nothing was to be done. The immediate surroundings were bare of trees, and in any case the lightning charge of the beast would have caught his victim unless the branches had happened to be fairly overhead.

The glowing eyes lowered. A rasping gurgling began deep in the animal's throat, rising and falling in tone with the inhaling and exhaling of the breath. This increased in volume. It became terrifying. The long tail stiffened, whacked first to one side, then to the other. The moment was at hand.

Kingozi stood erect, his hands clenched, every muscle taut. All his senses were sharpened. He heard the voices of the veldt, near and far, and all the little sounds that were underneath them. His vision seemed to pierce the darkness of the shadows, so that he made out the details of the lion's mane, and even the muscles stiffening beneath the skin.

And then at the last moment a kongoni, panic stricken, running blind, its nose up, broke through the thin bush to the left and dashed across the trail directly between the man and the lion.

African animals are subject to these strange, blind panics, especially at night. The individual so affected appears to lose all sense of its surroundings. It has been known actually to bump into and knock down men in plain and open sight. What had so terrified the kongoni it would be impossible to say. Perhaps a stray breeze had wafted the scent of this very lion; perhaps some other unseen danger actually threatened, or perhaps the poor beast merely awakened from the horror of a too vivid dream.

The diversion occurred at the moment of the lion's greatest tension. His body was poised for the attack, as a bow is bent to drive forth the arrow. Probably without conscious thought on his part, instinctively, he changed his objective. The huge body sprang; but instead of the man the kongoni was struck down!

Kingozi stooped low and ran hard to the left. When at a safe distance he straightened his back, and set his footsteps rapidly campward.

The incident had thoroughly awakened him. His brain was working clearly now, and under forced draught. The magic of moonlight had lost its power. Habits of years reasserted themselves. His usual iron common sense regained its ascendency; though, strangely enough, there persisted in his mind a mystic feeling for the symbolism of this missed danger.

"Settles it!" he said, in his usual fashion of talking aloud. "I'm on a job, and I must do it. Came near being a messy ass!"

He saw plainly enough that a mission such as his had no place in it for women—even such women as Bibi-ya-chui. She must go back—or stay here—didn't matter much which. The call of duty sounded very clear. By the time he had reached the level of the upper plateau his mind was fully made up. As far as he was concerned the Leopard Woman had definitely lost all chance of going alone.

The frosted moonlight still lay across the world. It meant nothing but illumination to Kingozi. By its light he discerned a paper lying against a bush; and since paper of any sort is scarce, he picked it up.

At camp he lighted his lantern and spread out his find on the table. It proved to be a map.

A glance proved to Kingozi that it was not his property. He remembered a sudden wind squall early in the afternoon. Evidently it had swept the Leopard Woman's table.

The map was in manuscript, very well drawn, and the text was German. From long habit Kingozi glanced first at the scale of miles, then raised his eyes to determine what country was represented. After a moment he arose, took his lantern into his tent, and there spread his find on his cot.

For it was a map of this very locality!

Kingozi examined it with great attention, finally getting out for comparison his own sketch maps. The German map was a more finished product; otherwise they were practically the same. Kingozi searched for and found records of the various waters along his back track. Each was annotated in ink in a language strange to him—probably Hungarian, he reflected. At the dry *donga* where he had overtaken and rescued the Leopard Woman's water-starved safari he found the legend *wasser* also.

"Explorations for this map made after the rains," he concluded.

Here the Leopard Woman had written the German word *nein !* underscored several times.

So far Kingozi's sketches and the German map were the same. But the German map furnished all details for some distance in advance. This village was indicated, and the mountains, and plains beyond. The three practical routes were plotted by means of red lines. These lines converged at the far side of the ranges, united in one, and proceeded out across the plains. Kingozi counted days' journeys by the indicated water-holes up to eleven. Then the map ceased; but an arrow at the end of the red line was explained by a compass bearing, and the name M'tela. And, as far as Kingozi could see, the sole purport of the whole affair was not topography but a route to the country of M'tela!

Here was a facer! As far as any one knew, the country he had just traversed was unexplored. Yet here was a good detailed map of just that route. Furthermore, a copy was in the hands of this woman who claimed she was out for sport

merely, and had no knowledge of the country. Yes—she
had made just that statement. Of course she might be
out merely for adventure, just as she said. If she were of
prominence and influence, she might easily enough have
obtained a copy of a private map. But then why did she
pretend ignorance? She seemed never to have heard of the
name of M'tela; yet this map's sole reason for being was
that it indicated at least the beginning of a route to M'tela's
country.

Could she be on the same errand as himself?

That sounded fantastic. Kingozi reviewed the circumstances. M'tela was a formidable myth, gradually taking shape as a reality. He was reported as a mighty
chief of distant borders. Tales of ten thousand spears
drifted back to official attention. Allowing the usual dis-
count, M'tela still loomed as a powerful figure. Nobody
had paid very much attention to him until this time, but
now his distant border had become important. Through
it a new road from the north was projected. The following
year the route was to be explored. The friendship of M'tela
and his umpty-thousand spears became important. His
hostility could cause endless trouble and delay. Kingozi's
present job was to lay the foundations for this friendship.

"You have a free hand, Culbertson," the very high official
had said to him. "We are not going to suggest or advise.
Choose your own men; take as many or as few as you please.

Take your own time and your own methods. But get the results."

"I appreciate your confidence, sir," Kingozi had replied.

"You and that man Winkleman are the best hands on earth with natives, and we know it. Requisition what you want."

This woman was a Hungarian: she possessed a German official map. Could she be on official business? It did not seem likely. Women are not much good at that sort of thing in Africa. What official business could she be on? The same as his own? That seemed still more unlikely; but if so, why should they not work together? Germany and England had an equal stake in the opening of this new route. An amical Boundary Commission had just completed a satisfactory survey between the German and British East African Protectorates. But she had lied to him, and she had acted lies of apparent ignorance! Why that?

Having examined the subject from all sides, and having discovered it as yet incapable of solution, Kingozi, characteristically, decided to go slow. If she were on the same mission as himself, that fact would develop in due time, and then they could work together. If she were still on some mission, but a mission other than his own, that fact, too, would in due time develop. If she were merely travelling in idle curiosity—well, she ought not to lie!

For Kingozi had changed his mind. No longer was he

determined that she must turn back at this point. Now he was equally determined that she must accompany him.

"I'll keep an eye on you, young woman," said he. "You pretend to be very eager to go on with me. We'll see! But now you'll find it difficult to quit this game. You may get more of it than you bargained for. If you are really out just for sport and curiosity, I'm sorry for you. But you shouldn't lie!"

He copied the map roughly; then returned it to the spot under the bushes where he had found it.

Next morning he announced to the Leopard Woman his changed decision. He was self-contained and direct. She smiled secretly to herself. She thought she understood both the change of decision and the brusqueness. One was the magic of the tropic moon; the other was the shy, half-ashamed reaction of the strong man whose emotions have controlled him. The proof—that she was going with him.

She was wrong!

CHAPTER XIV

OVER THE RANGES

When the day came for departure the Leopard Woman was indisposed, and could not travel. At the end of that period eight bags of *potio* disappeared. They had to be replaced. Kingozi occupied the time on the details of his preparations. Then three men deserted, and all loads had to be redistributed. At last they were off.

A horde of savages accompanied them at first. These dropped off one by one until there remained only the guides appointed. The trail led steeply upward. It soon shook free of the thorn tangle and debouched on grassy rolling shoulders from which a wide, maplike view could be seen of the country through which they had passed. Shortly they skirted a deep cleft cañon in which sang a brook; and at its head came to a forest. The trees were tall, their cover dense; long, ropelike vines hung in festoons. It was very still. A colobus barked somewhere in the tops; the small green monkeys swung from limb to limb, or scampered along the rope vines, chattering. Silent, gaudy birds swooped across dusky spaces. The dripping of water reached the ear; the smell of dampness the nostrils.

This was as far as they went the first day. The climb had been severe; and at the end of three and a half hours the woman announced that she was done up. Nothing remained but to make camp. This was done, therefore; and all the afternoon Kingozi lay flat on the cot he had caused to be brought into the open air, and blew smoke upward, and stared at the maze of limbs in the forest roof. The Leopard Woman kept her tent; but he did not offer to disturb her. He was thinking.

Next day they marched for hours through the forest, and at last came out on more rolling grass shoulders. Evidently this side of the mountains was not abrupt, but slanted off in a gentle slope to unknown distances. There the game began to reappear; and Kingozi dropped two hartebeeste for the safari. Here Cazi Moto came up in great perturbation to announce that two of the *memsahib's* porters were missing. The little headman did not understand how it happened, as he had zealously brought up the rear. Unless, of course, it was a case of desertion.

Kingozi looked thoughtful, then ordered camp to be pitched. Accompanied by Simba, Mali-ya-bwana, and three *askaris* he took the back track. At the end of an hour and a half of brisk walking he met the two missing porters. Their explanation was voluble. They had fallen out for a few moments, and when they had resumed their loads, the safari was ahead. Then they had hastened, but the road had divided. They had taken the wrong fork.

"Show me where the road divided," ordered Kingozi.

The loads were deposited by the side of the trail, and the delinquents, with every appearance of confidence, led the way back another hour's march to a veritable fork. Kingozi examined the earth for tracks.

"Could you not see that the safari had gone this way and not that way?" he asked.

"Yes, *bwana*," they said together; "we saw it after a little. That is why we came back."

Kingozi grunted, but said nothing. The nine men retraced their steps. Both porters were on a broad grin, laughing and talking in subdued tones to the *askaris*. The *bwana* strode on rapidly ahead. They followed at a little dogtrot, carrying their loads easily.

At camp Kingozi ordered them to place the loads in place beneath the tarpaulin.

"Simba," said he in a casual voice, "these men get *kiboko*."

"Yes, *bwana*. How many?"

"Fifty."

The bystanders gasped, and the shining countenances of the culprits turned a sickly gray. Fifty lashes is a maximum punishment, inflicted only for the gravest crimes. More cannot be administered without fear of grave consequences. The offence of straggling is generally considered not serious. Even Simba was not certain he had heard aright.

"How many, *bwana?*" he asked again.

"Fifty," repeated Kingozi tonelessly, and turned his blank, baleful glare in their direction.

The punishment was administered. When it was finished the porters, shaking like leaves, blankets drawn over their bleeding flanks, were brought to face the white man seated in his chair.

"*Bassi,*" he pronounced. The word went out into a dead silence, so that it was heard to the farthest confines of the hushed camp. "Let no man hereafter miss the trail."

He arose and entered his tent. Cazi Moto was there, unfolding the canvas bath tub, laying out the clean clothes. He looked up from his occupation, his wizened face contorted in a shrewd smile.

"No more will we make camp when the sun is only a few hours high," he surmised.

Kingozi looked at him.

"You and I have handled many safaris, Cazi Moto," he replied.

Delays from these causes ceased, but other delays supervened. Never were the reasons for them attributable to accident; but they were more numerous than ordinarily. Kingozi said nothing.

All the day's march he walked fifty yards ahead of the long procession. The Leopard Woman walked part of the time; part of the time she rode a donkey procured from the *sultani*. The two necessarily held little converse during

the day. At camp Kingozi had many tasks—camp to
arrange, meat to procure, sick to doctor, guides to interrogate. Only at the evening meal, which now they shared, did
he and his travelling companion resume their intimacies.

The relation had developed into a curious one. For one
thing, it was more expansive. They discussed many subjects of what might be called general interest, talking interestedly on books, world politics, colonial policies, even the
larger problems of life. In these discussions they explored
each other's intelligence, came to a mental approachment,
a cold, clear respect for each other's capacity and experience.
Never did they approach the personal. At no time in their
acquaintance had they talked so unrestrainedly, so freely,
with so much genuine pleasure; at no time did they touch
so little the mysteries of personality.

If the Leopard Woman felt this, or wondered at the
cloaked withdrawal, she gave no sign. Apparently she
was all candour. She seemed to throw herself frankly and
with pleasure into this relationship of the head, to have
forgotten the possibilities so richly though so momentarily
disclosed by the magic of the moon. She lounged in her
canvas chair, twisting her lithe body within her silks; she
smoked her cigarettes; the jewel of changing lights glowed
on her forehead; she talked in her modulated voice and
quaint, precise English. The man's pulses remained calm.
His eyes did not miss the beauty of her form, as frankly
defined beneath the silk as the forms of the naked *bibis* of

the village; nor the alluring paleness of her face in contrast to the red lips; nor the drowning passion of her wide eyes. But they did not reach his senses. Were the insulation of his plain duty—which to Kingozi meant quite sincerely his whole excuse for existence in this puzzling life—were this to be withdrawn—he never even contemplated the thought. Reminders from that night of the moon prevented him from doing so.

After this fashion they came to the grass plains of the uplands. Here ensued more delays. These did not spring from delinquencies in the safari: the exemplary punishment assured that. But things broke, and things were forgotten, and things had to be done differently. The guides, procured with difficulty from the little hunting peoples of the plain, disappeared at the end of the second day. They professed themselves afraid of Chaké, the Nubian. The latter vehemently denied having spoken a word to them. Day's marches were shortened because the woman could not stand long ones. Kingozi found it a great bother to travel with a woman.

Nevertheless, he made no attempts to separate the safaris. He had been watching closely. These difficulties, the delays, breakages, and abbreviations of day's journeys had, nine times out of ten, their origin in the camp of the Leopard Woman. In ordinary circumstances he would have put this down to inferior organization. But there was the mysterious, unmentioned map, whose accuracy, by the way, he found exact. Gradually he came to the conclusion that the delays were not entirely accidental. The conclusion became a conviction that the Leopard Woman was making as much of a drag and as big a nuisance of herself as possible.

Why?

She wanted to become such a burden that Kingozi would go on without her. Again, why? At the village she had vehemently refused to go back, and had pleaded to join forces with Kingozi. This puzzled him for some time. Then he saw. Of course she did not want to turn back. If, as he surmised, she had some errand with M'tela, like his own, she would not want to turn back, but she would like a plausible excuse to separate from him once the ranges of mountains were crossed. Why did she not drop off then on the excuse, say, of the wonderful new hunting grounds? That would be simple. Kingozi concluded that she wished the initiative to come from him. And the more convinced he was that she wanted to get rid of him, the more firmly he resolved that she must remain.

But it did make for slow travel.

What of it? There was no haste. There was plenty of game, the days passed pleasantly, the evenings were delightful. A moonbeam flashed in his brain showing him vistas—— He firmly shut the window!

Certainly if Bibi-ya-chui harboured any active desire to drive Kingozi into leaving her to her own devices, she concealed it well. Occasionally in the evening, when he stared into the distance, she twisted herself to look at him. Then her eyes widened, no one could have told with what emotion. In her fixed stare could have been many things— or nothing. Did she desire this man, as she had seemed to the night of the full moon, and did she but bide her time, knowing this was not the moment? Did she desire this man, and hate him because he had touched her only to turn away? Did the very simplicity and directness of his nature baffle her? Did she hate him for his mastering of circumstances but not herself? Any or all of these emotions might have lain beneath the smoulder in her eyes. One thing Kingozi would not have seen, had he turned his head suddenly enough, and that was indifference. But he continued to stare out into the veldt, and she continued to stare at him; while around them the chatter of men, the wail of hyenas, the thunder of lions, the shrill, thin cries of night birds, and the mighty brooding silence that took no account of them all attended the African night.

CHAPTER XV

THE SHARPENING OF THE SPEAR

Thus passed six weeks. By the end of this time the combined safaris had progressed out into the unknown country about a normal three weeks' journey. The rest was delay.

They had ventured out into the plain as into an enchanted sea. The mountains had dropped below the horizon behind them; none had as yet arisen before. The veldt ran in long, low undulations, so that always they walked up or down gentle slopes. It was as though a ground swell had set in toward distant, invisible shores. Here the short grass was still green from the rains. Water lay in pools at the bottom of *dongas*. By this good fortune travel was independent of the permanent water, and hence safe and easy. Game was everywhere. Not for a single hour in all that six weeks were they out of sight of it. Scattered over the sward like deer in a pack the beasts grazed placidly in twos or threes, or in great bands. Without haste, almost imperceptibly, they drew aside to allow the safari to pass, and closed in again behind it. Thus the travellers were always the centre of a little moving oasis of clear space

five hundred yards in diameter. Occasionally some unusual and unexpected crease in the earth or density of brush
in the *dongas* brought them in surprise fairly atop an un-
suspecting herd. Then ensued a wild stampede. This
communicated itself visually to all the animals in sight.
They moved off swiftly. And then still other remote
beasts, unaware of the cause of disturbance, quite out of
sight of the safari, but signalled by twinkle of stripe or
flash of rump, also took flight. So that far over the veldt, at
last, the game hordes shifted uneasily until the impulse died.

In this country were many lions. Most of the requisites
of a lion were here present—abundant game, water, the
cover of the low brush in the *dongas*. Only lacked a few
rocky kopje fastnesses to make it ideal; but that lack could
be, and was, overlooked. The members of the safari
often saw the great beasts sunning themselves atop ant
hills; walking with dignity across the open country; sitting
on their haunches to stare with great yellow eyes at these
strangers passing by. Here they had never been annoyed
or hunted; so here they had not become as strictly nocturnal
as nearer settlement. In all their magnificence they stalked
abroad, lords of the veldt. Kingozi's finger itched for the
trigger. There is no more exciting sport than that of lion
shooting afoot. It is a case of kill or be killed; for a lion,
once the issue is joined, never gives up. He fights literally
to the death; and when he is so crippled that he can no
longer keep his feet, he drags himself forward, and dies

facing his opponent dauntlessly. No other beast furnishes the same danger, the same thrill. His mere appearance stirs the most sluggish spirit.

"*Simba! Simba! Simba!*" the exclamation ran back the line of the safari, the sibilant hissed excitedly. Kingozi's heart bounded, and his knuckles whitened as he gripped his rifle.

"*Bwana hapana piga?*" Simba implored. "Is not *bwana* going to shoot?"

But Kingozi shook his head. The temptation was strong, but he resisted it. He refrained from shooting at the lions for exactly the same reason that he had insulated himself against the Leopard Woman's charms.

In all this wide country were no settled habitations. Your African native requires hills or forests; he will not dwell on open plains at any great distance from his natural protection. A few people there were, hunters and nomads, living on wild honey and game. They were solitaries and lived where night found them, a little race, shyer than the game. For days and days they flanked the safari before venturing to approach. Then one would appear a hundred yards away and open shouted negotiations with the porters. Perhaps after a few hours he would venture into camp. Invariably Kingozi interrogated these people. They stood before him palpitating like birds, poised, tense for flight. He asked them of water, of people, of routes. By means of kind treatment and little presents he tried to gain their confidence. Sometimes thus he induced them to talk freely, but never did he succeed in persuading them to guide him. The mere fact of interrogation rendered them uneasy. Probably they could not themselves have understood that uneasiness; but invariably at nightfall they disappeared. They made fire by the rubbing of sticks, shot poisoned arrows at game.

From them Kingozi gained little but chatter. They knew accurately every permanent water, to be sure. This information, in view of the abundance of rain pools, was not at present valuable; nevertheless Kingozi questioned them minutely, and made many marks on the map he was preparing. Always he mentioned M'tela. At first he introduced the name at any time in the course of the interview; but soon he found that this dried up all information. So then he reserved that subject for the last. They were afraid of the very syllables. They spoke them under their breaths, with side glances. M'tela was a great lord; a lord of terror, to be feared.

At first the information was most vague. M'tela was over yonder—a long distance—who knows how far? He possessed more or less mythical characteristics, ranging from a height of forty or fifty feet down to the mere possession of a charm by which he could kill at a distance. Then, as the journey went on, the vagueness began to define. M'tela took form as a big man with a voice like the lion at night. His surroundings began to be described. He lived in the edge of a forest; his people were many; he had forty wives, and the like. Still it was far, very far. Kingozi concluded that none of these people had in person visited the Kabilagani, but were talking at second hand.

And finally direct information came to him—in the form of fear. M'tela was a great lord, a lord of many spears, his hand was heavy, he took what he desired, his warriors were fierce and cruel and could not be gainsaid. Told under the breath, with furtive glances to right and to left. And not far: a three days' journey. Kingozi translated this into terms of safari travel and made it about eight days. And, indeed, though no mountains as yet raised their peaks above the horizon, fleets of clouds setting sail from the distant ranges winged their way joyously down a growing wind.

The Leopard Woman fell ill and kept her tent. Kingozi waited two days, then sought her out. His patience over delay was about gone. The headaches to which physical exhaustions always made him subject had annoyed him greatly of late, had rendered him irritable. His eyes bothered him—a reflex from his run-down condition, he thought, combined with a slight inflammation due to the glare of sun or yellowing grass. Boracic acid helped very little. The halo he had noticed around the light that evening when they had first arrived at the *sultani's* village returned. He saw it about every campfire, every lantern flame, even around the brightest of the stars. Altogether he approached the interview in a strongly impatient mood.

The Leopard Woman lay abed beneath silken sheets. This was the first time Kingozi had ever seen sheets of any kind on any kind of a safari.   In reality the Leopard Woman was an enticing, luring vision, but Kingozi, through the lenses of his mood, saw only the silkiness and "sheetiness" of those covers.   He began to comprehend the numerous tin boxes.

"I'm going to leave you here and push on," he began abruptly.   "You will be all right with the men I shall leave you.   When you feel able to do so, follow on.   I'll leave a plain trail."

She objected feebly; but immediately, seeing that this would not touch his mood, she asked him the reason of his haste.

"I'll tell you," he replied, "about a week distant is a chief named M'tela.   Did you ever hear of him?"

"M'tela?" she repeated the name thoughtfully.   "No—but I don't know much about native tribes."

Remembering her map Kingozi's lips compressed under his beard.   What earthly object could she have in lying?—unless her errand was as secret as his own.

"Well, he is described as being very powerful.   And of course he will hear of us.   It is well to make friends with him before he has had a chance to think us over too long.   I'll just go on and see him."

"When will you start?" she asked, conceding the point without discussion.

"To-morrow morning. I shall make the distance in about five days, probably: you should be able to do so in eight or ten. How are you feeling to-day?"

"Better. I wondered would you ask."

He picked up her wrist.

"Pulse seems steady. Any fever?"

"A little early and late."

"Well, keep on with the hydrochlorate. You'll pull out in a day or so."

But the Leopard Woman pulled out in a second or so after Kingozi's departure. As soon as he was safe away, she threw back the covers and swung to the edge of the cot. At her call Chaké, the Nubian, appeared. To him she immediately began to give emphatic directions, repeating some of them over and over vehemently. He bent his fuzzy head listening, his yellow eyeballs showing, his fang-like teeth exposed in a grin of comprehension. When she had finished he nodded, said a few words in his own tongue, and glided from the tent.

At his own camp he stooped and picked up a weapon. This was a spear, and belonged to him personally. He had brought it all the way from Nubia. It differed from any of the native spears of East Africa both in form and in weight. Its blade was broad and shaped like a leaf; its haft was of wood; and its heel was shod with only the briefest length of iron. Chaké kept this spear in a high state of polish, so that its metal shone like silver. He lifted it, poised it, made as though to throw it, to thrust with it. Then with a sigh of renunciation he laid it aside. From behind one of the porters' tents he took another spear, one typical of this country that had been traded for only a day or two before. This Chaké considered clumsy and unnecessarily heavy. Nevertheless he bore it out into the long grass where he squatted in concealment; and, producing a stone, began painstakingly to sharpen the point and edges. As the slow labour went on he seemed to work himself gradually to a pitch of excitement. A little crooning song began to rise and fall, to flow and ebb. His eyes flashed, his back bent to a tense crouch. Every few moments he clashed the spear against an imaginary shield, poised it, thrust with it strongly, the chant rising. Then abruptly his voice fell, his muscles relaxed, he resumed the rythmical whetting with the stone.

All afternoon he squatted, passing the stone over the steel; polishing long after the point and edges were as sharp as they could be made. When the sun grew large at the world's edge he threw himself flat on his belly and wormed his way to a position a few yards from Kingozi's tent. There he left the spear. When he had gained a spot a hundred yards away, he arose to his feet and walked quietly into camp. A moment later he was sitting on his heels before his fire, eating his evening meal.

CHAPTER XVI

THE MURDER

That night Kingozi was restless and could not sleep. His vision had been blurring badly during the day, and now his eyeballs ached as though they had been seared. After his solitary evening meal he wandered about restlessly, gripping his pipe strongly between his teeth. Shortly after dark he entered his tent with the idea of turning in early; but the pain drove him out again. He remained only long enough to substitute his mosquito boots for his day boots. The Nubian, lying in the long grass beside the newly sharpened spear, settled himself to wait.

Kingozi's figure lost itself among the men of the camp. The strong, clean wind that blew every day from distant ranges, was falling with the night. A breath of coolness came with it. Chaké shivered and wished he had brought his blanket. The time was very long; but back of Chaké were generations of men who had lain patiently in wait. He gripped the haft of the heavy spear.

Black night descended in earnest. The little fires were dying down. Still Kingozi, tortured by his headache, wandered about. Upward of two hours passed. Then at last the crouching Nubian saw dimly the silhouette of the white man returning, caught in the glimmer of coals the colour of the khaki coat he wore. The moment was at hand. Chaké arose to his knees, his spear in his right hand. As soon as his victim should lie down on the cot, it was his intention to thrust him through the canvas. It must be remembered that the cot was placed close to the wall, and that the body of the sleeper was defined against it.

But unexpectedly the wearer of the khaki coat passed the tent door and proceeded to the rear where he reached upward to the rear guy rope where hung a towel, or some such matter. This brought him to within four feet of the kneeling Nubian, the broad of his back exposed, both arms upraised. Without hesitation Chaké drove the spear into his back. The sharp long blade slipped through the flesh as easily as a hot knife into butter. The murdered man choked once and pitched forward headlong on his face. Chaké, leaving the weapon, glided swiftly away.

Once well beyond the chance of a fire glimmer he arose to his feet and quickly regained his own camp. This was exactly on the opposite side of the circle. The four men with whom he shared his tiny cotton tent, *askaris* all as beseemed his dignity, were sound asleep. He squatted on his heels, pushed together the embers of his fire, staring into the coals. His ugly face was as though carved from ebony. Only his wild savage eyes glowed and flashed with a brooding lambent flame; and his wide nostrils slowly expanded and contracted as though with some inner heaving emotion.

Thus he sat for perhaps ten minutes. Then on the opposite side of the circle a commotion began. Some one cried out, figures ran to and fro, commands were given, brands were snatched from dying fires, torches were lit. Elsewhere, all about camp, sleepers were sitting up, were asking one another what was the matter. The *askaris* in Chaké's tent grumbled, and turned over, and asked what it was all about. Chaké shook his mop of hair, staring into the fire.

From the Leopard Woman's tent came a sharp summons. The Nubian arose and stalked boldly across the open space. At the closed tent he scratched his fingernail respectfully against the canvas.

"*Karibu, karibu!*" summoned his mistress impatiently. He slipped between the flaps and stood inside.

The Leopard Woman was seated upright in her cot. On the tin box near the head of the bed burned a candle in a mica lantern. By its dim light her face looked paler than ever, and deep black circles seemed to have defined themselves under her eyes. The Nubian and the white woman stared at each other for a moment.

"It is done?" she asked finally, in a hoarse whisper.

"It is done, *memsahib*," he replied calmly.

For another pause she stared at him, her eyes widening.

"You have done well. *Bassi!*" she enunciated at last.

The tent flaps still quivered behind the Nubian's exit, when she threw herself face downward on the cot. Her body shook with convulsive dry sobs. After a moment she twisted on her side. Both hands clutched her throat, as though she strangled for air. Her eyes were round and rolling. It was as if some mighty pent force were struggling for release. Suddenly the release came. She began to weep, the tears streaming down her face. Shortly she commenced to mutter little short disjointed phrases in her own language. She wrung her hands.

"I had to do it!" she gasped in German. "I had to do it! It was the only way! Tell me it was the only way!" she seemed to appeal to some one invisible. And then she resumed her lament in the Hungarian.

But all at once something dried this emotion as the sear of a flame would dry water over which it passed. The tears ceased, her eyes flashed, she jerked her body upright, listening. The commotion of pursuit and investigation was sweeping past her tent.

Distinctly she heard the voice of Kingozi giving commands.

An instant later Chaké darted into the tent and fell to the ground. His face was the sickly gray of a negro in terror, his eyes rolled in his head, his teeth chattered, his every muscle trembled.

"*Memsahib! Memsahib!*" he gasped.

Her eyes were blazing with an anger the more fierce in that some of it was reaction.

"Fool!" she spat at him.

"I killed him, *memsahib!* I drove the *shenzi* spear through his back! I left him lying there! He is a god! He has come back from the dead!"

"Fool!" she repeated, and swung her feet to the floor. "Stay here! Do not go out!" she commanded, when she had assumed her mosquito boots. She slipped out between the tent flaps.

Torches were everywhere flickering about. She stopped one of the men as he passed.

"A *shenzi* has killed Mavrouki with a spear," the man answered her question.

She stood for some time watching the torches. Then she saw Kingozi himself take his place by the pile of loads.

"Fall in!" he commanded sharply.

She returned to her tent.

"Here!" she addressed the crouching Nubian. "It is as I said. You have been a fool. You have killed a porter by mistake. Now the *bwana* has ordered to *fall in*. He wishes to see if any are missing. Go take your place, and answer to your name."

"Oh, *memsahib!* Oh, *memsahib!*" the man was groaning.

"Go, I say!" she cried. "And hold up your head. If this is suspected of you, you will surely die."

Kingozi called the roll by the light of a replenished fire.

As each man was named, he was required to step forward to undergo Kingozi's scrutiny.

Most were uneasy, many were excited. Kingozi passed them rapidly in review. But when Chaké came forward, he paused in the machine-like regularity of his inspection.

"Hullo, my bold buccaneer," said he in English, "what ails you?"

The Leopard Woman had drawn near. Kingozi glanced at her over his shoulder.

"I know these Fuzzy-Wuzzies pretty well," he remarked. "This man has the blood look in his eye."

"He's been sick all day," she ventured.

"Sick, eh? Have you had him about you all evening?"

The Leopard Woman hesitated the least appreciable portion of a second.

"No," she answered, "he was sick; I let him sleep in his own camp."

She withdrew a pace, almost as though washing her hands of the affair. Kingozi whirled and levelled his forefinger at the Nubian.

"Why did you use a *shenzi* spear?" he demanded.

Over Chaké's face had come the blank, lifeless expression of the obstinate savage. Kingozi recognized it, and knew that further interrogation was a matter of much time and patience. His eyes and head ached cruelly.

"Very well," he answered the Nubian's unspoken opposition. "You'll keep. Simba, get me the hand irons and the leg irons. Guard this man. To-morrow we will look into it." He turned away without waiting to see his commands carried out. "I've got a beastly headache," he remarked to Bibi-ya-chui. "This affair—this whole affair—will keep. Cazi Moto, I want two men with guns—my men—to stand by my tent, one in front, one in the rear."

The Leopard Woman watched his drooping, wearied form making its way to his tent. He walked shuffling, almost stumbling. The habitual masking stare of her eyes changed. Something softer, almost yearning, crept into them. When the tent flaps had fallen behind him she threw both arms aloft in a splendid tragic gesture, careless of the staring men. Her face was convulsed by strong emotion. She turned and fled to her own tent, where she threw herself face down on her cot.

"It must be done! It must be done!" she groaned to her pillow.

CHAPTER XVII

THE DARKNESS

Kingozi retired again to his cot; but for a long time he could not get to sleep. Little things annoyed him. A fever owl in a thorn tree somewhere nearby called over and over again monotonously, hurriedly, without pause, without a break in rhythm. Kingozi knew that the bird would thus continue all night long, and he tried to adjust his mind to the fact, but failed. It seemed beyond human comprehension that any living creature could keep up steadily so breathless a performance. Some of the men were chatting in low voices. Ordinarily he would not have heard them at all; now they annoyed him. He stood it as long as he could, then shouted "*Kalele!*" at them in so fierce a tone that the human silence was dead and immediate. But this made prominent other lesser noises. Kingozi's headache was worse. He tossed and turned, but at last fell into a half-waking stupor.

He was brought to full consciousness by the entrance of Cazi Moto. He opened his eyes. It was still night—a very black night, evidently, for not a ray of light entered the tent.

"What time is it, Cazi Moto?" he asked.

"Five o'clock, *bwana*."

It was time to rise if a march was to be undertaken. Kingozi waited a moment impatiently.

"Why do you not light the candle?" he demanded.

"The candle is lighted, *bwana*," replied Cazi Moto, with a slight tone of surprise.

Kingozi reached his outspread hand across to his tin box. His fingers encountered a flame, and were slightly scorched. He lay back and closed his eyes.

"The men have struck their tents?" he asked Cazi Moto after a moment.

"Yes, *bwana*, all is prepared."

Then there must be a dozen little fires, and the tent must be filled with flickering reflections. Kingozi lay for some time, thinking. He could hear Cazi Moto moving about, arranging clothes and equipment. When by the sounds Kingozi knew that the task was finished and Cazi Moto about to depart, he spoke.

"We shall not make safari to-day," he said. Cazi Moto stoppped.

"*Bwana ?*"

"We shall not make safari to-day."

Cazi Moto's mind adjusted itself to this new decision. Then, without comment, he glided out to reverse all his arrangements.

Left alone Kingozi lay on his back and bent his will power to getting control of the situation.

He was blind.

At first the mere thought sent so numbing a chill through all his faculties that he needed the utmost of his fortitude to prevent an insensate and aimless panic. Gradually he gained control of this.

Then he groped for the candle. By experiment he found that at a distance of a foot or so the illumination registered. Then there was no paralysis of the nerve itself. Desperately he marshalled his unruly thoughts, striving to look back into the remote past of his student days. Fragments of knowledge came to him, but nothing on which to build a theory of what was wrong.

"It's mechanical; it's mechanical," he muttered over and over to himself, but could not seem to progress beyond this point. All he could conclude was that it was *not* ophthalmia or trachoma. He had seen a good deal of these two plagues of Egypt. and their symptoms were absent here. He concentrated until his mind was weary, and his will slipped. At last in despair he relaxed and in an unconscious gesture rubbed his eyes with his forefingers and thumbs. The contact brought him to with a jerk.

The eyeballs, instead of feeling soft and velvety under the lids, were as hard as marbles.

The shock of this phenomenon rang a bell in his memory. A distinct picture came to him of his classroom and old Doctor Stokes. He could fairly hear the slow, impressive voice.

"There is one symptom," the past was saying to him "one symptom, young gentlemen, that is not always present; but when present establishes the diagnosis beyond any doubt. I refer to a peculiar hardening of the eyeball itself——"

" Glaucoma! " cried Kingozi aloud.

His thoughts, like hounds on a trail, raced off after this new scent. Desperately he tried to recollect. In snatches he captured knowledge. Of its accuracy he was sometimes in doubt; but little by little that doubt grew less. To change the figure, the latent images of his past science developed slowly, like the images on a photographic plate.

Glaucoma—a hardening, an enlarging of the pupil, a change in the shape and consistency of the iris—yes, he had it fairly well. Treatment? Let's see—an operation on the iris, delicate. That was it. Impossible, of course. But there was something else, a temporary expedient, until the surgeon could be reached—an undue expansion of the pupil——

"Why," shouted Kingozi aloud, sitting up in bed. "Pilocarpin, of course!"

What luck! He fervently blessed the shortage of phenacetin that had forced him to take pilocarpin as a sweating substitute for fever.

"Cazi Moto!" he called. Then, as the headman hurried up: "Get me the box of medicines, quick!"

He waited until he heard the little man reënter the tent.

"Place it here," he commanded.   "Now go."

He groped for the case, opened it——

The bottles it contained were all of the same shape.   He remembered that the pilocarpin was at the right-hand end—or was it the left?   Hastily he uncorked the left-hand bottle, and was immediately reassured.   It contained tablets.   The right-hand bottle, on the contrary, held the typical small crystals.   But a doubt assailed him.   At the same end of the case were the receptacles also of the atropin and the morphia.   He remembered the Leopard Woman's remarking how much alike they all were.   Kingozi seemed to see plainly in his mind's eye the precise arrangement, to visualize even the exact appearance of the labels on the bottles—first the morphia, next to it the pilocarpin, and last the atropin.   But while he contemplated this mental image, it shifted.   The pilocarpin and atropin changed places.   And this latter recollection seemed as distinct to him as the first had been.

He fingered the three bottles, his brows bent.   And across his mental travail floated another thought that brought him up all standing.

Pilocarpin and atropin had exactly the opposite effect.

"Here, this won't do!" he said aloud.   "If I get the wrong stuff in my eyes it will destroy them permanently."

He raised his voice for Cazi Moto.

"When Bibi-ya-chui is awake," he told the headman, "I want to see her.   Tell her to come."

CHAPTER XVIII

THE LEOPARD WOMAN CHANGES HER SPOTS

Kingozi washed, dressed, had his breakfast, and sat quietly in his chair. In the open he found that he had a dim consciousness of light, but that was all. There was no pain.

After a while Cazi Moto came to report that the Leopard Woman was out and about. Kingozi's message had been delivered.

"She says you shall come to her tent," concluded Cazi Moto.

Kingozi considered. To insist that she should come to him might lead to a downright refusal, unless he sent her word of his condition. This he did not wish to do. His recollections of the classroom were now distinct. He knew that the pilocarpin would restore his vision within a few hours; and while the alleviation would be temporary, it might last some months, or until he could get the proper surgical aid. Therefore it would be as well not to let the men know anything was even temporarily the matter.

"Take my chair," he ordered Cazi Moto. Then when the latter started off, he followed, touching lightly the folded seat. As he felt the shade of the tree under which the

176

Leopard Woman's tent had been pitched, he chanced a "good morning." Her reply gave him her direction, and he seated himself facing her.

"I am stupid this morning," he said. "Had a bad night. I wanted you to do something for me—read a label, as a matter of fact—and it never occurred to me that I might bring the label to you. Cazi Moto, go get my box of medicines."

"I do not quite understand," replied the Leopard Woman. "What is it you would have me do?"

"Read a label—on a bottle."

"Why is it you do not read it yourself?"

"My eyes do not focus well this morning."

"I see," she said slowly. "And you would have me indicate for you the remedy. That is it?"

"Yes, that is it. I've stupidly forgotten which the bottle is I want."

He heard her moving slightly here and there. He strained his ears to understand what she was about.

"You are blind!" she cried suddenly.

"Temporarily—until I get my remedy. How did you know?"

"The look of you; and just this moment I thrust suddenly at your face."

Cazi Moto arrived with the medicine chest which he placed at his master's feet, and opened. Kingozi extracted the three bottles.

"The table is directly in front of you," came the Leopard Woman's voice.

He reached out, and after a moment deposited the vials on the table.

"It's one of these," he said, "but I don't know which. Just read them for me."

"This remedy will cure you?"

"It will give me my sight. I have what is known as glaucoma. It is an undue expansion of the pupil. This remedy contracts it again. The only real cure is an operation."

A silence ensued.

"Well?" asked Kingozi at length.

"It interests me," came her voice. "Suppose you had not this remedy?"

"I should remain blind," replied Kingozi simply.

"Until you obtained the remedy?"

"Probably for always. One must not let glaucoma run or it becomes chronic. It's God's own luck that I have this stuff with me—it's the pilocarpin I told you of. The other stuff—atropin—would blind me for sure!"

He thrust forward the three bottles.

"Here," he urged.

"If you had not the remedy—this what-you-call—pilocarpin, what would you do?" An edge of eagerness had crept into her tones.

"Do?" said Kingozi, a little impatiently. "I'd streak it for a surgeon. I have no desire to lose my sight."

Another pause.

"I shall not read your labels," she decided. Her voice now was low and decided.

"What!" cried Kingozi.

He could hear the rustle of her clothes as she leaned forward.

"Listen," she said. "Why should I do this for you? You have treated me as a man treats his dog, his horse, his servant, his child—not as a man treats a woman. Do you think because I have been the meek one, the quiet one, that I have not cared?"

"But this—my sight——"

"Your sight is safe. You tell me so yourself. Go back to your surgeon. And if you suffer inconvenience on the way—or pain—or humiliation—or anger—why that is what you have made me suffer."

"I——?"

"You! You have treated me with scorn, with contempt, like a little child, as though I did not exist! You have—what-you-call—ridden over—overridden what I propose, what I try to do. You and your lordly way! You are not a man—you are a fish of cold blood; a statue of iron! You have nothing but the head! You 'know nothing whatever about vegetables'—nor women! Bah! Shall I read your labels and give you your sight? Ah, no! ah, *non !*"

Kingozi was stunned. Idly his hand slid forward across the table. It encountered and closed upon her wrist. Instantly she struggled to be free, whereupon mechanically he tightened his clasp. She made a desperate effort to do something. His other hand sought hers. It grasped one of the three bottles, and even as he determined this fact, she tried again to hurl it to the ground. Frustrated, she relaxed her grip, and he released her.

He could hear the fling of her body as she stood upright; could catch the indrawing of her breath.

"Read them for yourself!" was her parting shot as she withdrew.

Kingozi sat very still for a long time. Then he arose abruptly and commanded Cazi Moto to return with him to his own camp. There he caused his chair to be placed in the shade.

"Cazi Moto," said he, "listen well. You are my other hands; now you must be something else. I am sick in the eyes; I can see nothing. In one of these bottles is the medicine that will cure me, and in one of them is the medicine that will make me blind forever. I do not know which it is; and I cannot read the *barua* because I cannot see it. And Bibi-ya-chui cannot read it. So you must be my eyes. Take a stick, and make on the ground marks exactly like those on the *barua*. Make them deep, so that I may feel them with my hands."

Cazi Moto sharpened a stick, smoothed out a piece of earth, and squatted beside it.

The Central African native is untrained either to express himself or to see pictorially. We have been so trained since the building blocks of our infancy, so that a photograph of a scene is to us an exact replica of that scene in miniature. As a matter of fact, it is only an arbitrary and conventional arrangement of black and white. A raw native sees nothing more than that even in a portrait of himself.

So Cazi Moto went at this task absolutely unequipped both of brain and of hand. In addition the label was rather difficult. The printed body of it contained the firm name of the chemists and their address; the drug itself was written, Kingozi remembered with exasperation, in his own not very legible script.

"Dashed fool!" he told himself aloud in his usual habit. "Deserve what you've got. Ought to have segregated the drugs—ought to have printed the labels—no use thinking of that now."

Cazi Moto worked painstakingly, his shrewd and wizened face puckered in absorption. He accomplished a legible *Borroughs & Wellcome* after many trials. Then he proceeded with the script. It seemed impossible to make a start; he did not even begin at the beginning, but was inclined to view the work as an entity and to begin drawing it at the top of the middle. Kingozi corrected that. At

last the white man's fingers made out distinctly a capital
M. He erased it with a sweep of the hand.

"That part of the *barua* again," he ordered.

After a time Cazi Moto repeated the feat.

"Once more."

This was quicker.

Kingozi dropped that bottle into his side pocket with a
sigh of relief.

"Evidently the morphine," he said. "We'll try it again
later to be sure. Wish I didn't scribble such a rotten hand.
My capital As and Ps are something alike."

He had a new idea. For fifteen minutes he tried to get
from Cazi Moto at first the number of letters on each label;
and later, when the flowing script proved this impractical,
an idea of the relative lengths of the words. Neither method
was certain enough; another argument for printing your
labels, thought Kingozi.

"We'll get it, old sportsman!" he cried aloud in English.
"We'll try for the first letter."

He bent forward, but the lesson went no further.

For an hour the Leopard Woman had been watching,
curious as to what these two were doing so quietly in the
shade of the tree. At last she evidently made up her mind
she must find out. Quietly she drew near them unnoticed,
so that at last she was standing only a few feet to one side.
There she witnessed the final triumph as to the morphine,
and heard Kingozi's last confident speech. As he leaned

forward to place another bottle for Cazi Moto to copy from, she gathered her forces, rushed forward between them, snatched the vial, and dashed it violently against a rock, where it naturally broke into innumerable pieces. Cazi Moto stared up at her, astounded into immobility. Kingozi, without a trace of emotion, leaned back in his chair.

"I think I am losing my wits," he remarked. "I have been criminally stupid through this whole affair. I might have foreseen something of the kind."

She stood there panting excitedly, her hands clinched at her sides.

"I will read your label for you now—the bottle you hold in your hand! It is atropin—atropin——" She laughed wildly.

"I thank you, madam," he said ironically.

"Now you must go back!"

"Yes. Now I must go back. I thank you."

"You may well thank me. I have saved your life!" she cried hysterically, and was gone.

Kingozi did not examine the meaning of this; indeed, it hardly registered at all as it was to him evidently the product of excitement.

He forgot even the scandalized Cazi Moto squatting at his feet. For a long time he stared sightlessly straight ahead. He could not explain this woman. The whole outburst, the complete about-face in what had been their apparent relations, overwhelmed him. He had had no idea

of the slow damming back of resentments; in fact, he really
had no idea that there were causes for resentment at all!
He had done the direct, obvious, efficient thing in a number
of instances when naturally her powers or abilities were inadequate.   Characteristically, he forgot utterly the night
of the full moon!

First of all, it was evident that he must turn back if he
was to save his eyesight.   As he remembered glaucoma, it
ought to be surgically treated within two months, at most.

The second point was whether he could turn back.   His
mission was a simple one.   Would it wait?   He could not
see why not.   He had been sent to gain the friendship and
active alliance of M'tela and his spears; and had been given
carte blanche in the matters of equipment, methods, and
time.   Inside a year or so the International Boundary
Commission would be running boundary lines through that
country.   Until then the Kabilagani could very well go
on as they probably had gone on for the last five hundred
years.

Very well; as far as his job was concerned, he could go
back; as far as his eyes were concerned, he must go back.

Remained the problem of Bibi-ya-chui.

Why was she in the country?   For the same purpose as
himself?   It seemed unlikely; she appeared to have slight
qualifications for such a task.   Indeed, in the candour of
his own inner communings Kingozi acknowledged that he
and the German, Winkleman, alone could be held really

fitted for that sort of negotiation. But if she were? Why did she not say so? Their object would be the same. It was as much to Germany's interest to pacify, to make friendly this hinterland before the advent of the Boundary Commission. All this was a puzzle. But there was the indubitable secret map, and the indubitable concealment of purpose; and—to Kingozi's mind—the indubitable attempt to make travelling so tedious that he would split safaris and permit her to go alone.

This led to another conclusion. He could not see the reason for it all, but one thing was clear: she must not even now be allowed to take her own course. Whatever she was up to, she did not intend to let him know about it; ergo it was something inimical to him, either personally or officially. Probably personally, Kingozi thought with a grim smile. He was no fool about women when his mind was sufficiently disengaged from other things; and now he remembered the inhibited promise of the tropic moon. Still he could take no chances. He could turn back; he must turn back; and as a corollary the Leopard Woman must turn back with him!

CHAPTER XIX

THE TRIAL

He remembered Cazi Moto squatting, undoubtedly horrified to the core.

"Cazi Moto, are you there?"

"Yes, *bwana*."

"Where has the *memsahib* gone?"

"Into her tent, *bwana*."

"Listen well to me. She has destroyed the medicine. Now we must go back to where *Bwana* Marefu can come to fix my eyes. We shall go with all the men as far as the people of the *sultani*. There we will leave many porters and many loads. With a few men we will go to Bwana Marefu. When he has fixed my eyes, then we will come back. I will fix a *barua* for *Bwana*. This must be sent on ahead of us so he can come to meet us. Pick two good men for messengers. Is all that understood?"

"Yes, *bwana*."

"Tell me, then, what is to be done?"

Cazi Moto repeated the gist of what had been said. Kingozi nodded.

"That is it."

"*Bwana ?*" Cazi Moto hesitated.

"Yes. Speak."

"That woman. Shall she be *kibokoed* or killed?"

Kingozi caught back a chuckle.

"No," he said gravely. "That will wait for later. But see that she is watched; do not permit her to talk to her men; take all her guns and pistols, and bring them to me."

"And this Chaké?"

"Of course." Kingozi had really forgotten the man in the concentrations of the past few hours. "Let him be brought before me an hour before sundown."

He found himself all at once overcome with sleep. Hardly was he able to stagger to his cot before he fell into a deep, refreshing slumber.

At the appointed hour Cazi Moto scratched on his tent door. Kingozi arose and walked confidently into the opening. Cazi Moto deftly indicated the location of the chair. Kingozi sat down.

Although he could not see, he visualized the scene well enough. Immediately in front of him, and ten feet away, stood the manacled Nubian, with an armed man at either elbow. Behind them, in turn, were grouped silently all the combined safaris. At his own elbows stood Cazi Moto and Simba—possibly Mali-ya-bwana.

He allowed an impressive wait to ensue. Then abruptly he began his interrogation. He had been thinking over the circumstances, off and on, since last night, and had determined on his line. Ordinarily he would have called for witnesses of various sorts, but this would have been not at all for the purpose of piling up evidence against the accused. That is the civilized fashion; and is superfluous among savages. Kingozi's witnesses would have been called solely for the purpose of furnishing information to himself. He needed only one piece of information here, and that only one witness could furnish him—the man before him.

"Why did you kill Mavrouki?" he demanded.

"I did not kill Mavrouki, *bwana*."

"That is a lie," rejoined Kingozi calmly.

Chaké became voluble.

"All night I sat by my fire cooking *potio* and meat," he protested. "This the *askaris* will tell you. And my spear lay in the tent with the *askaris*," he went on at great length, repeating these two points, babbling, protesting, pleading. Kingozi listened to him in dead silence until he had quite run down.

"Listen," said he impressively, "all these words are lies. This is what happened: from one of the *shenzis* you traded a spear, or a spear was given you. Your own spear you left in the tent. All day you sat in the grass and sharpened the *shenzi* spear." This was a wild guess, based on probabilities, but by the uneasy stir in the throng Kingozi knew he had scored. "Then at night you waited, and you speared Mavrouki with the *shenzi* spear, and you left it in his back, for you said to yourself, 'men will think a *shenzi* has done this thing.' Then you went quietly to your fire, and cooked *potio*, and your own spear was all the time where the *askaris* were lying."

Kingozi paused. He knew without Cazi Moto's whispered assurance that every shot had told. It was a simple bit of deduction, but to these simpler minds it seemed miraculous.

"Why did you wish to kill me?" he demanded.

The Nubian, taken completely by surprise, began to chatter with fright.

"I did not wish to kill you, *bwana*. I wished to kill Mavrouki."

"That is a lie," said Kingozi equably. "Why should you wait for Mavrouki near my tent? Was Mavrouki my gun bearer, or even my cook, that he should come to my tent? Mavrouki was a porter, and if you wished to kill Mavrouki you would wait by the porters' camp."

He said these words slowly, without emphasis, in almost a detached manner. By the murmur he knew that this amazing reasoning had, as usual, struck the men with deep astonishment. The African native is a simple creature. He waited a full minute.

"Mavrouki wore a khaki coat. He and I were the only people of all the safari who had khaki coats. That is why in the darkness you mistook Mavrouki for me. That is why you killed Mavrouki."

He said this in a firm voice, as though making an indisputable statement.   The buzz of low-voiced comment increased.   This time he did not pause.

"Why did you wish to kill me?" he repeated.

But again he sensed the fact that Chaké had taken refuge in the dull stupidity that is an acknowledgment of defeat. He knew that he would get no more replies.   After waiting a few moments he went on.   His voice had become weighty with authority and measured with doom.

"You will not tell.   Let it be so.   And now listen; and you other safari men listen also.   Because you have wished to kill me, you shall have two hundred lashes with the *kiboko;* and then you shall be hanged."

A moment of horror was followed by a low murmur of comment.   Not a man there but realized that the unfortunate Nubian would never live to be hanged.   A punishment of twenty-five is as much as the most stoical can stand in silence; fifty as much as can be absorbed without permanent injury; seventy-five an extreme resorted to on a very few desperately rare occasions.   Beyond that no experience taught the result.   Kingozi's sentence was equivalent to death by torture.

He leaned forward in his chair, listening intently.   He heard his victim's gasp, the mutter of the crowd.   They passed him by.   Then he sank back, a half smile on his lips. He had caught the rustle of silks, the indignant breathing of a woman.   He knew that Bibi-ya-chui stood before him.

"But this is atrocious!" she cried. "This cannot go on!"

"It shall go on," he replied steadily. "Why not?"

"He is my man. I forbid it!"

"He is my man to punish when he attempts my life."

"I shall prevent this—this—oh, this outrage!"

"How?" he asked calmly.

She turned to the men and began to talk to them in Swahili, repeating emphatically what she had just said to Kingozi in English, uttering her commands. They were received in a dead silence.

"You have heard the *memsahib* speak, you men of the *memsahib's* safari," remarked Kingozi; then: "You, Jack, whom I made chief of *askaris*, you speak."

"What does the *bwana* say of this?" came Jack's deep voice after a moment.

"You have heard."

"What the *bwana* says is law."

"Does any man of you think differently? Speak!"

No voice answered. Kingozi turned to where, he knew, the Leopard Woman stood.

"You see?"

He heard only a choked sob of rage and impotence. After waiting a minute he resumed:

"Do my command. Let three men, in turn, give the *kiboko*. You, Simba, see that they strike hard."

A faint clink of manacles indicated that the guards had laid hands on their victim.

"Wait!" cried the Leopard Woman in a strangled voice. Kingozi raised his hand.

"You—you brute!" she cried. "You shall not do this! Chaké is not to blame! It is I—I, who speak. I did this. I ordered him to kill you. I alone should be punished!"

He drew a deep breath.

"I thought so," he said softly; then in Swahili: "These are my orders. Let this man be well guarded. Let him be treated well, and given *potio* and meat. He shall be punished later. And now," he turned to Bibi-ya-chui in English again, "let us drop the excitement and the hysterics. Let us sit down calmly and discuss the matter. Perhaps you are now ready to tell me why you have lied to me; why you have concealed your possession of a secret map and other information; why you have deliberately delayed my march; and, above all, why you have refused to aid my blindness and have attempted to kill me."

CHAPTER XX

KINGOZI'S ULTIMATUM

But she did not immediately answer this. She was on fire with a new thought.

"This is another of your—what you call—traps!" she cried. "You never intended to kill this man with the *kiboko!* You intended to make me speak—as I did!"

"That's as may be," he rejoined. "At least I should have tried how far he would have been faithful to you before telling what he knew—if you had not spoken."

"He is faithful—to the death," she asseverated with passion.

"I am inclined to believe you are right. But that is neither here nor there. I am waiting answers to my questions."

"And you shall wait," she took him up superbly. "I shall not answer!"

He shrugged his shoulders wearily.

"That is your affair. I must confess that I am curious to know, however, why you did not shoot me. You have a pistol."

"Your men took that pistol."

"But not until late this morning. You had plenty of chance."

"I could not," she said, her voice taking on a curious intonation; "there was no need."

"You mean since I went blind there was no need," he interjected quickly.

She hesitated whether to reply. Then:

"Yes, that is it," she assented.

Kingozi leaned forward, gripping the arms of his chair.

"I must tell you that my blindness is not going to help you in the way you believe," he said.

"What do I believe?" The animation of curiosity crept into her voice.

"For one thing, you believe I am no ivory hunter; and you know perfectly why I am in this country."

"Do I?"

"Do you not?"

"Well—yes."

"Why is it, tell me."

She pondered this, then made up her mind.

"I do not know why not. The time for fencing is over. I know perfectly that you are sent by your government to make treaty with M'tela. And I know," she added with the graciousness of one who has got back to sure ground, "that no one could do it better; and no one as well."

"Except Winkleman," said Kingozi simply.

"Except Winkleman—perhaps."

"As you say, the time for fencing is over," pursued Kingozi. "That is true. And it is true also that you are not merely travelling for pleasure. You are yourself on a mission. You are Hungarian, but you are in the employ of the German Government."

She laughed musically.

"*Bravo!*" she cried. "That is true. But go on—how do you make the guess?"

"Your maps, your—pardon me—equivocations, and a few other matters of the sort. Now it is perfectly evident that you are trying to forestall me in some manner."

"Point number two," she agreed mockingly.

"I am free to confess I do not know why; and at present I do not care. That's why I tell you. You are so anxious to forestall me—for this unknown reason—that when smaller things fail——"

"You are of an interest—what smaller things?"

"Various wiles—some of them feminine. Delays, for example. Do you suppose I believed for a moment those delays were not inspired? That is why my punishments were so severe—and other wiles," he concluded vaguely.

She did not press the point.

"When smaller things failed," he repeated, "you would have resorted even to murder. Your necessity must have been great."

"Believe me—it was!" she answered.

He brought up short at the unexpected feeling that

vibrated in her voice. His face expressed a faint surprise, and he returned to his subject with fresh interest.

"And when my eyes failed me, and you could have given me my sight by the mere reading of a label, you refused; you condemned me to the darkness. And, further, when I had a chance to learn my remedy for myself, you destroyed it. I wonder whether that cost you anything, too?"

He sat apparently staring out into the distance, his sightless eyes wide with the peculiar blank pathos of the blind. The Leopard Woman's own eyes were suffused with tears!

"I remember now something you said when you broke the bottle of pilocarpin," he said slowly. "I did not notice it at the time; now it comes to me. 'I have saved your life,' you said. I get the meaning of that now. You would have killed me rather than not have forestalled me; but the blindness saved you that necessity. You know, I am a little glad to learn that you did not *want* to kill me."

"Want!" she cried. "How could I want?"

Kingozi chuckled.

"You told me enough times just what you thought of me."

Her crest reared, but drooped again.

"No women likes to be treated so. And if you had your eyes, so I would hate you again!"

"I don't know why you want to prevent me from reaching M'tela, nor why you want to reach him first, nor why in its wisdom your government sent you at all. I'd like to know, just as a matter of curiosity. But it doesn't really matter, because it does not affect the essential situation in the least."

"You are going to M'tela just the same?" she inquired anxiously.

"Bless you, no. I have no desire to go blind. It's the beastliest affliction can come to an active man. And glaucoma is a tricky thing. I'd like to get to McCloud tomorrow. But still you are not going to get to M'tela before me."

"No?"

"I am sorry; but you will have to go with me."

"You have the force," she acknowledged after a moment.

Somewhat surprised at her lack of protest—or was it resignation to the inevitable?—Kingozi checked himself. After a moment he went on.

"Somehow," he mused, "in spite of your amiable activities, I have a certain confidence in you. It would be much more comfortable for both of us if you would give me your word not to try to escape, or to go back, or to leave my camp, or cause your men to leave my camp, or anything like that."

"Would you trust my word?"

"If you would give it solemnly—yes."

"But to do what I wished to do—as you say just now yourself—I am ready to use all means—even to killing.

Why do you not think I would also break my word to do my ends?"

"I think you would not."

"But do you think I would, what you call—consider your trust in me more great than my government's trust in me?"

"No. I do not think that either."

"Well?"

"I do not think you will give your word to me unless you mean to keep it. If you do give it, I am willing to rely upon it."

The Leopard Woman moved impulsively to his side.

"Very well. I give it," she said with a choke.

"That you go with my safari, without subterfuge, without sending word anywhere—in other words, a fair start afresh!"

"Just that," she replied.

"That is your word of honour?"

"My word of honour."

"Give me your hand on it."

She laid her palm in his. His hand closed over hers, gripping it tightly. Her eyes were swimming, her breast heaved. Slowly she swayed toward him, leaned over him. Her lips touched his. Suddenly she was seized hungrily. She abandoned herself to the kiss.

But after a moment she tore herself away from him, panting.

"This must not be!" she cried tragically. "I know not what I do! This is not good! I am a woman of honour!"

Kingozi, his blind face alight, held out his arms to her.

"Your honour is safe with me," he said.

But he had mistaken her meaning. Step by step she recoiled from him until she stood at the distance of some paces, her hands pressed against her cheeks, her eyes fixed on him with a strange mixture of tenderness, pity, and sternness.

"What is it?" he begged, getting uncertainly to his feet. "Where are you?"

But she did not answer him. After a moment she slipped away.

CHAPTER XXI

THE MESSENGERS

The return trip began promptly the following morning, and progressed uninterruptedly for two weeks. One by one they picked up the water-holes found on the journey out.

A few details had to be adjusted to compensate for Kingozi's lack of eyes. The matter of meat supplies, for example.

"Good luck I gave some attention to your shooting, old sportsman," he remarked to Simba in English, then in Swahili: "Here are five cartridges. Go get me a zebra and a kongoni."

Simba was no shot, but Kongozi knew he would stalk, with infinite patience and skill, fairly atop his quarry before letting off one of the precious cartridges.

In the matter of rhinoceros and similar dangers, they simply took a chance.

Kingozi marched at the end of a stick held by Simba. He gave his whole energies to getting over the day's difficulties of all sorts. His relations with the Leopard Woman swung back. Perhaps vaguely, in the back of his mind, he looked forward to the interpretation of that unpremeditated kiss; but just now a mixed feeling of responsibility and delicacy prevented his going forward from the point attained. During the march they walked apart most of the time. The weariness of forced travel abridged their evenings.

Chaké walked guarded, and slept in chains.

Whenever the location of water-holes permitted, the safari made long jumps. The two messengers sent out with a scrawled letter to Doctor McCloud—whom they knew as Bwana Marefu—were of course far ahead. With any luck Kingozi hoped to meet the surgeon not far from the mountains where dwelt the *sultani* of the ivory stockade.

Thus the march went through a fortnight. The close of the fourteenth day found them camped near water in a *donga*. The dim blue of mountains had raised itself above the horizon ahead. This rejoiced the men. They were running low of *potio*, and they knew that from the *sultani's* subjects in these mountains a further supply could be had. As a consequence, an unwonted *kalele* was smiting the air. Each man chatted to his next-door neighbour at the top of his lungs, laughing loudly, squealing with delight. Kingozi sat enjoying it. He had been so long in Africa that this happy rumpus always pleased him. Suddenly it fell to silence. He cocked his ear, trying to understand the reason.

Across the open veldt two figures had been descried.

They were coming toward the camp at a slow dogtrot; and as they approached it could be seen that save for a turban apiece they were stark naked; and save for a spear and a water gourd apiece they were without equipment. One held something straight upright before him, as medieval priests carried a cross. The turbans were formed from their blankets; mid-blade of each spear was wound with a strip of red cloth; the object one carried was a letter held in the cleft of a stick.

By these tokens the safari men knew the strangers to be messengers.

The mail service of Central Africa is slow but very certain. You give your letter to two reliable men and inform them that it is for *Bwana* So-and-so. Sooner or later *Bwana* So-and-so will get that letter. He is found by a process of elimination. In the bazaars the messengers inquire whether he has gone north, south, east, or west. Some native is certain to have known some of his men. So your messengers start west. Their progress thenceforward is a series of village visits. The gossip of the country directs them. Gradually, but with increasing certainty, their course defines itself, until at last—months later—they come trotting into camp.

These two jogged in broadly agrin. Cazi Moto and Simba led them at once to Kingozi's chair.

"These men bring a *barua* for you, *bwana*," said Cazi Moto.

Kingozi took the split wand with the letter thrust cross-wise in the cleft.

"Who sent them?" he asked.

"The *Bwana* M'Kubwa*, *bwana.*"

"Have they no message?"

"They say no message, *bwana.*"

"Take them and give them food, and see that they have a place in one of the tents."

"Yes, *bwana.*"

"And send Bibi-ya-chui to me."

The Leopard Woman sent word that she was bathing, but would come shortly. Kingozi sat fingering the letter, which he could not read. It was long and thick. He could feel the embossed frank of the Government Office. The situation was puzzling. It might contain secret orders, in which case it would be inadvisable to allow the Leopard Woman a sight of its contents. But Kingozi shook off this thought. At about the time he felt the cool shadow of the earth rise across his face as the sun slipped below the horizon, he became aware also by the faint perfume that the Leopard Woman had come.

"I am in a fix," he said abruptly. "Runners have just come in with this letter. It is official, and may be secret. I am morally certain you ought not to know its contents; but I don't see how I am to know them unless you do. Will you read it to me, and will you give me your word not

---

**Bwana M'Kubwa*—the great lord, i. e., the chief officer of any district.

to use its contents for your own or your government's purposes?"

She hesitated.

"I cannot promise that."

"Well," he amended after a moment, "you will stick to the terms of your other promise—that you will not attempt to leave my safari or send messages until we arrive."

"The fresh, even start," she supplied. "That promise is given."

He handed her the envelope.

A crackle of paper, then a long wait.

"I shall not read you this," she said finally in a strangled, suppressed voice.

"Why not?" he demanded sharply.

"It contains things I would not have you know."

He felt the paper thrust into his hands, reached for her wrists, and pinioned them. For once his self-control had broken. His face was suffused with blood and dark with anger.

But his speech was cut short by an uproar from the camp. Cries, shrieks, shouts, yells, and the sound of running to and fro steadily increased in volume. It was a riot.

In vain Kingozi called for Cazi Moto and Simba. Finally he grasped his *kiboko* and started in the direction of the disturbance. The Leopard Woman sprang to his side, and guided him. He laid about him blindly with the *kiboko*, and in time succeeded in getting some semblance of order.

"Cazi Moto! Simba!" he shouted angrily.

"Bwana?" "Sah?" two panting voices answered.

"What is this?"

They both began to speak at once.

"You, Cazi Moto," commanded Kingozi.

"These men are liars," began Cazi Moto.

"What men?"

"These men who brought the *barua*. They tell lies, bad lies, and we beat them for it."

"Since when have you beaten liars? And since when have I ceased to deal punishment? And since when has it been permitted that such a *kalele* be raised in my camp?" pronounced Kingozi coldly. "For attending to such things you are my man; and Simba is my man; and Mali-ya-bwana is my man; and Jack is my man. Because you have done these things I fine you six rupees each one."

"Yes, *bwana*," said Cazi Moto submissively.

"These other men—what manner of 'lie' do they tell? Bring them here."

The messengers were produced.

"What is it you tell that my men beat you for telling lies? They must be bad lies, for it is not the custom of men to beat men for telling lies."

"We tell no lies, *bwana*," said one of the messengers earnestly. "We tell the truth."

"What is it you tell?"

"We said what has happened: that across the Serengëtti

came white men from the country of Taveta, and that these
white men were many, and had many *askaris* with them,
and our white men from Nairobi met them, and fought so
that those from Taveta were driven back and some were
killed.   And down the N'Gouramani River many of our
white men with *Mahindi** fought with strange white men
on a hill below Ol Sambu, but were driven off.   And many
Mahindi are coming in to Mombasa, all with guns, and all
the *askaris* are brought into Nairobi.   And we told these
safari men that the white men were making war on the
white men, so they cried out at this, and beat us."

Kingozi had listened attentively.

"Well, Cazi Moto?" he demanded.

"But this is a lie; a bad lie," said Cazi Moto, "to say
that white men make war on white men!"

"Nevertheless it is true," rejoined Kingozi quietly.
"These other white men are the *Duyches†*, and they make
war."

He turned and walked back to his camp unassisted.   He
groped for his chair and sat down.   His hand encountered
the letter.

"You do not need to read this to me now," he told the
Leopard Woman quietly.   "I know what it tells."   He
thought a moment.   "It is clear to me now.   You knew
this war was to be declared."

*Mahindi—East Indians.
†Duyches—Germans.

She did not reply.

"You know about *when* this war was to be declared," he pursued his thought. "Yes, it fits."

Her silence continued.

"You should have killed me," he thought aloud. "That alone could have accomplished your mission properly. You might have known I would make you go back, too. Or perhaps you thought you could command your own men in spite of me?"

"Perhaps," she said unexpectedly.

He raised his voice:

"Cazi Moto!"

The chastened headman came running.

"To-morrow," Kingozi told him, "the men go on half *potio*. There will be plenty of meat but only half *potio*."

"Yes, *bwana*."

"And if any man grumbles, or if any man objects even one word to what I do or where I go, bring him to me at once. Understand?"

"Yes, *bwana*."

"*Bassi*."

"What is it you intend to do now?" asked the Leopard Woman curiously.

"Go back, of course."

"Back—where?"

"To M'tela."

She gasped.

"But you cannot do that! You have not considered; you have not thought."

He shrugged his shoulders.

"But it means blindness; blindness for always!"

"I know my duty."

"But to be blind, to be blind always; never to see the sun, the wide veldt, the beasts, and the birds! Never to read a book, to see a man's face, a woman's form; to sit always in darkness waiting—you cannot do that!"

He winced at her words but did not reply. Her hands fluttered to his shoulders.

"Please do not do this foolishness," she pleaded softly; "it is not worth it! See, I have given my word! If you had thought I would go ahead of you to M'tela, all that danger is past. A fresh start, you said it yourself. Do you think I would deceive you?"

She was hovering very close to him; he could feel her breath on his cheek. Firmly but gently he took her two wrists and thrust her away from him.

"Listen, my dear," he said gently, "this is a time for clear thinking. My country is at war with Germany; and my whole duty is to her. You are an Austrian."

"My country, too, is at war," she said unexpectedly.

"Ah, you knew that would happen, too," he said after a startled pause. "I know only this: that if in times of peace

it was important to my government that M'tela's friendship be gained, it is ten times as important in time of war.
I must go back and do my best."

"But why?" she interjected eagerly. "This savage
tribe—it is in the remote hinterland; it knows nothing of
the white man or the white man's quarrels. What difference can it make?"

"That is not my affair. For one thing, he is on the
border."

"But what difference of that? The border means nothing. The fate of their colonies will be fought in Europe, not
here. What happens to this country depends on who wins
there below."

"Can you state positively of your own knowledge that
no invasion or movement of German troops is planned
across M'tela's country? On your sacred word of honour?"
propounded Kingozi suddenly.

"On my word of honour," she repeated slowly, "no such
movement."

"Do you know what you are talking about?"

She was silent.

"It doesn't sound reasonable—an invasion from that
quarter—what could they gain either on that side or on
this?" Kingozi ruminated. A sudden thought struck him.
"And that there is no reason whatever, from my point
of view as a loyal British subject, against my going out at
this time? On your word?"

"Oh!" she cried distressedly, "you ask such questions! How can I answer——"

He stopped her with grave finality.

"That is sufficient. I go back."

She did not attempt to combat him.

"I have done my duty, too," she said dully. "Mine is not the Viennese conscience. My parole; I must take that back. From to-morrow I take it back."

"I understand. I am sorry. To-morrow I place my guard."

"Oh, why cannot you have the sense?" she cried passionately. "I cannot bear it! That you must be blind! That I must kill you if I can, once more!"

Kingozi smiled quietly to himself at this confession.

"So you would even kill me?" he queried curiously.

"I must! I must! If it is necessary, I must! I have sworn!"

"Don't you suppose I shall take precautions?"

"Oh, I hope so! I do hope so!" she cried.

Her distress was so genuine, her unconsciousness of the anomaly of her attitude so naïve that Kingozi forbore even to smile.

"I must go on," he concluded simply.

CHAPTER XXII

THE SECOND MESSENGERS

The return journey began. A remarkable tribute to Kingozi's influence, not only over his own men, but over those of the new safari, might have been read from the fact that there was brought for correction not one grumble, either over the halving of the *potio* or the apparently endless counter-marching. As far as the white members were concerned the journey was one of doggedness and gloom. Kingozi's strong will managed to keep to the foreground the details of his immediate duty; but to do so he had to sink all other considerations whatever. The same effort required to submerge all thought of the darkened years to come carried down also every recollection of the past. The Leopard Woman ceased to exist, not because she had lost importance, but because Kingozi's mind was focussed on a single point.

And she. Perhaps she understood this; perhaps the tearing antagonism of her own purposes, duties, and desires stunned or occupied her—who knows? The outward result was the same as in the case of her companion. They walked apart, ate apart, lived each in his superb isolation, going forward like sleep-walkers to what the future might hold.

Thus they travelled for ten days. In mid-march, then, Cazi Moto came to tell Kingozi that two more messengers had arrived.

"They are not people of our country," he added. "They are *shenzis* such as no man here ever saw before."

"What sort of *shenzis* ?"

"Short, square men. Very black. Hair that is long and stands out like a little tree."

"What do they say?"

"*Bwana*, they speak a language that no man here understands. And this is strange: that they do not come from the direction of Nairobi."

"Perhaps they are men from M'tela."

"No, *bwana*, that cannot be, for they carry a *barua*. They came from a white man."

"That is strange, very strange," said Kingozi quickly. "I do not understand. Is there water near where we stand?"

"There is the water of the place we called *Campi ya Korungu* when we passed before."

"Make camp there."

"The sun is at four hours*, *bwana*."

"It makes no difference."

When camp had been pitched Kingozi caused the new messengers to be brought before him. A few moments'

---

*10:00 o'clock.

questioning elicited two facts: one, that there existed no medium of communication known to both parties; two, that the strangers were from some part of the Congo basin. The latter conclusion Kingozi gained from catching a few words of a language root known to him. He stretched his hand for the letter.

It was in a long linen envelope, unsealed, and unembossed.

Not from the government. He unfolded the sheets of paper and ran his fingers over the pages. Written in pencil; he could feel the indentations where the writer had borne down. Some private individual writing him from camp on the Congo side. Who could it be? Kingozi's Central African acquaintance was wide; he knew most of the gentlemen adventurers roaming through that land of fascination. A good many were not averse to ivory poaching; and the happy hunting ground of ivory poaching was at that time the French Congo. It might be any of them. But how could they know of his whereabouts in this unknown country? And how could they know he was in this country at all? These last two points seemed to him important. Suddenly he threw his head back and laughed aloud.

"Self-centred egotist!" he addressed himself. "Cazi Moto, tell Bibi-ya-chui I wish to see her."

Cazi Moto departed to return immediately with the Leopard Woman who, at this hour, was still in her marching clothes. If she felt any surprise at this early abandonment of the day's march she did not show it. Two *askaris*, confided with the task of guarding her, followed a few paces to the rear. She glanced curiously at the bushy savages.

"Here," said Kingozi, holding out the letter, "is a *barua* for you—from your friend Winkleman in the Congo."

The shock of surprise held her speechless for a moment.

"Your blindness is well! You can see!" she cried then.

Kingozi raised his head sharply, for there was a lilt of relief and gladness in her voice.

"No," he answered, "just ordinary deduction. Am I right?"

He heard her slowly unfolding the paper.

"Yes, you are right," she said in sober tones, after a moment. She uttered a happy exclamation, then another; then ran to his side and threw her arms around his neck in an impulsive hug. Kingozi remembered the waiting men and motioned them away. She was talking rapidly, almost hysterically, as people talk when relieved of a pressure.

"Yes, it is from Winkleman. He has come in from the Congo side. When this letter was written he was only ten days' march from M'tela."

"How do you know that?" interjected Kingozi sharply.

"Native information, he says. Oh, I am so glad! so glad! so glad!"

"That was the plan from the start, was it?" said Kingozi. "I don't know whether it was a good plan or that I have

been thick. My head is in rather a whirl. It was Winkleman right along, was it?"

She laughed excitedly.

"Oh, such a game! Of course it was Winkleman. Did
you think me one to be sent to savage kings?"

"It didn't seem credible," muttered Kingozi. "It is a
humiliating question, but seems inevitable—were you
actually sent out by your officials merely to delay *me* ?"

"So that Winkleman might arrive first—surely."

"I see." Kingozi's accent was getting to be more for-
mally polite. "But why you? Why did not your most
efficient employers dispatch an ordinary assassin? I do
not err in assuming that you all knew that this war was to
be declared at this time."

"That is true." Her voice still sang, her high spirits un-
subdued by his veiled sarcasm.

"Then since it is war, why not have me shot and done
with it? Why send a woman?"

"That was arranged, truly. A man of the Germans was
following you. He was as a sportsman, for it would not
do to rouse suspicion. Then he had an accident. I was
in Nairobi. I heard of it. I did not know you, and this
German did not know you. It seemed to us very simple.
I was to follow until I came up with you. Then I was to
delay you until I had word that Winkleman had crossed
the *n'yika.*"

"All very simple and easy," murmured Kingozi.

"It was not simple! It was not easy!" she cried in a sudden flash of resentment. "You are a strange man. When you go toward a thing, you see down a narrow lane. What is either side does not exist." Her voice gradually raised to vehemence. "I am a woman. I am weak and helpless. Do you assist me, comfort me, sustain me in dreadful situation? No! You march on, leaving me to follow! I think to myself that you are a pig, a brute, that you have no chivalry, that you know not the word gentleman; and I hate you! Then I see that I am wrong. You have chivalry, you are a true gentleman; but before you is an object and you cannot turn your eyes away. And I think so to myself that when this object is removed, is placed one side for a time, then you will come to yourself. Then will be my chance. For I study you. I look at your eyes and the fire in them, and the lips, and the wide, proud nostril; and I see that here is no cold fish creature, but a strong man. So I wait my time. And the moon rises, and the savage drums throb, throb like hearts of passion, and the bul-buls sing in the bush—and I know I am beautiful, and I know men, and almost I think you look one side, and that I win!"

"So all that was a game!" commented Kingozi.

"A game? But yes—then!"

"For the sake of winning your point—would you—would you——"

"For the sake of winning my point did I not command

to kill you—you—my friend?" she commented, her manner falling from vehemence to sadness. "If I could do that, what else would matter!" She paused; then went on in a subdued voice: "But even then your glance but wavered. You are a strong man; and you are a victim of your strength. When an idea grips hold of you, you know nothing but that. And so I saw the delaying of you was not so simple, so easy. It was not as a man to a woman, but as a man to a man. It was war. I did my best," she concluded wearily.

Kingozi was staring in her direction almost as though he could see.

"Why do you tell me all this?" he asked at length.

"I want you to know. And I am so glad!" The lilt had crept back into her voice.

"I congratulate you," he replied drily.

"Stupid! Oh, stupid!" she cried. "Do you not see why I am glad? It is you! Now you shall not sit forever in the darkness. You shall go back to your doctor, who will arrange your eyes."

"Why?" asked Kingozi.

"Why!" she repeated, astonished. "But it is 'why not!' Listen! Have you thought? Winkleman is now but a week's march from M'tela. And here, where we stand, it is perhaps twenty days, perhaps more. Winkleman would arrive nearly two weeks ahead of you. Tell me, how long would it take you to win M'tela's friendship so it would not be shaken?"

Kingozi's face lit with a grim smile.

"A week," he promised confidently.

"You see! And Herr Winkleman is equal to you; you have said so yourself. Is not it so?"

"It's so, all right."

"Then—you see?"

"I see."

"Then we shall go back to the doctor. Oh, do you not see it is for that I am glad—truly, truly! You must believe me that!"

"I believe you," said Kingozi. "Nevertheless, I do not think I shall go back."

"But that is madness. You cannot arrive in time. And it is to lose your eyes all for nothing, for a foolish idea that you do your duty!"

Kingozi shook his head. She wrung her hands in despair.

"Oh, I know that look of you!" she cried. "You see only down your narrow lane!"

CHAPTER XXIII

THE COUNCIL OF WAR

That evening Kingozi called to him Cazi Moto, Simba, and Mali-ya-bwana. He commanded them to build a little fire, and when the light from the leaping flames had penetrated his dull vision, he told them to sit down before him. Thus they knew that a serious council was intended. They squatted on their heels below the white man in his chair, and looked up at him with bright, devoted eyes.

"Listen," he said. "The matter is this: the *Inglishee* are at war with the *Duyche*. Over from the Congo comes a *Duyche* known as *Bwana* Nyele.* It is his business to reach this *shenzi* king, M'tela, and persuade M'tela to fight on the side of the *Duyche*. It is our business to reach M'tela and persuade him to fight on the side of the *Inglishee*. Is that understood?"

"It is understood, *bwana*," said they.

"But this *Duyche*, *Bwana* Nyele, is only one week's march from M'tela; and he undoubtedly has many gifts for M'tela and the Kabilagani. And we are many days' safari distant, and I am blind and cannot hurry."

---

* *Bwana* Nyele—the master with the mane, i. e., beard or hair.

The three uttered little clucks of sympathy and interest.

"But for all that we may win. You three men are my eyes and my right hand. I have a plan, and this is what you must do: Cazi Moto must stay with me to be headman of safari, and to be my eyes when we come to M'tela's land. You Simba, and you Mali-ya-bwana, must go with six of the best men to where *Bwana* Nyele is marching. These two strange *shenzis* will guide you. Then when you are near the safari of *Bwana* Nyele you must arrange so that these *shenzis* can have no talk with any of the safari of *Bwana* Nyele. That is understood?"

"Yes, *bwana*," said Simba. "Do we kill these *shenzis* ?"

"No, do not kill them. Tie them fast."

"Yes, *bwana*, and then?"

"This is the most difficult. You must get hold of *Bwana* Nyele, and you must tie him fast also, and keep him from his safari. He is a *m'zungu**, yes—but he is a *Duyche*, and my enemy, and these things are right, because I command it."

"Yes, *bwana*."

"Then you must keep *Bwana* Nyele and these two *shenzis* close in camp, hidden where their safari cannot find them. And after two weeks you must send two men to M'tela's to find me, and to tell me where you are hidden. Now is all that understood? You, Simba, tell me what you are to do."

* *M'zungu*—white man.

"Mali-ya-bwana, myself, six men and these *shenzis* travel to where the safari of *Bwana* Nyele marches. When we are near that safari we tie up the two *shenzis*. Then we get *Bwana* Nyele and tie him up in a secret camp. Then after two weeks we send two men to tell the *bwana* where we are. But, *bwana*, how do we get *Bwana* Nyele?"

"That I will tell you soon. One thing you forgot: you must reach the *Duyche* before he gets into M'tela's country. This means travel night and day—fast travel. Can this be done?"

"We shall pick good men, *bwana*, runners of the Wa-kamba. We shall do our best."

"Good. Each man four days' *potio*, and what biltong he can use. Simba, take my small rifle and fifty cartridges. Take some snuff, beads, and wire—only a little—to trade for *potio* if you meet with other people. Understood?"

"Yes, *bwana*."

"Cazi Moto," he directed. "bring me the small box of wood from my *sandoko*."

He slid the cover off this box when it was delivered into his hands, fumbled a moment, and held up an object.

"What is this?" he asked.

"It is a bone, *bwana*."

"Yes, it is a bone; but it is more. It is a magic. With this you will take *Bwana* Nyele."

He could sense the stir of interest in the three men before him.

"Listen carefully. This is what you must do. When you have come near to this safari, you must follow it until it has put down its loads and is just about to make camp. Not a rest period on the road; not after camp is made— just at the moment when the men begin to untie the loads, when they begin to pitch the tents. That is the magic time. Understand?"

"Yes, *bwana*," they chorused breathlessly.

"Simba must be ready. He must take off his clothes, and he must oil his body and paint it, and put on the ornaments of a *shenzi* of this country. For that pur- pose he must take with him the necklace, the arm- lets, anklets, and belt that I traded for with the *shenzis*, and which Cazi Moto will get from my tent. Do you know the style of painting of these *shenzis* of the plains, Simba?"

"Yes, *bwana*."

"It is important that you make yourself a *shenzi*. This magic is a bad magic otherwise. Then at the moment I have named, Simba as a *shenzi* will take this magic bone and hold it out to *Bwana* Nyele saying nothing. *Bwana* Nyele will say words, perhaps in Swahili which Simba will understand; perhaps in some other language which he will not understand. Simba must point thus; and then must start in that direction. *Bwana* Nyele will follow a few steps. Then Simba will say: 'Many more, *bwana*, over there only a little distance.'" Kingozi uttered this last sentence in atrocious Swahili. "You must say it in just that way, like a *shenzi*. Say it."

Simba repeated the words and accent.

"Yes, that is it. Then say nothing more, no matter what he asks; and do not let him touch the magic bone. Point. He will follow you; and when he has followed out of sight of the safari you will all seize him and tie him fast. The rest is as I have commanded."

"How does *bwana* know how these things will happen thus?" breathed Simba in awestricken tones.

"It is a magic," replied Kingozi gravely.

Over and over he drilled them until the details were thoroughly understood. Then he dismissed them and leaned back with a sigh. The plan was simple, but ought to work. At the moment of making camp Winkleman would be less apt than at any other time to take with him an escort —especially if his interest or cupidity were aroused—for every one would be exceedingly busy. And no fear about the interest and cupidity! The "magic" bone Kingozi had confided to Simba was a fragment of a Pleistocene fossil. Kingozi himself valued it highly, but he hoped and expected to get it back. It made excellent bait, which no scientist could resist. Of course there might be a second white man with Winkleman, but from the reported size of the latter's safari he thought not. All in all, Kingozi had great reliance in his magic.

At the end of fifteen minutes Simba came to report.

"All is ready, *bwana*," he said, "and we start now. But if *bwana* could let me take a lantern, which I have in my hand, we could travel also at night."

The lantern, as Kingozi well knew, was not for the purpose of casting light in the path, but as some slight measure of protection against lions.

"Let me have it," he ordered. It was passed into his hands, and proved to be one of the two oil lanterns kept for emergencies.

But Kingozi sent the headman for one of the candle lanterns in everyday use, and a half-dozen short candles.

"These are better," he said; "and *qua heri*, Simba. If you do these things well, large *backsheeshi* for you all."

"*Qua heri, bwana,*" said Simba, and was gone.

CHAPTER XXIV

M'TELA'S COUNTRY

To the bewilderment of the Leopard Woman the pace of the safari now slackened. Heretofore the marches had been stretched to the limit of endurance; now the day's journey was as leisurely as that of a sportsman's caravan. It started at daybreak, to be sure, but it ended at noon, unless exigencies of water required an hour or two additional. As a matter of fact, Kingozi knew that he had done everything possible. If Simba & Co. succeeded, then there was no immediate hurry; if they failed, hurry would be useless.

Bibi-ya-chui noticed the absence of two such prominent members of the safari as Simba and Mali-ya-bwana, of course, but readily accepted Kingozi's explanation that he had sent them "as messengers."

The little safari for the third time crawled its antlike way across the immensities of the veldt. Cazi Moto managed to keep them supplied with meat, but at an excessive expenditure of cartridges. As he used the Leopard Woman's rifle, this did not so much matter, for she was abundantly supplied. At last the blue ranges rose before them; each day's journey defined their outlines better. The foothills began to sketch themselves, to separate from the ranges, finally to surround the travellers with the low swells of broken country. Running water replaced the still water-holes. Cazi Moto reported herds of goats in the distance. One evening several of the goatherds ventured into camp. They spoke no Swahili, but at the name M'tela they nodded vigorously, and at the mention of Kabilagani they pointed at their own breasts.

"I wish I had eyes!" cried Kingozi petulantly. "What kind of people are they?"

The Leopard Woman told him as best she could—tall, well-formed, copper in hue, of a pleasing expression, clad scantily in goat skins.

"Their ornaments, their arms?" cried Kingozi with impatience.

"They are poor people," replied Bibi-ya-chui. "They have armlets of iron beaten out, and necklaces of shell fragments or bone. They carry spears with a short blade, broad like a leaf."

"Their armlets are not of wire? They have no cowrie shells?"

"No, it is beaten iron——"

"Good!" cried Kingozi. "There has been little or no trading here!"

One of the goatherds went with them as guide to M'tela.

"Without doubt," Kingozi surmised, "others have run on to warn M'tela of our coming."

Their way led on a gentle, steady up grade without steep climbs. The hills, at first only scattered, low hummocks, became higher, more numerous, closed in on them; until, before they knew it, they found themselves walking up the flat bed of a cañon between veritable mountains. The end of the view, the Leopard Woman said, was shut by a frowning, unbroken rampart many thousands of feet high.

"Then we are due for a climb," sighed Kingozi. "These native tracks never hunt for a grade! When they want to go up, why up they go!"

But the head of the cañon, instead of stopping against the wall, bent sharply to the left. A "saddle" was disclosed.

Toward this the hard-beaten track led. Shortly it began to mount steeply, and shortly after it entered a high forest growing on the abrupt slopes. Here it was cool and mysterious, with green shadows, and the swing of rope vines, and the sudden remoteness of glimpsed skies. The earth was soft and moist under foot; so the dampness of it rose to the nostrils. Vines and head-high bracken and feather growths covered the ground. In every shallow ravine were groves of tree ferns forty feet tall. A silence dwelt there, a different silence from that of the veldt at night; compounded of a few simple elements, such as the faint, incessant drip of hidden waters and occasional loud, hollowly echoing noises such as the bark of a colobus or the scream of a hyrax. There were birds, rare, flashing, brilliant, furtive birds, but they said nothing.

Through this forest on edge the path led steeply upward. Sometimes it was almost perpendicular; sometimes it took an angle; sometimes—but rarely—it paused at a little ledge wide enough to rest nearly the whole safari at once.

For an hour and a half they climbed, then topped the rim of the escarpment and emerged from the forest at the same time.

Immediately they were a thousand leagues from the Africa they knew. A gently rolling country stretched out before them with sweeps of green grass shoulder high, and compact groves of trees as though planted. For miles it undulated away until the very multitude of its low, peaceful hills shut in the horizon. Cattle grazed in the wide-flung hollows, and little herds of game; goats and sheep dotted the hills. The groves of trees were very green. Everything breathed of peace and plenty. Almost would one with proper childhood recollections listen for a church-going bell, search for spires and cottage roofs among the trees. Slim columns of smoke rose straight into the motionless air. The very sun seemed to have abated its African fierceness, and to have become mild.

Some of these things Kingozi learned from Cazi Moto; some from the Leopard Woman; each after his kind.

About a half-mile away a number of warriors in single file walked across the wide valley and disappeared in the forest to the left. They carried heavy spears and oval shields painted in various designs. A fillet bound long ostrich plumes that slanted backward on either side the head; and as they walked forward in the rather teetery fashion of the savage dandy these plumes waved up and down in rhythm.

"M'tela," said the *shenzi* goatherd waving his hand abroad.

They camped at the edge of a pleasant grove near running water. The donkey that the Leopard Woman rode fell to the tall lush grasses with a thankfulness beyond all expression. All the safari was in high spirits. They saw *potio* in sight again; and, immediately, long grass for beds.

Visitors came in shortly—a dozen armed men, like the warriors seen earlier in the day, and a dignified older man who spoke a sufficient Swahili. Kingozi received these in a friendly fashion, did not permit them to sit, but at once began to cross-question them. The Leopard Woman emerged from her tent.

"Stay where you are," Kingozi called to her in decided tones. "You must in this permit me to judge of expediencies. I forbid you to hold any communication with these people. I hope you will not make it necessary for me to take measures to see that my wishes are carried out."

She showed no irritation, not even at the "forbid," but smiled quietly, and without reply returned to her tent.

"Yes," said the old man, "this was M'tela's country, these were M'tela's people." He disclaimed having been sent by M'tela.

At this point Kingozi, apparently losing all interest, dismissed them into the hands of Cazi Moto. The latter, previously instructed, took his guests to his own camp. There he distributed roast meat, one *balauri* of coffee to the old man, and many tales, some of them true. These people had never before laid eyes on a white man, but naturally, at this late date in African history, all had heard more or less of the phenomenon. Cazi Moto found that the distinction between *Inglishee* and *Duyche* was known. He left a general impression that Kingozi was the favourite son of the King, come from sheer friendship and curiosity to see M'tela, whose fame was universal. For two hours the warriors squatted, or walked about camp examining with carefully concealed curiosity its various activities and strange belongings. Then all disappeared. No more people appeared that day.

Kingozi knew well enough that this was a spying party sent directly from M'tela's court; and that, pending its report, nothing more was to be done. Cazi Moto's detailed description of what had been said and done cheered his master wonderfully. By all the signs the simplest of the white man's wonders were brandnew to the visitors; *ergo* Winkleman could not have arrived. If he were not yet at M'tela's court, the chances seemed good that Simba and the magic bone had succeeded.

Nothing at present could be done. Kingozi sent Cazi Moto out to kill an abundance of game. The little headman returned later to report the extraordinary luck of two zebra to two cartridges (at thirty yards to be sure!) and that after each kill very many *shenzis* gathered to examine the bullet wound, the gun, and the distance. They were immensely excited, not at all awestricken, entirely friendly. There was no indication of any desire to rob the hunters. Evidently, Kingozi reflected, they were familiar with fire-arms by hearsay, and were deeply interested at this first-hand experience.

The safari remained encamped at this spot all the next day, and the day succeeding. Natives came into camp, at first only the men, hesitatingly; then the women. A brisk little trade sprang up for yams, bananas, *m'wembe* meal, eggs, and milk. No shrewder bargainer exists than your African safari man, and these soon discovered that beads and wire possessed great purchasing power in this unsophisticated country. The bartering had to be done in sign language, as Swahili seemed to be unknown; and no man in the safari understood this unknown tongue. Kin-gozi sat in state before his tent, smoking his pipe—which he still enjoyed in spite of his blindness—and awaiting events in that vast patience so necessary to the successful African traveller. Occasionally a group of the chatting natives would drift toward his throne, would fall into awestricken silence, would stare, would drift away again; but none ad-dressed him. The Leopard Woman, obeying rules that Kingozi had managed to convey as very strict, held apart.

Only in the evening, after the lion-fearing visitors had all departed, did they sit together sociably by the fire. The nights at this elevation were cool—cold they seemed to the heat-seasoned travellers.

There was not much conversation. Kingozi was lost in a deep brooding, which she respected. The occasion was serious, and both knew it. During the moment of decision the man's duty and principle had been the most important matters in the world. Once the decision was irrevocably made, however, these things fell below the horizon. There loomed only the thought of perpetual blindness. Kingozi faced it bravely; but such a fact requires adjustment, and in these hours of waiting the adjustments were being made.

Only once or twice did Bibi-ya-chui utter the thoughts that continually possessed her.

"It seems so foolish!" she complained to him. "You are making yourself blind for always; and you are going to be a prisoner for long! If you would go back, you would not be captured and held by Winkleman when you reach M'tela!"

But such expostulations she knew to be vain, even as she uttered them.

At about nine o'clock of the third day Cazi Moto reported a file of warriors, many warriors—"like the leaves of grass!" armed with spears and shields, wearing black ostrich plumes, debouching from the grove a mile across the way.

At the same instant the Leopard Woman, her alarm causing her to violate her instructions, came to Kingozi's camp.

"They attack us!" she cried. "They come in thousands! How can we resist so many—and you blind! Tell me what I shall do!"

"There is no danger," Kingozi reassured her. "This is undoubtedly an escort. No natives ever attack at this hour of the day. Their time is just at first dawn."

She sighed with relief. Then a new thought struck her.

"But if they had wished to attack—at dawn—we have had no extra guards—we have not fortified! What would prevent their killing us all?"

"Not a thing," replied Kingozi calmly. "We are too weak for resistance. That is a chance we had to take. Now please go back to your tent. Cazi Moto, strike camp, and get ready to safari."

The warriors of M'tela debouched on the open plain, seemingly without end. The sun glinted from their upraised, polished spears; their ostrich plumes swayed gently as though a wind ruffled a field of sombre grain tassels; the anklets and leg bracelets clashed softly together to produce in the aggregate a rhythmic marching cadence. Their front was nearly a quarter of a mile in width. Rank after rank in succession appeared: literally thousands. Drums roared and throbbed; and the blowing of innumerable trumpets, fashioned mostly from the horns of oryx and sing-sing, added to the martial ensemble.

The members of the safari were gathered in little knots, staring, wide eyed with apprehension. Upon them descended zealous Cazi Moto. Even his *kiboko* had difficulty in breaking up the groups, in setting the men at the commonplace occupations of breaking camp. Yet that must be done, in all decent dignity; and at length it was done.

The first ranks were now fairly at the outskirts of camp; the last had but just left the woods. The plains were literally covered with spearmen. A magnificent sight! They came to a halt, raised their spears horizontally above their heads; the horns and drums redoubled their din; a mighty, concerted shout rent the air. Then abruptly fell dead silence.

From the front rank a tall, impressive savage stepped forward, pacing with dignified stride. He walked directly to Kingozi's chair.

"*Jambo, bwana!*" He uttered his greeting in deep chest tones that rumbled like distant thunder.

"*Jambo, n'ympara,*" responded Kingozi in a mild tone. By his use of the word *n'ympara*—headman—he indicated his perfect understanding of the fact that this man, for all his magnificence, for all the strength of his escort, was not M'tela himself, but only one of M'tela's ministers.

"*Jambo, bwana m'kubwa!*" rolled the latter.

"*Jambo,*" replied Kingozi.

"*Jambo, bwana m'kubwa-sana!*"

"*Jambo.*"

"*Jambo, bwana m'kubwa-sana!*"

"*Jambo.*"

Having thus climbed by easy steps to the superlative greeting, the minister uttered his real message. As befitted his undoubted position in court, he spoke excellent Swahili.

"I am come to take you to the *manyatta* of M'tela," he announced.

"That is well," replied Kingozi calmly. "In one hour we shall go."

CHAPTER XXV

M'TELA

They set off through the beautiful country in their usual order of march. The warriors of M'tela accompanied them, walking ahead, behind, and on either flank. The drums roared incessantly, the trumpets of horn sounded. It was a triumphal procession, but rather awe-inspiring. The safari men did their best to imitate Kingozi's attitude of indifference; and succeeded fairly well, but their eyes rolled in their heads.

The Leopard Woman sat her donkey, and surveyed it all with appreciative eyes. In spite of Kingozi's reassuring words, the impression of savage power as the warriors debouched from the wood had been vivid enough to give emphasis to a strong feeling of relief when their intentions proved peaceful. The revulsion accentuated her enjoyment of the picturesque aspects of the scene. The shining, naked bodies, the waving ostrich plumes, the glitter of spears, the glint of polished iron, the wild, savage expression of the men, the throb of barbaric music appealed to her artistic sense. In a way her mind was at rest. At least the striving was over. Kingozi had made his decision; it was no use to struggle against it longer. She had no doubt that now they were virtually prisoners, that they were being conducted in this impressive manner to a chieftain already won over by Winkleman. The latter had had more than the time necessary to carry out his purpose. Kingozi's persistence was maddeningly futile; but it was part of the man, and she could not but acquiesce.

They marched across the open grassy plain, and into the woods beyond. A wide, beaten track took them through, as though they walked in a lofty tunnel with green walls through which one could look, but beyond which one might not pass. Then out into the sunlight again, skirting a swamp of plumed papyrus with many waterfowl, and swarms of insects, and birds wheeling swiftly catching the insects, and other larger birds soaring grandly above on the watch-out for what might chance. This swamp was like a green river flowing bank high between the hills. It twisted out of sight around wooded promontories. And the hills, constantly rising in height, crowned with ever-thickening forests, extended as far as the eye could reach.

At the end of the straight vista they turned sharp to the right and climbed a tongue of land—what would be called a "hog's-back" in the West. It was grown sparsely with trees, and commanded a wide outlook. Now the sinuous course of the papyrus swamp could be followed for miles in its vivid green; and the tops of the forest trees lay spread like a mantle. The top of the "hog's-back" had been flattened, and on it stood M'tela's palace.

The Leopard Woman stared curiously. There was not much to be seen. A high stockade of posts and wattle shut off the view, but over it could be distinguished a thatched roof. It was rectangular instead of circular and appeared to be at least forty feet long—a true, royal palace. Smaller roofs surrounded it. Outside the gate stood several more of the gorgeous spearmen, rigidly at attention. Not another soul was in sight.

But whatever seemed to lack either in the cordiality or curiosity of the inhabitants was more than made up for by the escort. With admirable military precision, a precision that Kingozi would have appreciated could he have seen it, they deployed across the wide open space at the front of the plateau. The drums lined up before them. In the echoing enclosure of the forest walls the noise was prodigious. And then abruptly, as before, it fell. In the silence the voice of the old headman was heard:

"Here will be found the way to the guest houses," he urged gently.

The ragged safari, carrying its loads, plunged again into a forest path, walking single file, a tatterdemalion crew. And yet a philosophic observer might have caught a certain nonchalance, a faint superiority of bearing on the part of these scarecrows; ridiculous when considered against the overwhelming numbers, the military spruceness, the savage formidability of the wild hordes that surrounded them. And if he had been an experienced as well as a philosophic observer he could have named the quality that informed them. Even in these truly terrifying, untried conditions it persisted—the white man's *prestige*.

The forest path, wide and well-trodden, led them a scant quarter mile to a cleared wide space on the very edge of the hill, which here fell abruptly away. A large circular guest house occupied the centre point, and other smaller houses surrounded it at a respectful distance. To the right hand were the tops of trees on a lower elevation; to the left and at the rear the solid wall of forest; immediately in front a wide outlook over the papyrus swamp and the partly clothed hills beyond.

Their guides—for there were several—indicated the guest houses, and silently disappeared. The safari was alone with its own devices.

Kingozi's practical voice broke the slight awe that all this savage magnificence had imposed.

"Cazi Moto!" he commanded, "tell me what is here."

He listened attentively while the wizen-faced little headman gave a detailed account, not only of the present dispositions, but also of what had been seen during the short march to M'tela's stronghold. At the conclusion of this recital he called to the Leopard Woman.

"I am here, near you," she answered.

"You must be my eyes for this," he told her. "Look

into the large guest house. Is it clean? Is it fairly new?"

She reported favourably as to these points.

"I am sorry, but I must take it over for myself," he said. "Matter not of comfort, but of *prestige*. You would do best to pitch your tent somewhere near. Cazi Moto, let the men make camp as usual."

"Very well," she agreed to her part of this program. Her manner was very gentle; and she looked on him, could he have known it, with eyes of a tender compassion. His was a brave heart, but Winkleman must long since have arrived——

She moved slowly away to superintend the placing of her tent, reflecting on these matters. It was decent of Winkleman to keep himself in the background just at first. Time enough to convince poor blind Kingozi that the game was up when he had to some extent recovered from the strain and fatigue of the long journey. But Winkleman was a good sort. She knew him: a big, hearty, bearded Bavarian, polyglot, intensely scientific, with a rolling deep voice. He must have had ten days—a week anyway—to use his acknowledged arts and influence on the savage king. Kingozi had said a week would be enough—and Kingozi knew! She sighed deeply as she thought of the doom to which his own obstinacy had condemned that remarkable man. Her eyes wandered to where he sat in his canvas chair, superintending through the ever-efficient Cazi Moto the

details of the camp.   His shoulders were sagging forward
wearily, and his face in repose fell into lines of infinite sadness.   Her heart melted within her; and in a sudden revulsion she flamed against Winkleman and all his diabolical
efficiency.   After all, this little corner of an unknown land
could not mean so much to the general result, and it would
be so glorious a consolation to a brave man's blindness!
Then she became ashamed of herself as a traitor.   Her tent
was now ready; so she entered it, bathed, clad herself in
her silks, and hung the jewel on her forehead.   Once more
the serene mistress of herself, she came forth to view the
sights.

It was by now near the setting of the sun.   The forest
shadows were rising.   Colobus were calling, and birds.
Up a steep trail from the swamp came a long procession of
women and little girls.   They were all stark naked, and
each carried on her head an earthen vessel or a greater or
lesser gourd according to her strength.   They passed near
the large guest house, and there poured the water from
their vessels into a series of big jars.   Thus every drop of
water had to be transported up the hill, not only for the
guest camp, but for all M'tela's thousands somewhere
back in the mysterious forest.   These women were of every
age and degree of attractiveness; but all were slender, and
each possessed a fine-textured skin of red bronze.   Except
the very old, whose breasts had fallen, they were finely
shaped.   The rays of the sun outlined them.   They seemed

quite unaware of their nakedness. Their faces were good humoured; and some of them even smiled shyly at the white woman standing by her tent. Having poured out the water, they disappeared down the forest path.

Thence shortly appeared other women with huge burdens of firewood carried by means of a strap, after the fashion of the Canadian tump-line; and still others with *m'wembe*, bananas, yams, eggs, *n'jugu* nuts, and gourds of smoked milk. Evidently M'tela did not do things by halves.

The customary routine of the camp went on. Supper was served as usual; and as usual the Leopard Woman joined Kingozi for the meal. The occasion was constrained on her side, easy on his. He asked her various questions as to details of the surroundings which she answered accurately but a little absently. She spoke from the surface of her mind. Within herself she was listening and waiting— listening for the first sound of shod feet, waiting for the moment when Winkleman should see fit to declare himself and end the suspense.

So high was this inner tension that she fairly jumped from her chair as a demoniac shrieking wail burst from the forest near at hand. It was answered farther away. Other voices took up the cry. It was as though a thousand devils in shuddering pain were giving tongue.

"Tree hyraxes," Kingozi reassured her.

"Those tiny beasts!" she cried incredulously.

"Just so. Sweet voices, haven't they? Some of these people must be wearing hyrax robes."

And indeed she remembered seeing some of the soft, beautiful karosses.

But now from the direction of M'tela's palaces arose a confused murmur that swelled as a multitude drew near. The drums began again. Soon, the Leopard Woman described, torches began to flash through the trees. At the same moment Cazi Moto came to report.

"Build up a big fire," commanded Kingozi. He turned to the Leopard Woman.

"This is likely to be an all-night session," he said resignedly. "If you want to get out of it, I advise you to go now. Not that you'll be able to get any sleep. But if you stay, you must stick it out. It would never do to leave in the middle of the performance. Some of it you won't like."

"What is it to be?"

"Ceremonial dances, I fancy."

"I think I shall stay," she said slowly.

In her heart she thought it extremely unlikely that the performance would last all night. Indeed her own opinion was that Kingozi would be a prisoner within an hour.

Kingozi settled himself stolidly in his chair before the fire that was now beginning to eat its way through an immense pile of fuel, where, during all subsequent events, he remained in the same attitude.

The Leopard Woman, on the contrary looked with all her eyes. The torches came nearer. People began to pour out from the woods. There were warriors in full panoply; lithe, naked men carrying only wands peeled fresh to the white; women hung heavily with cowries; other women with neither garment nor ornament, their bodies oiled and glistening. A deep, rolling chant arose from hundreds of throats, punctuated and carried by a sort of shrill, intermittent ululation. The drums were there, but for the moment they were not being beaten in cadence, only rubbed until they roared in undertone to the men's chanting.

All these people divided to right and left in the clearing of the guest camp, and took their stations. More and more appeared. The space filled, filled solidly, until at last there was no break in the mass of humanity except for a circle forty feet in diameter about the fire.

Suddenly a group of fifteen or twenty men detached themselves from the main body and leaped into this cleared space. The great chant still rolled on; but now a varied theme was introduced by a chorus of the nearby women. The dancers were oiled to a high state of polish, naked except for a single plume apiece and a sort of tasselled tail hung to a string belt. They clustered in a close group near the fire, facing a common centre. In deep chest tones they pronounced the word *goom*, at the same time half crouching; then in sharp staccato head tones the word *zup*, at the

same time rising swiftly up and toward their common centre.
It was like the ebb and surge of a wave, the alternate
smooth crouch and spring over and over again—*goom,
zup! goom, zup! goom, zup!*—and behind it the twinkle
of torches, the gleam of eyes, the roll of the deep-voiced
chanting.

Endlessly they repeated this performance. The Leopard
Woman, watching, at last had to close her eyes in order to
escape the hypnotic quality of it. In spite of herself her
senses swam in the rhythmic monotony. All outside the
focus of the dancers turned gray—*goom, zup! goom, zup!*
—was it never to end? And then it seemed to her that it
never would end, that thus it would go on forever, and
that so it was just and right. The men were tireless. The
sweat glistened on their bodies, but their eyes gleamed
fanatically. She floated off on a tide of irrelevant thoughts.

Hours later, as it seemed to her, she came to herself
suddenly. Kingozi still sat stolidly in his chair. The
dancers were retiring step by step, still with unabated vigour,
continuing their performance. They melted into the
crowd.

Now a pellmell of bizarre figures broke out. They
were bedecked fantastically: some of them were painted
with white clay; one was clad in the skins of beasts. There
was no rhythm or order to their entrance; but immediately
they began to dash here and there shouting.

"It is the Lion Dance, *memsahib*," Cazi Moto told her

in a low voice. "That one is the lion; and they hunt him with spears in the long grass."

The chase went forward with some versimilitude, and yet with a symbolic syncopation that indicated the Lion Dance was a very ancient and conventional ceremony. These dancers gave way to a chorus of singers. For interminable hours, so it seemed, they chanted a high, shrill recitative, carried in fugue by deeper voices. The burden of the song was evidently an impromptu. Occasionally some peculiarly apt or pleasing phrase was caught up for endless repetition. And in the background, against the farther background of the undistinguished masses, those who had formerly carried on their performances in the full glare of front-row publicity and the campfire, now continued their efforts almost unabated. The impressive utterers of the *goom-zup* shibboleth, the slayers of the symbolical lion, carried on still. Indeed as the night wore on, and one group of dancers succeeded another, the homogeneous crowd began to break into varied activity. Each took his turn as principal, then fell back to form part of the variegated background. Each dance was different. Warriors fully armed clashed shield and spear; witch doctors crouched and sprang; women stamped in rhythm; the elephant was hunted, the crops sown and gathered, all the activities of community and individual life were danced, the frankness of some saved from obscenity only by the unconscious earnestness of their exposition and the evidence of their symbolism that they were not the expression of the moment but very ancient customs.

The Leopard Woman watched it all with shining eyes. The emotion of the picturesque, the call of savage wildness, the contagion of a mounting community excitement caused the blood to race through her veins. The drums throbbed against her heart as the pulse throbbed against her temples. She resisted an actual impulse to rise from her chair, to throw herself with abandon into an orgy of rhythm and motion. Perfectly she understood those who, having reached the breaking point, dashed madly through the fire scattering embers and coals, or who darted forward to kiss ecstatically the white man's feet, or who reached a wild paroxysm of nerves to collapse the next instant into exhaustion. She was brought to herself by Kingozi's calm voice.

"Sweet riot, isn't it?" he remarked. "They're working themselves up to a high pitch. It's always that way. You would think they'd drop from sheer weariness."

"How long will they keep it up?" she asked, drawing a deep breath, and trying to speak naturally.

"So it got you, too, a little, did it?" he said curiously.

"What do you mean?"

"The excitement. It's contagious unless you are accustomed to it. I've seen safe and sane youngsters go quite off their heads at these shows, and dash down and caper around like the maddest *shenzi* of them all. Felt it myself at first. It draws you; like wanting to jump off

when you look down from a high place." He was talking
evenly and carelessly. "Enough of this sort of thing will
make a crowd see anything. Devil-worshippers for in-
stance, they see red devils, after they work up to it, not a
doubt of it."

"Thank you," she answered his evident purpose of bringing her to herself.

"All right now, eh?"

"Yes."

"Well, to answer your question; I've known dances to
last two days."

"Heaven!" she cried, dismayed.

"But this is to prepare a suitable entrance for his majesty. We'll hear from him along toward daylight." He
held out his wrist watch toward her. "What time now?"

Somehow the simple action seemed to her pathetic.
Her eyes filled, and she stooped as though to kiss the out-
stretched hand. Never again would the worn old wrist
watch serve its owner, except thus, vicariously!

"It is ten minutes past the twelve," she answered in a
stifled voice.

"We must settle down to it. If you want tea or something to eat, tell Cazi Moto."

He resumed his stolid demeanour.

The dancing continued. Every once in a while women
threw armfuls of fuel on the blaze. The tree hyraxes, out-
screeched and outnumbered, fell into silence or withdrew.

Above the stars shone serenely; and all about stood the trees of the ancient forest. Outside the hot, leaping red light they drew back aloof and still. They had seen many dances, many ebbs and flows of men's passions; for they were very old.

The Leopard Woman's vision blurred after a time. She was getting drowsy. Her thoughts strayed. But always they circled back to the same point. She found herself wondering whether Winkleman would appear to-night.

A few hours earlier than Kingozi had predicted, in fact not far after two o'clock, the wild dancing died to absolute immobility and absolute silence, and M'tela arrived.

He appeared walking casually as though out for a stroll, emerging from the end of the wide forest path. Central African natives are never obese—comic papers to the contrary notwithstanding. Nevertheless, M'tela was a large man, amply built, his muscles overlaid by smoother, softer flesh. He possessed dignity without aloofness, a rare combination, and one that invariably indicates a true feeling of superiority. As he moved forward he glanced lazily and good-humouredly to right and left at his people, in the manner of a genial grown-up among small children. He wore a piece of cotton cloth dyed black, so draped as to leave one arm and shoulder bare, a polished bone armlet, and a tarboush that must have been traded through many hands.

"The *sultani, bwana*," murmured the ever-alert Cazi Moto.

M'tela wandered to where Kingozi sat. The white man did not move, but appeared to stare absently straight before him. At ten paces M'tela stopped and deliberately inspected his visitor for a full half-minute. Then he advanced and dropped to the stool an obsequious and zealous slave placed for him.

"*Jambo*, papa," he said casually.

His manner was perfect. The thousand or so human beings who crowded the clearing might not have existed. Himself and Kingozi, two equals, were settling themselves for an informal little chat in the midst of solitudes. His large intelligent eye passed over the Leopard Woman, but if her appearance aroused in him any curiosity or other interest no flicker of expression betrayed the fact.

As he heard the form of address a brief gleam of satisfaction crossed Kingozi's face. Whether it has been transferred from the English, or has been adopted more directly from the babbling of infants, "papa" is perfectly good Swahili. When M'tela addressed Kingozi as "papa" he not only acknowledged him as a guest, but he admitted the white man to the intimacy that exists between equals in rank.

M'tela was friendly.

CHAPTER XXVI

WAITING

Two days passed. By the end of that time it had been borne in on the Leopard Woman that Winkleman had not yet arrived. Kingozi and M'tela circled each other warily, like two strange dogs, though all the time with an appearance of easy and intimate cordiality. As yet Kingozi had neither confided to the savage the fact of his blindness nor visited the royal palace. The latter ceremony he had evaded under one plea or another; and the infliction he had managed to conceal by the simple expedient of remaining in his canvas chair. Later would be time enough to acknowledge so great a weakness; later when the subtle and specialized diplomacy he so assiduously applied would have had time to do its work.

For M'tela was initially friendly. This was a great satisfaction to Kingozi, though none knew better than he how any chance gust of influence or passion could veer the wind. Still it was something to start on; and something more or less unexpected and unhoped for. M'tela himself supplied the reason in the course of one of their interminable conversations.

"I am pleased to see the white man," he said. "Never has the white man come to my country before; but always I knew he would come. One time long ago my brother who is king of the people near the Great Water said these words to me: 'My brother, some day white men will come to you. They will be few, and they will come with a small safari, and their wealth will look small to you. But make no mistake. Where these few white men who look poor come from are many more—like the leaves of the grass—and their wealth is great and their wonders many; and for each white man that is speared ten more come, without end, like water flowing down a hill. I know this to be so, for I am an old man, and I have fought, and of all those who fought the white man in my youth only I remain.' So I remembered these words of my brother always."

"You are a wise man, oh, King," said Kingozi, "for those words are true."

Hourly Kingozi cursed his eyes. With this man so well-disposed a day—a single hour—of the white man's miracles would have cemented his friendship. But Kingozi was deprived at a stroke of the great advantages to be gained by cutting out paper dolls, making coins disappear and appear again, and all the rest of the bag of tricks. He had not even the alternative advantage of a store of rich gifts with which to buy the chief's favour. This crude alternative to subtle diplomacy he had scorned when making out a small safari for a long journey.

To be sure he was not doing badly. A box of matches and instructions in the use thereof went far as an evidence of munificence. Sparingly he doled out his few treasures—the gaudy blankets; coils of brass, copper, and iron wires; beads; snuff; knives, and the like. They were received with every mark of appreciation. In return firewood, water, and food of all sorts came in abundantly. But these, Kingozi well knew, were only temporizing evidences of good feeling. Time would come when M'tela would ceremoniously bring in his real present—assuredly magnificent as beseeming his power. Then, Kingozi knew, he should be able to reciprocate in degree. He could not do so; he could not use his accustomed methods; he could not even exhibit his trump card—the deadly wonder of the weapon that could kill at a distance.

Nevertheless he would have awaited the outcome with serene indifference could he have been certain of a clear field. The arrival of Winkleman would, he secretly admitted, upset him completely. Winkleman—another white man, possessed of powers he did not possess, of wonders he did not own, of knowledge equal to his—would have no difficulty in taking the lead from him. Certainly Winkleman had not yet arrived, and he was long overdue. On the other hand, neither had Simba nor Mali-ya-bwana reported; and they were equally overdue. These were ticklish times; and Kingozi had great difficulty in sitting calmly in his canvas chair listening to the endless inconsequences of a savage.

The Leopard Woman could not understand how he did it. Her inner nervous tension, due as much to a conflict as to suspense, drove her nearly frantic. She knew that Winkleman's appearance spelled defeat for Kingozi; she knew that she should hope for that appearance—and deep in her heart she knew that she dreaded it! But as time went on without tangible results, she began to long for it as a relief. At least it would be over then. And Kingozi—oh, brave heart! oh, pathetic figure—if anything could make it up to him——!

The morning of the third day came. Usual camp activities carried them on until nine o'clock. Kingozi was settled in his chair awaiting what the day would bring forth. The Leopard Woman coming across from her tent to the guest house stopped short at what she saw.

Across the way, a half or three-quarters of a mile distant, beyond the green papyrus swamp, on the slope from the edge of the forest, appeared a long file of men bearing burdens on their heads. Even at this distance she made out the colour of occasional garments of khaki cloth, or the green of canvas on the packs.

She arrived at Kingozi's side simultaneously with Cazi Moto.

"A safari comes, *bwana*," said the latter. "It is across the swamp."

Kingozi's figure stiffened.

"What kind of a safari?" he asked quietly.

The Leopard Woman answered him. There was no note of jubilation in her voice.

"It is a white man's safari," she told him. "I can see khaki—and they are marching as a white man's safari marches."

"Get my glasses," he told Cazi Moto. Then to her, his voice vibrating with emotion too long controlled: "Look and tell me, fairly. I must know. Whatever the outcome you must tell me truth. It will not matter. I can do nothing."

"I will tell you the truth," she promised, raising the glasses.

For some moments she looked intently.

"It is Winkleman's safari," she announced sadly. "I have been able to see. It is a very large safari with many loads," she added.

Kingozi's face turned gray. He dropped his face into his hands. Gently she laid her hand on his bowed head. Thus they waited, while the safari, evidently under local guidance, plunged into some hidden path through the papyrus, and so disappeared.

CHAPTER XXVII

THE MAGIC BONE

Let us now follow Simba, Mali-ya-bwana, and their six men and the two strange *shenzis* who were to act as guides.

They started off across the veldt at about four o'clock of the afternoon and travelled rapidly until dark. The gait they took was not a run, but it got them over the ground at four and a half to five miles an hour. Shortly after sundown they stopped for an hour, ate, drank, and lay flat on their backs. Then they arose, lighted a candle end in the mica lantern, and resumed their journey. Thus they travelled day and night for three days. There seemed to be neither plan nor regularity to their journeying. Whenever they became tired enough to sleep, they lay down and slept for a little while; whenever they became hungry, they ate; and whenever they thirsted, they drank, paying no attention whatever to the time of day, the state of their larder, or the distance to more water. No ideas of conservation hampered them in the least. If the water gave out, they argued, they would be thirsty; but it was as well to be thirsty later from lack of water than to be thirsty now from some silly idea of abstention. No white man could

have travelled successfully under that system. Nevertheless, the little band held together and arrived in the fringe
of hills fit and comparatively fresh.

Here they encountered people belonging to M'tela's
tribes; but their guides seemed to vouch for them, and
they passed without trouble. Indeed they were here
enabled to get more food, and to waste no time hunting.
At noon of another day, surmounting a ridge, they looked
down on a marching safari. The two *shenzi* guides pointed
and grinned, much pleased with themselves. Their pleasure was short lived; for they were promptly seized, disarmed,
and tied together. The grieved astonishment of their expressions almost immediately faded into fatalistic stolidity.
So many things happen in Africa!

Mali-ya-bwana and one of the other men proceeded rapidly ahead on the general line of march. The rest paralleled
the safari below. After an hour the scouts returned with
news of a water-hole where, undoubtedly, the strange safari
would camp. All then hurried on.

Concealed in a thicket Simba proceeded with great zest
to make himself over into a *shenzi*. In every savage is a
good deal of the small boy; so this disguising himself pleased
him immensely. Taking the spear in one hand and the
"sacred bone" reverently in the other, he set out to intercept the safari.

It came within the hour. Simba almost unremarked
regarded it curiously. There were over a hundred men,

all of tribes unknown to him with the exception of a dozen who evidently performed the higher offices. The common porters were indeed *shenzis*—wild men—picked up from jungle and veldt as they were needed; and not at all of the professional porter class to be had at Mombasa, Nairobi, Dar-es-salaam, or Zanzibar. Simba's eyes passed over them contemptuously, but rested with more interest on the smaller body of *askaris*, headmen, and gun bearers. These also were of tribes strange to him; but of East African types with which he was familiar. They were all dressed in a sort of uniform of khaki, wore caps with a curtain hanging behind, and arm bands gayly emblazoned with imperial eagles. All this was very impressive. Simba conceived a respect for this white man's importance. Evidently he was a *bwana m'kubwa*. The supposed savage experienced a growing excitement over the task he had undertaken. All his training had taught him to respect the white man, as such; and now he was called upon to abduct forcibly one of the sacred breed—and such a specimen! Only Simba's undoubted force of character, and the veneration his long association with Kingozi had inculcated, sustained him.

For Winkleman was a big man in every way: tall, broad, thick, with a massive head, large features, and such a tremendous black beard! Well had he deserved his native name of *Bwana* Nyele—the master with the mane.

Simba awaited the moment of greatest confusion in the placing and pitching of the camp, and then advanced

timidly, holding out the bone Kingozi had given him. His
courage and faith were very low. They revived instantly
as he saw the immediate effect. It was just as Kingozi
had told him it would be; and as there was nothing on earth
in a bit of dry bone that could accomplish such an effect
except magic, Simba thenceforward went on with his adventure in completed confidence.

For at sight of the bone *Bwana* Nyele's eyes lit up, he uttered an astonishing bellow of delight, and sprang forward
with such agility for so large a man that he almost succeeded
in snatching the talisman from Simba's hands. Acting
precisely on his instructions the latter backed away, pointing over the hill.

"Where did you get that?" Winkleman demanded.

Simba continued to point.

"Give it me."

Simba started away, still pointing. Winkleman followed a few steps.

"There is more?" he asked. "Do you speak Swahili?"

"Many more, *bwana*," Simba replied in the atrocious
Swahili Kingozi had ordered. "Over there only a little
distance."

Everything turned out as Kingozi had promised. *Bwana*
Nyele asked several more questions, received no replies,
finally bellowed:

"But lead me there, *m'buzi !* I would see!"

Simba guided him up the hill. At the appointed spot

they fell upon him and bore him to the earth in spite of his strength, and bound his hands behind his back. Then Simba wrapped the magic bone reverently in its cloth. Certainly it was wonderful magic.

Winkleman put up a good fight, but once he felt himself definitely overpowered he ceased his struggles. He was helped to his feet. A glance at his captors taught him that these were safari men and not savages of the country; and, with full knowledge of the general situation, he was not long in guessing out his present plight. But now was not the time for talk.

A half-hour's walk took the party to a second water-hole, the indications for which Simba had already noted on his little scouting tour. There they proceeded to make camp. The six porters began with their swordlike *pangas* to cut poles and wattles, to peel off long strips of inner bark from the thorn trees which would serve as withes. Then they began the construction of a *banda*, one of the quickly built little thatched sheds, open at both ends. At sight of this Winkleman swore deeply. He was fairly trapped, and knew it; but the *banda* indicated that he was to be held prisoner in this one spot for at least some days. However, wise man in native ways, he said nothing and made no objection. But his keen wide eyes took in every detail.

When the *banda* was finished and a big pile of the dried hay had been spread as a couch Simba approached respectfully but firmly, took *Bwana* Nyele's helmet from his head, his spine-pad from his back, and his shoes from his feet. In this strategy Winkleman with reluctance admired the white man's hands. Without head and spine covering of some sort he could not travel a mile under the tropic sun; without foot covering or a light he would be helpless at night. Of course these things could be improvised; but not easily. He stretched himself on the hay and awaited events.

The men built a fire and gathered around it. They were cooking, but at the same time the two whom Winkleman recognized as leaders conferred earnestly and at great length. Had he been at their elbows he would have heard the following:

"The magic of this bone is a very great magic," Simba was saying. "All happened exactly as *Bwana* Kingozi told us. Now is the fifth day. There remain now nine days to wait until we must bring this *m'zungu* to *Bwana* Kingozi at the *manyatta* of M'tela."

"It is indeed great magic," agreed Mali-ya-bwana. "How many days is the *manyatta* ?"

"I do not know. These *shenzis* should know; but they talk only monkey talk. Here, let us try." He drew one of the prisoners one side. "M'tela," he enunciated slowly.

The savage nodded, and pointed the direction with his protruded lower lip.

Simba indicated the sun, and swept his hand across the arc of the heavens. Then he looked inquiringly at the other and held up in rapid success first one, then two, then three fingers. The savage was puzzled. Simba went through the movements of a man walking, pronounced the name of M'tela, pointed out the direction, and then repeated his previous pantomime. A light broke on the *shenzi*. He held up four fingers.

Simba next called to Mali-ya-bwana to interrogate the other prisoner apart. As the latter also reported M'tela four days distant—when he understood—this was accepted as the truth.

"Then we remain in camp five days," they concluded, after working out the subtraction.

"But," intervened one of the porters, "we have no more *potio*."

"I have the *bwana's* gun," Simba pointed out, "and also the gun of this *m'zungu*. There is here plenty of game."

"To eat meat always is not well," grumbled the porter.

"To eat *kiboko* (whip) is always possible," replied Simba grimly.

"Nevertheless," said Mali-ya-bwana, who as co-leader was privileged to more open speech, "*potio* and meat are better than meat only."

Simba looked at him inquiringly.

"You have a thought?"

Mali-ya-bwana leaned forward.

"It is this: If the bone has such great magic that thus we can take prisoner a mighty *bwana* like this, surely it is powerful enough to fight also against safari men."

Simba pondered this.

"Every one knows that a white man is a great Lord," urged Mali-ya-bwana, "and that it is useless for the black man to fight against him. This is true always. Every man knows this."

"Black men have killed white men," Simba objected.

"Only when the numbers were many. Even then many more black men also have died, so that the painting for mourning went through many tribes. Never before have men like us taken a white man thus easily."

"That is true."

"Then since this magic bone can subdue for us a great lord of a *m'zungu*, surely it will also subdue for us a safari of black men like ourselves, a safari that the *m'zungu* has held in his hand."

"That is true."

"And that safari must have much *potio*."

"That also is true."

"Let you—or me, it does not matter—take the magic bone, and with it take also this safari and its *potio*."

"I will do it," assented Simba after a moment. "You will stay here to carry out the *bwana's* orders."

CHAPTER XXVIII

SIMBA'S ADVENTURE

In the course of the evening Winkleman, conceiving that the right moment had come, set himself seriously to establishing a dominance over these members of an inferior race. He was a skilled man at this, none more so; nevertheless he failed. For in the persons of Simba and Mali-ya-bwana he was dealing not with natives, but with another white man as shrewd and experienced as himself. Kingozi had from the abundance of his knowledge foreseen exactly what methods and arguments the Bavarian would use, and in his final instructions he had dramatized almost exactly the scene that was now taking place. Simba had his replies ready made for him. When an unexpected argument caught him unaware, he merely fingered surreptitiously his magic bone, and remained serenely silent. Winkleman might as well have talked at a stone wall. He soon recognized this, as also that the man had been coached minutely.

"Who is your *bwana*?" he asked at length.

"He is a very great *bwana*," Simba replied.

"His name?"

"He has many names among many people."

"What name do you call him?"

"I call him *bwana m'kubwa* (great master)," replied Simba blandly.

Winkleman gave up this tack and tried another.

"What is his business? What does he do here?"

"His business is to fight."

"Ah!" ejaculated Winkleman. "To fight!"

"Yes. His business is to fight the elephant."

Winkleman swore. He could get at nothing this way. He must give his mind to escape.

Early the next morning Simba started. He took with him, of course, his magic bone; but, like a canny general, he carried also the rifle. Mali-ya-bwana was left sufficiently armed by Winkleman's weapon and the sixteen cartridges captured on his person.

By the water-hole Simba found the safari encamped. At sight of his khaki-clad figure several men ran to meet him. Their countenances were of a cast unfamiliar to Simba. He looked at them calmly.

"Does some one speak Swahili?" he inquired.

"*N'dio !*" they assented in chorus.

Simba looked about him. This was indeed a great safari, and a rich *bwana*. The tent, of green canvas, was what is known as a "four-man tent"; that is, it took four men to carry it. The pile of loads in the centre of the cleared space was high. There were three tin boxes and many chop boxes among them.

The group moved slowly across the open space, stared at by curious eyes, and came to a halt before a drill tent slightly larger than the little kennels assigned to the ordinary porters. Here over a fire bubbled a *sufuria*, the African cooking pot, tended by a naked small boy. A clean mat woven in bright colours carpeted the ground; on this all seated themselves.

It would be tedious to relate each step of the ensuing negotiations. These simple Africans would have needed no instruction from civilization to carry on the most long-winded submarine controversy in the most approved and circuitous manner. At the end of one solid hour of grave and polite exchange it developed that the white man was not at present in camp. Somewhat later Simba permitted it to be understood that his own white man was not in the immediate neighbourhood. These gems of knowledge were separated by much leisurely chatter, and occasional and liberal dippings into the *sufuria*. And thus was the beginning and the end of the first day.

At noon of the second day, after a refreshing night's sleep, Simba moved up his forces.

"Your white man is known to me," said he.

Some one remarked appropriately.

"He is a prisoner in my camp."

"In the camp of your white man."

"In my camp. I myself have taken him prisoner," insisted Simba.

"You are telling lies," said the headman of the safari.

Simba took this calmly. In Africa to call a man a liar is no insult.

"It is the truth," said he. "With my own hands I took him; and he lies bound in my camp."

"These are lies," persisted the headman. "How can such things be? That you took a white man, a great *bwana*? That is foolishness. That has never been and could never be. How could you accomplish such a feat?"

"I have a magic."

"Ho!" cried the headman derisively. "Everybody knows that a magic is not good against the white man. That has been tried many times!"

"This is a white man's magic."

The statement made a visible impression.

"Let us see it," they demanded.

But Simba refused. He was entirely at ease. In his ordinary habit he would have become excited over being doubted, he would have wrangled, have shouted—in short, would have been but one unit among many equals. But the possession of the magic bone gave him a confidence from outside himself. For the time being he slipped genuinely into the attitude of the white man; became a super-Simba, as it were. This dignity and sureness commenced to have its effect. Almost they began to believe that Simba's words might be true!

At three o'clock the battle closed in.

"My men need *potio*," said Simba. "Let ten loads be put aside, and let ten of these *shenzis* be told to carry them where I shall say."

But the headman leaped to his feet.

"Who are you to give orders?" he cried. "These things belong to my white man."

"Your white man is my property," replied Simba superbly; and with no further parley he shot the headman dead.

Here indeed showed the super-Simba. The dispute might in the ordinary course of events have come to shooting; but only after hours of excited wrangling, and as a climax worked up to in a crescendo of emotion. This expeditious nipping in the bud was a thoroughly white-manly proceeding.

The headman whirled about under the impact of the high-power bullet at so close a range, and collapsed face down. Simba sat calmly in his place. He did not even trouble to place himself in a better defensive attitude against possible attack. His confidence in his magic bone was growing to sublimity as he noted how efficiently it carried him through every crisis. All over the camp the porters, startled, leaped to their feet. But at the headmen's fire no one moved. They would ordinarily have been afraid neither of Simba nor Simba's weapons. Firearms were familiar to them. The usual sequence to Simba's deed would have been an immediately defunct Simba. But his serene confidence in his magic caught their credulity.

The white man's *prestige* and privileges were invested in him.

"Yours is undoubtedly a great magic," said Winkle-man's gun bearer politely. "Let us talk."

They talked at great length, without bothering to remove the dead headman. The result was finally a continued respect for Simba, his magic bone, and his ready rifle; but a lingering though polite incredulity as to the matter of Winkleman—*Bwana* Nyele. It was possible that Simba had killed the latter, of course. But to have taken him alive—and to be holding him prisoner——

It was suggested that the various upper men of this safari accompany Simba to the place of incarceration. Declined for obvious reasons. Proposition modified to exclude all visitors but one. Still declined.

The debate summarized in the above short paragraph consumed six hours. What is time in the face of an African eternity? And in Africa, as every one knows, the feeling of eternity is an accompaniment of every-day life.

After some refreshments the sitting rose. Simba did not spend the night in camp. That did not seem to him wise. Instead he withdrew to a place he had already marked, deftly built himself a withe platform in the spread of an acacia, and slept soundly above the danger line.

Next morning the discussion was resumed. It was all on an amicable basis. A bystander would have seen merely a group of lazy native servants gossiping idly. And, indeed, for one word of relevance were a dozen of sheer chatter. That is the African way.

Since it was impossible to visit *Bwana* Nyele, why could not *Bwana* Nyele be brought to within sight? Simba considered this; but finally rejected it. The risk was too great, magic bone or no magic bone.

"It is probable you speak lies," said the gun bearer at last. "You say you want *potio* and that you hold *Bwana* Nyele prisoner. But you do not bring us orders from *Bwana* Nyele for *potio*. Nor do you give us proof. We must have proof before we believe or before we obey."

"I will bring you *Bwana* Nyele's gun; or his coat; or anything that is his that you may see that I hold him prisoner."

"Those things prove nothing," the gun bearer pointed out. "They might have been taken from a dead man."

They negotiated further. One gifted with the power of seeing only essential things would have found here a strange parallel. For these two men, talking cautiously, clinging with tenacity to single points, yielding grudgingly, would have been the same to him as two shrewd business men coming together on the phrases of a contract, or two diplomats framing the terms of a treaty.

Thus well into the third day. By that time an agreement had been reached. It was very simple and direct and practical, when one thinks of it; covered the situation fully; involved few compromises; and gained each man his point.

Simba demanded *potio* and obedience because he held the mighty *m'zungu* prisoner. The gun bearer wanted indubitable proof not only that Simba held the white man, but that he held him alive.

It was agreed that Simba was to return to his own camp, was to procure the proof agreed upon, and was promptly to return. The said proof was to be one of *Bwana* Nyele's fingers, which all agreed would be easily recognizable both as to identity and freshness!

The divulgence of this simple little plan by a Simba quite in earnest dissipated Winkleman's last hope of doing anything by means of persuasion. He knew his African well enough to realize that this fantastic method of identification seemed quite a matter of course. In fact, Simba was at the moment sharpening his hunting knife in preparation. Winkleman swore heartily and fluently, then grinned. He was at heart a good soul, Winkleman, with a sense of amusement if not of humour, and a philosophy of life denied most of his inexperienced and theoretical countrymen. And also he realized that he had his work cut out to prevent the program being carried through. The African is slow to come to a definite conclusion, but once it is arrived at it is apt to look to him like a permanent structure. It was a wonderful tribute to Winkleman that it took him only four hours to persuade Simba that there might be another way;

and two hours more to convince him that there might even be a better way. When Simba reluctantly and a little doubtfully sheathed his knife, the big Bavarian wiped his brow with genuine thankfulness.

The reader need not be wearied by a detailed report of the interminable conferences that led up to the substitute plan. It would be a picture of a big bearded man smoking slowly—for until affairs were decided he could get no more of his own tobacco—leaning on his elbow beneath the roof of the *banda*. Before him squatted on their heels in the posture white men find so trying Mali-ya-bwana and Simba, entirely respectful, their shining black eyes fixed on the white man. The open ends of the *banda* gave out on a dry boulder-strewn wash and the parched side of a hill. All else was sky. Morning coolness was succeeded by the blaze of midday, when the very surface of the ground danced in the shimmer; then slowly the shadows crept out, the veils of mirage sank to earth, a coolness wandered in from some blessed region; darkness came suddenly; over the parched hill—now looming mysterious in black garments—the tropic stars blazed out. Then outside some one lighted a fire. The flames cast lights and shadows within the *banda* where still the white man leaned on his elbow, the black men squatted on their heels, and the murmur of talk went on and on.

But Winkleman got his way. At an appointed hour and at an appointed place Winkleman, Mali-ya-bwana, and two of the carriers met Simba conducting the gun bearer from the other camp. The interview was very short. Indeed it had all been carefully rehearsed. Winkleman said only what he had agreed to say; and thereby earned his finger.

"This man holds me prisoner," he told the gun bearer. "What he says is true. Do what he asks you to do. It is my command."

"Yes, *bwana*," agreed the gun bearer.

Then they parted. The immediate result was five loads of *potio* brought by safari men to "somewhere in Africa," and thence transported by Simba's men to Simba's camp. As game was thereabout abundant and undisturbed everybody was happy.

Thus passed a week, which brought time forward to the moment when Simba, following his instructions, was to report to Kingozi at the village of M'tela. Therefore Simba set forth, taking with him, according to African custom, one of the porters as companion. He carried Kingozi's rifle, but left that belonging to Winkleman with Mali-ya-bwana.

Winkleman watched Simba go with considerable satisfaction. Mali-ya-bwana was a man much above average African intelligence, but he had not the experience, the initiative, the *flaire* of Simba. Ncr had he Simba's magic bone. Simba took that with him. Winkleman knew nothing of the supposed virtues of that property; and in consequence entertained a respect for qualities of Simba that were not entirely inherent in that individual. He began to flatter Mali-ya-bwana; to fraternize just enough; to assume complete resignation to his plight—in short, to use just those tactics a clever man would use to lull the alertness of any bright child. Naturally he succeeded. At sundown of the second day he began to complain of the irksomeness of his bonds.

"This is foolishness, so to treat a *m'zungu*," said he. "Nothing is gained. I cannot sleep; and the skin of my wrists is sore. He who watches has only to keep the fire bright. I cannot go like smoke."

To Mali-ya-bwana, in his flattered and unsuspicious mood, this seemed reasonable. He was no such fool as to turn Winkleman loose to his own devices; but he compromised by untying the Bavarian's wrists, and doubling the thongs by which the latter's ankles were hitched to the larger timbers of the *banda*. Also he instructed the sentinel to keep the fire bright, to watch *Bwana* Nyele, and to stop instantly any and all movements of the hands toward the feet.

The early watches passed quietly. A second sentinel replaced the first. Up to this time Winkleman had slept quietly. Now he began to shift position often, to twist and turn, finally to groan softly. The sentinel came to the end of the *banda* and looked in. To him *Bwana* Nyele raised a face so ghastly that even the half-savage porter was startled. The man's eyes seemed to have sunk into his head, deep seams to have creased his brow and jaws. Apparently Winkleman was on the point of dissolution.

"*Magi ! nataka magi !*"* he gasped.

The sentinel took the canteen from the peg where it hung and bent over the dying man. Instantly his throat was clasped by a pair of heavy and powerful hands.

Two minutes later Winkleman rose to his feet free. The porter's knife in his hand, he looked down on that unfortunate securely bound and gagged. Treading softly Winkleman stepped through the sleeping camp into the clear. He drew a deep breath. Then unconsciously wiping from his face the mixture of grease and ashes that had constituted his "make-up," he strode grimly away toward his own safari.

---

*Water! I want water!

CHAPTER XXIX

WINKLEMAN'S SAFARI ARRIVES

The Leopard Woman watched the safari file down the distant hill and lose itself beneath the green plumes of the papyrus swamp. By all right she should have rejoiced. Against every probability she had succeeded. The stars had worked for her. Though the prearranged plan had not carried in any of its details, nevertheless the sought-for result had been gained. She had herself done little to detain Kingozi; yet he had been detained; and here was Winkleman, belated but in time, to carry out triumphantly the wishes of the Imperial Government. But her heart was like lead.

After the first droop Kingozi had straightened beneath the blow, and now sat bolt upright, staring straight before him, as a king might have sat alone on his throne. Whatever was coming, he would front it serenely.

The head of the safari appeared at the foot of the slope. It seemed a trifle uncertain as to where to go next, but catching sight of Kingozi's tents, it turned up the hill. Cazi Moto's keen eyes were searching out every detail; those of the Leopard Woman had suddenly become suffused with tears.

"It is a rich safari, *bwana*," Cazi Moto reported; "many loads." His voice sharpened with surprise, but he did not raise his tones. "Simba is there," said he.

"Simba! So they caught him," muttered Kingozi. "Well, that play failed. Do you see the white man?" he asked.

"No, *bwana*. The white man has not yet come. But Simba now sees us, and is coming."

"He is guarded?"

"No, *bwana;* he is alone."

"*Jambo, bwana*," said Simba's voice a moment later.

Something in his tone caught Kingozi's ear.

"Yes, Simba?" was all he replied.

"All has been done as you ordered, *bwana*. This is the fourteenth day, and I am here to tell you."

Kingozi caught his breath sharply.

"*Bwana* Nyele was captured?"

"Mali-ya-bwana holds him prisoner at a certain water."

"There was no trouble?"

"None, *bwana*. All happened as you told. This magic is a very great magic," said Simba piously.

Kingozi paused.

"The safari," he suggested at last. "I am told of a safari; indeed, I can hear it. What of that? No orders were given as to a safari."

"That is true, *bwana*," explained Simba earnestly, "but this is a very great safari. It has tents and *potio*, and *chakula,** and blankets and beads and wire and many other things to a quantity impossible to say. And it came to my mind that *shenzis* like these things, as do all men, and that in this *shenzi* country my *bwana* might make use of them; so I brought them with me for your use, *bwana*."

"You had no trouble bringing this great safari?" asked Kingozi.

"I used again the magic bone," replied Simba.

"Simba, you jewel!" cried Kingozi in English, "you've saved the day! I should think *shenzis* did like these things! And oh, haven't I needed them! You old tar-baby, you!"

And Simba replied as usual to this incomprehensible gibberish with his own full stock of English:

"Yes, suh!"

"You have done well, very well," Kingozi shifted to Swahili. "I am pleased with you. For this work you shall have much *backsheeshi*—a month's wages extra, and twenty goats for your farm, and any other thing that you want most. What is it?"

Simba appeared to hesitate and boggle.

"Speak up! I am very pleased."

"This is a very great thing I would ask," said Simba in a low voice.

"It is a great thing you have done."

"*Bwana*," cried Simba earnestly. "It is this: I would

*Chakula—white man's food.

have the magic bone for my own. For it is a very great magic," he added wistfully.

Kingozi choked back an impulse to shout aloud.

"It is yours," he said gravely.

"Oh, *bwana! bwana!*" choked Simba. "*Assanti! assanti sana !*"

His sob was echoed at Kingozi's elbow.

"Oh," cried the Leopard Woman, "I know I should be sorry that this has come this way! But I'm not; I am glad!"

CHAPTER XXX

WINKLEMAN APPEARS

With the riches thus unexpectedly placed at his disposal, and legitimately his by the fortunes of war, Kingozi was enabled to proceed to the final grand exchange of gifts that assured his friendship with M'tela and sealed the alliance. He was spurred to his best efforts in this by the news, brought in by an alarmed Mali-ya-bwana, that Winkleman had escaped. However, by dint of rich presents, supplementing the careful diplomatic negotiations that had gone before, he arrived at an understanding.

"And now, oh, King, I must tell you this," he said boldly. "Of white men there is not merely one but many kinds, just as among the African peoples. There are strong men and weak men, good men and bad men, and men of different tribes. Of the tribes are the *Inglishee* to which I belong, which is the most powerful of all—like your own people of the Kabilagani in this land—and also another tribe called the *Duyche*, only a little less powerful. These two tribes are now at war."

"Ā-ā-ā-ā," observed M'tela interestedly.

"One of the *Duyche* is in your country, oh, King. I have met him and defeated him by my magic. Some of these people you see here were his people; and of his goods I have everything."

"But it may be," suggested M'tela with a slight cooling of cordiality, "that many more *Duyche* will follow this one."

"They cannot prevail against my magic. Talk with Simba, with my men, and know what virtue is in my magic. But beyond that, oh, King, have you not heard of the wars of the Wakamba? of Lobengula? of the Matabele and the Basuto? has not news come to you from the north of the battles of the Sudan? Have you not heard of Lenani, the king of all Masai, and of his advice to his people? All these wars were won by *Inglishee;* Lenani's words of wisdom spoke of *Inglishee.* Have you ever heard of the victories of the *Duyche ?* No. There were no such victories!"*

After an hour's elaboration of this theme Kingozi judged the moment propitious to return to the original subject. M'tela offered the opportunity.

"This *Duyche* whom you have conquered—you killed him?"

*Kingozi here took shrewd advantage of the fact that German East Africa was peacefully occupied without necessity of the spectacular tribal wars of Matabeland, Zululand, Basutoland, and the Wakamba district of British East Africa. Lenani's advice to his people was given at the close of the Wakamba war. Said he: "There is no doubt that the Masai are a greater people than the Wakamba, and in case of war we could fight the white man harder than the Wakamba fought him. Undoubtedly, too, my people could kill a great many of the English. But this I have noticed: that when a Wakamba is dead, he remains dead; but when a white man is dead ten more come to take his place." In consequence of this advice the Masai—one of the most warlike of all the tribes—negotiated with the English, and to-day remain both at peace and unconquered.

"He escaped."

"Ā-ā-ā-ā."

"He is still alive and in your land. Let order be given to search him out."

"That shall be done," said M'tela after a moment's thought.

Mali-ya-bwana and Simba set out with a posse of M'tela's men. They had no great difficulty in getting track of the missing Bavarian. Winkleman had arrived to find the camping site deserted. He had, indomitably, set out on the track of his safari. To eat he was forced at last to beg of the wild herdsmen. M'tela's dread name elicited from these last definite information. The search party found Winkleman, very dirty, quite hungry, profoundly chagrined, but still good humoured, seated in a smoky hut eating soured smoky milk. He wore sandals improvised from goatskin, a hat and spine-pad made from banana leaves ingeniously woven.

"*Ach!*" he cried, recognizing Kingozi's two men. "So it is you! What have you done with my safari?"

"I led it to my *bwana*," replied Simba.

"Where you may now lead me," said Winkleman resignedly. "By what means have you thought of these things, N'ympara?"

"By the magic of this," replied Simba with becoming modesty, producing the precious bone.

"*Ach* the *saurian!*" cried Winkleman. "I remember.

It had gone from my mind. It is a curious type; I do not quite recognize. Let me see it."

But Simba was replacing carefully the talisman in its wrappings. He had no mind to deliver the magic into other hands—perhaps to be used against himself!

They led Winkleman directly to Kingozi's camp. Winkleman followed, looking always curiously about him. His was the true scientific mind. He was quite capable of forgetting his plight—and did so—in the interest of new fauna and flora, or of ethnological eccentricities. Once or twice he insisted on a halt for examination of something that caught his notice, and insisted so peremptorily when the savages would have forced him on, that they yielded to his wish.

It was early in the morning. Kingozi, as ever, sat in his canvas chair atop the hill. He was alone, for the Leopard Woman, always on the alert and always staring through her glasses, had caught sight of the little group before it plunged into the papyrus; and had retired to her tent. Winkleman plowed up the hill blowing out his cheeks in a full-blooded hearty fashion.

"Oho!" he cried in his great voice when he had drawn near. "This is not so bad! It is Culbertson!"

"I am sorry about this," said Kingozi briefly—"a man of your eminence—very disagreeable."

Winkleman dropped heavily to the ground.

"That is nothing," he waved aside the half-apology,

"though it would not be bad to have the bath and change these clothes. But fortunes of war—it is but the fortunes of war—I would have done worse to you. How long is it that you have arrived?"

"Long enough," replied Kingozi briefly. "Oh, Cazi Moto, bring tea! I have had your tent pitched, Doctor Winkleman; and you must bathe and change and rest. But before you go we must understand each other. This is war time, and you are my prisoner. You must give me your parole neither to try to escape nor to tamper with my men, with M'tela, or any of his people. If you feel you cannot do this I shall be compelled to hold you closely guarded."

Winkleman laughed one of his great gusty laughs.

"I give it willingly. What foolishness otherwise. What foolishness anyway, all this. War is nonsense. It destroys. It interferes. Consider, my dear Culbertson, here was I safely in the Congo forests, and for two, three months I have lived there, like a native quietly; and of all the world there is to amuse me only the fauna and the flora—which I know like my hand. But I discover a new species—a *papilio*. But all the time I live quiet, and I wait. And at last the people, the little forest people, little by little they get confidence; they come to the edge of the forest, they venture to camp, slow. Suppose I wave my hand like that—pouf! They have run away. But I wait; and they come forth. So I camp by myself in the forest—for I leave my safari

away that it may not frighten this people. And by and by
we talk. I am beginning to learn their language. Culbertson, I find these people speak the true click language,
but also I find it true sex-denoting language most resembling
in that respect the ancient Fula!"

"Where was this? Impossible!" cried Kingozi, interested
and excited.

"Ah!" roared Winkleman with satisfaction. "I thought
I would your interest catch! But it is true; and in the central Congo."

"But that would throw the prehistoric Libyan and
Hamitic migrations farther to the west than——"

"Pre-cisely!" interrupted Winkleman.

"What sort of people were they? Did they show Hamitic characteristics particularly? or did they incline to the
typical prognathous, short-legged, stealopygous type of the
Bushmen?"

But Winkleman reverted abruptly to his narrative.

"That is a long discussion to make. It will wait. But
just as I get these people where I can put them beneath
my observation, so, there comes an ober-lieutenant with
foolishness in the way of guns and uniform and *askaris* and
that nonsense; and my little people run into the forest
and are no more to be seen."

"Hard luck!" commented Kingozi feelingly.

"Is it not so? This ober-lieutenant is a fool. He knows
nothing. *Dumkopf !* All he knows is to give me a letter

from the *Kaiserliche dumkopf* at Dar-es-salaam. I read it
It tells me I must come here, to this place, with speed, and
get the military aid of this M'tela and so forth with many
details. It was another foolishness. I know this type of
people well. There is nothing new to be learned. They
are of the usual types. It is foolishness to come here. But
it is an order, so I come, and I do my best. But now I am
a prisoner, while I might be with the little people in the
Congo. I talk much."

"I fancy we are going to have a good deal to talk about,"
interjected Kingozi.

"*Ach!* that is true! That is what I said—that I am glad
this is Culbertson who catches me. Yes! We must talk!"

Cazi Moto glided to them.

"Bath is ready, *bwana*," said he.

Winkleman puffed out his chest and protruded his great
beard.

"This war—foolishness!" he mumbled.

"Yes, we have much to talk about. Nevertheless," said
Kingozi with slight embarrassment, "it is necessary that I
do my duty according to my orders. And my orders were
much like yours—to get the alliance of this M'tela. But
I have told him that you are my enemy; and he sent his
men with mine to find you; and now, as you can well comprehend, I must——"

But Winkleman's quick comprehension leaped ahead of
Kingozi's speech.

"I must play the prisoner, is it not?" he cried with one of his big laughs. "But so! Of course! That is comprehend. How could it be otherwise? I know my native! I know what he expects. I shall be humble, the slave, your foot upon my neck. Of course! Do you suppose I do not know?"

"That is well," said Kingozi, much relieved, "I shall tell him that you are a man of much wisdom and great magic; and that I have saved your life to serve me."

"So!" cried Winkleman delightedly; and departed to his tent and the waiting bath. A few moments later he could be heard robustly splashing in the tent. A roar summoned Cazi Moto.

"Tell your *bwana* I want *n'dowa*—medicine—understand? Need some boric acid," he yelled at Kingozi. "Eyes in bad shape."

Kingozi ordered Cazi Moto to take over the entire medicine chest; then sent a messenger for M'tela, who shortly appeared.

"This enemy of mine is taken, thanks to your men, oh, King. I have him here in the tent, well guarded."

"How shall we kill him, papa?" inquired M'tela.

"That has not yet been decided," replied Kingozi carelessly. "He must, of course, be taken to the great King of all *Inglishee*."

M'tela looked disappointed.

"In the meantime," pursued Kingozi, "as he has much

knowledge, and great magic, I shall talk much with him, and get that magic for the benefit of us both, oh, King. He cannot escape, for my magic is greater than his."

This M'tela well believed, for the reports industriously circulated by Simba anent his magic bone had reached the King, and had not lost in transit.

So when Winkleman came swashbuckling up the hill M'tela was prepared. The blue-black beard and hearty, deep-chested carriage of the Bavarian impressed him greatly.

"But this is a great *bwana*, papa," he said to Kingozi. "Like you and me."

"This is the prisoner of which I spoke to you," said Kingozi in a loud voice.

Winkleman, a twinkle in his wide eyes, but with his countenance composed to gravity, stepped forward, salaamed, and placed his forehead beneath Kingozi's hand in token of submission. Thus proper relations were established. Winkleman seated himself humbly on the sod, and kept silence, while high converse went forward. At length M'tela departed. Winkleman immediately plunged into the conversational gap around which, mentally, he had been impatiently hovering for an hour.

"But this articulation of the *saurus*," he broke out. "What of it?"

"The magic bone," chuckled Kingozi.

"Pouf! Pouf! It resembled much the *cinoliosaurus*, but that could not be."

"Why not?" demanded Kingozi quickly.

"It has been found only in the lias formations of the Jurassic," stated Winkleman dogmatically, "and that type of Jurassic is not here. It is of England, yes; of Germany, yes; of the Americas, yes. Of central Africa, no!"

"Nevertheless——" interposed Kingozi.

"But the *cryptoclidus*—that greatly resembles the *cinoliosaurus*—perhaps. Or even a subspecies of the *plesiosaurus*——"

"Simba," called Kingozi.

"Suh!"

"Bring here the magic bone. The *bwana* wishes to look at it. No; it is all right. I myself tell you; no harm can come."

Reluctantly Simba produced the bone, now fittingly wrapped in clean *mericani* cloth, and still more reluctantly undid it and handed it to Winkleman. The latter seized it and began minutely to examine it, muttering short, disconnected sentences to himself in German.

"Now here is what I have said," he spoke aloud. "See. By this curve——"

He broke off, staring curiously into Kingozi's face. The latter sat apparently looking out across the hills, paying no attention to the fact that Winkleman had thrust the bone fairly under his nose. The pause that ensued became noticeable. Kingozi stirred uneasily, turning his eyes in the direction of the scientist.

"Glaucoma!" ejaculated Winkleman.

Kingozi smiled wearily.

"Yes. I wondered when you would find it out."

"You are all blind?"

"I can distinguish light." Kingozi straightened his back, and his voice became incisive. "But I can still see through eyes that are faithful to me! Make no mistakes there."

"My dear friend; have I not given my parole?" gently asked the Bavarian.

"Beg your pardon. Of course."

"It is serious. You should have a surgeon. But why have you not used the temporary remedy? Of course you know the effect of drugs?"

"I know that atropin is ruin, right enough," said Kingozi grimly.

"But the pilocarpin——"

"Of course. I only wish I had some."

"But you have!" came Winkleman's astonished voice. "There is of it a large vial!"

Kingozi gripped the arm of his chair for a full minute. Then he spoke to Cazi Moto in a vibrating voice.

"Bring me the chest of medicines. Now," he went on to Winkleman, when this command had been executed, "kindly read to me the labels on all these bottles; begin at the left. All, please."

He listened attentively while Winkleman obeyed. The pilocarpin was present; the atropin was gone.

"You have not deceived me?" he cried sharply. "No —why should you—wait——"

He thought for some moments. When he raised his face it was gray.

"One of the bottles was broken. I had reason to believe it the pilocarpin," he said quietly. "Can I trespass on your good nature to make the proper solution for my eyes?"

"It is but a temporary expedient," warned Winkleman. "It is surgery here demanded. I know the operation, but I cannot perform. One makes a transverse incision above the cornea——"

"I know, I know," interrupted Kingozi. "But the pilocarpin will give me my sight. Let us get at it."

CHAPTER XXXI

LIGHT AGAIN

Three hours later Kingozi stepped into the open, his vision cleared. Such is often the marvellous—though temporary—effect of the proper remedies in this disease. He looked about him with a thankfulness not to be understood save by one whose sight has been thus unexpectedly restored. Winkleman followed him full of deep sympathy.

"But I understand," he repeated over and over, "but it is like water on a weary march, *nicht wahr.* But this is bad, very bad! You say it has been going on for a month? And a month back! Too late. *Ach, schrecklich!* It is so much a pity! You have the youth, the strength, the knowledge! You could so far go! But you must learn the dictation; the great book, the *magnum opus*, it is there. Cheer up, my boy! Work, much work! That is what will cure your sick courage even if it cannot cure your sick eyes. Now, while we have the sight—see—the bone—this curve clearly indicates to me——"

Winkleman produced the *saurian* bone. And for the first time Kingozi noticed Simba hovering anxiously near.

Request and blandishments had proved of no avail in getting the magic bone from *Bwana* Nyele.

"It is all right," Kingozi reassured him. "We but use the magic for a little while. See; it has given me back my eyes."

"Ā-ā-ā-ā!" ejaculated Simba, deeply astonished.

"We will use it but a little while longer," Kingozi concluded. "Then you shall have it again."

"But to give this specimen to a gun bearer!" cried Winkleman in English. "That is craziness! It is a museum piece."

"It belongs to him; and I have promised," said Kingozi.

Winkleman subsided with deep rumblings. After a moment he renewed his discussion.

Kingozi only half heard him. His mind was occupied by another, more human problem. The discovery that the atropin and not the pilocarpin had been destroyed agitated him profoundly; not, as might be believed, because it enabled him at a critical time to regain the use of his sight, but because it threw before him an insistent question. Did, or did not, Bibi-ya-chui know? He recalled the incident in all its little details—himself in his chair and Cazi Moto squatting before the three bottles set up before them, carefully tracing in the sand with a stick the characters on the labels; the Leopard Woman's sudden dash forward; the tinkle of smashed glass, and her voice panting with excitement: "I will read your labels for you now—the bottle you hold in your hand! It is atropin, atropin"—and her wild laugh.

Did she *know*, or was she guessing or bluffing?

It hurt him, hurt him inconceivably to think that she might have deceived him thus; might have broken the wrong bottle, and then deliberately have kept him in darkness with the very remedy at hand. That would seem the refinement of cruelty.

But he must be fair. She was then fighting, fighting with all her power against odds, for her sworn duty. Deceit was her natural weapon. And at that time such deceit seemed very likely to win for her her point. No, he could not blame her there; he could not consistently even feel hurt. The few moments' reasoning brought him to the point where he did not feel hurt. After a little he even admired the quickness of wit.

The instinctive depression vanished before this reasoning. He suddenly became light-hearted.

But immediately the dark mood returned. Granted all this; how about the last two days? Before that it might well be that her sense of duty to her country, her firmness of spirit, her honour itself would impel her to cling to the last hope of gaining her end. Until his influence over M'tela was quite assured, Winkleman's arrival would probably turn the scale. She had not prevented Kingozi's arriving before the Bavarian; but she might hold the Englishman comparatively powerless. That was under-

standable. Kingozi felt he might even love her the more
for this evidence of a faithful spirit. But the last few days!
It must have become evident to her that her cause was lost;
that M'tela's friendship had been gained for the English.
If she had cared for him the least in the world would not
she have hastened to produce the pilocarpin for his relief?
What could she hope to gain by concealing it? And then
the other words insisted on his recollection, bitter words—
when, first blinded, he had asked her to read the labels on
the bottle that would have given him sight. "Why should
I do this for you? You have treated me as a man treats
his dog, his horse, his servant, his child—not as a man
treats a woman!" What real reason—besides his hopes
—had he for thinking she did not still hate him, or at least
remain indifferent to him? So indifferent that even after
her chance had passed she still neglected to inform him that
the pilocarpin was not destroyed after all.

Winkleman talked on and on about his *saurian*. Would
he never stop and go away?

"I agree with you; you are probably right," said Kingozi at last, driven by sheer desperation to the endorsement
of he knew not what scientific heresy. Winkleman snorted
heavily in triumph, and returned the bone to a vastly relieved Simba. Kingozi interposed in haste before the introduction of a new topic.

"Undoubtedly you will wish to see the palace of M'tela,"
said he with deep wile. "Of course you are supposed to be

my prisoner, so I must send you under guard. You might take a small present to M'tela from me. I have not yet visited his place of course. This might be considered a preliminary to my first visit. Does it appeal to you?"

"But yes! And I shall behave. I have given my parole. I shall be the good boy!"

"Of course. I understand that. Do you eat at noon? No? Well, good luck. Cazi Moto, take Mali-ya-bwana and two *askari* guns, and go with *Bwana* Nyele to the palace of M'tela."

Scarcely had the group disappeared down the forest path when Kingozi was at the tent door of the Leopard Woman.

"*Hodie ?*" he pronounced the native word of one desiring entrance.

"Who is there?" she asked in Swahili.

" I—Culbertson."

A slight pause; then her voice:

"Come."

He drew aside the tent flaps and entered. She was half reclining on the cot, her back raised by pillows stuffed with sweet grass. Her silk garment, carelessly arranged, had fallen partly open, so that the gleam of her flesh showed tantalizingly here and there. The blood leaped to Kingozi's forehead. She did not alter her pose. Suddenly he realized: of course, she thought him blind!

The embarrassment met his sterner mood in a head-on

collision, so that for a moment the impulsive speech failed him. She spoke first.

"That was Winkleman, I suppose," she said. "I did not want to appear. What is decided?"

"Decided?" he stammered, not knowing where to look, but unable to keep his eyes from straying.

"Yes. Is it too late? Can he prevail with this M'tela after all?"

"He is my prisoner; he has given his parole."

"Oh!" she exclaimed, raising herself on her elbow in excitement. The abrupt movement dropped the robe from her shoulder. "You can see!" she cried; and huddled the garment about her in a panic. "You can see!" she repeated amazedly. "How is that? What has happened?"

The words brought him to himself and to his need for definite knowledge.

"Winkleman read the labels on my bottles," he said sternly. "I have simply used the pilocarpin."

"The pilocarpin! But that was destroyed!"

So unmistakably genuine was her cry of amazement that Kingozi's heart leaped with joy. She had not known! He took a step toward the couch.

But at this moment a wild hullabaloo broke out in the camp. Men yelled and shouted. Some one began to blow a horn. There came the sound of many running to and fro. "Damn!" ejaculated Kingozi fervently; and ran out of the tent.

CHAPTER XXXII

THE COLOURS

The whole camp was gathered about a number of M'tela's people, who were all talking at once. The din was something prodigious. Kingozi pushed his way rather angrily to the centre of disturbance.

"Here, what is this?" he demanded to know.

But a dead, astonished silence fell upon them all. They stared at him gaping.

"What is it?" repeated Kingozi impatiently.

"But *bwana !*" cried Cazi Moto. "You see!"

"That is a magic," replied Kingozi curtly. "Now what is all this *kalele* about?"

"Bwana, these people say that messengers have come in telling of many white men and *askaris* marching in this direction."

"From where? But that does not matter—are they *Inglishee* or *Duyche* ?"

"These *shenzis* do not know the difference."

"That is true. How far away are they?"

"Very near, *bwana.*"

"Get my gun. Have Simba follow me. Here, you lead the way."

They marched rapidly through the forest path and past the palace of M'tela, which Kingozi had never seen. The savage king came out, and Winkleman and his bodyguard soon followed.

"Oh, King," said Kingozi. "Now is the time to show to me that your friendship is true. As you know, other white men are coming, with warriors. I do not know yet whether these are *Inglishee*, who are my friends—and yours —or *Duyche*, who are my enemies. If they are *Duyche* they must be attacked and killed or captured, for we are at war."

He watched M'tela carefully while he spoke, and felt satisfaction at what he saw.

"Have no fear, papa," replied M'tela easily. "I will cause the great drums to be beaten. My warriors are as the leaves of the grass; and these are few."

"Nevertheless they will kill many of yours," said Kingozi with great earnestness; "for they have guns that kill many times and at a long distance. When your warriors hear the great noise they make, and see the dead men, they will run."

"You do not know the warriors of M'tela," replied the king with dignity. "Should the half of them fall, the other half will give these to the hyenas. Yes, even if they had the thunder itself as weapon!"

"How many are there, oh, King?" asked Kingozi, greatly relieved.

"My men report thirty-one white men and many black men."

"I go now," advised Kingozi, "to look upon these men. Give me guides, and a messenger to send back with news of what I find."

M'tela issued the orders. A moment later Kingozi started on. Winkleman, who had spoken no word, waved him a friendly good-bye. Before they had reached the forest edge the great war drums began to roar.

The guides took them swiftly down the forest path and across the rolling country with the groves. Kingozi looked at it all with curiosity and delight. It seemed to him that never in all his wanderings had he seen so beautiful and variegated a prospect. His blindness had overtaken him, it must be remembered, out on the open dry veldt, between the Great and the Little Rains. It was as though he had awakened from a sleep to find himself in this watered, green, and wooded paradise.

At the top of a hill the guide stopped and pointed. Kingozi gathered that through the distant cleft he indicated the strangers must come. All sat down and waited.

An hour passed. Simba uttered an exclamation. Kingozi raised his glasses. Tiny figures on foot were debouching from the forest. They spread in all directions, advancing in fan-formation. Evidently the scouts. Then more tiny figures, figures on horseback. Kingozi counted them. There were, as M'tela had said, just thirty-one; a gallant

" At the top of the hill the guide stopped and pointed. Kingozi gathered that through the distant cleft he indicated the strangers must come"

little band, but at this distance indistinguishable. They rode out some distance. And at last the first files of the black troops appeared. Kingozi dropped his glasses to the end of its thong with a cheer. Drooping in the still air the colours were nevertheless easily recognized. The flag was of England.

"*Inglishee! Inglishee!*" he repeated to M'tela's messengers, and made a motion back toward the palace. The men departed at a lope. Kingozi and Simba took the other direction.

They met the newcomers halfway across the long, shallow dish between the wooded hills. On catching sight of them the mounted white men spurred forward. A confusion of greetings stormed them.

"It's Culbertson!" "Where did *you* rain down from?" "We've been looking for you without end! Isn't this a lark, old man!"

In the meantime, in the personal attendants of these white men, Simba had discovered acquaintances; among them the two messengers Kingozi had despatched back in quest of Doctor McCloud.

Kingozi stood in the middle of the group, his heart overflowing. It was good to see so many white faces again; it was good to see the faces of friends; it was good to know that his labours had not been in vain, and that the border was assured. And underneath it was a great exaltation. He walked on air. For she had not known! The blank astonishment of her face had proved that to him beyond a doubt. She really thought that she had destroyed the pilocarpin; she had not deliberately held from him the light of day!

His high spirits expressed themselves in an animation and volubility so unlike the taciturn Culbertson that many of his acquaintances stared.

"Seems quite bucked up," commented one to another. "Must have had a deuce of a time back here."

"What is this arm of His Majesty's Service, anyway?" Kingozi was asking in general. "I mean the mounted and disreputable portion, not the decent infantry."

"This, my son, is the Settlers' Own Irregulars; and we've come out for to hunt the shy and elusive German."

"Good heads scarce up this way," rejoined Kingozi. "I've aught one specimen myself, however."

"Specimen of what?"

"German. Ever hear of Winkleman?"

"Rather! The native *fundi*?* You don't mean to say you've got him!"

"I've got him. He's the only specimen in these parts. But I can show you several thousand of the best fighting men in Africa—all loyal British allies."

"Good man!" cried a grizzled old settler. "I told 'em you'd do it!"

"But the war?" demanded Kingozi eagerly. "What of the war? Tell me? I know nothing whatever."

*Fundi—expert.

One of the younger men dismounted and insisted on delivering his animal to Kingozi.

"Do me good to stretch my legs," said he. "And you've walked your share."

Riding in a little group of the officers Kingozi listened attentively to an account of affairs as far as they were known. The Marne, and the Retreat from Mons straightened him in his saddle. It was worth it; he had done his bit! Whatever the price, it was worth it!

The account finished, Captain Walsh began questioning in his turn.

"Excellent!" he greeted Kingozi's account. "Couldn't be better! We have reasons to believe that the waterholes on this route are mapped by the Germans."

"They are," interrupted Kingozi.

"And that the plan contemplated coming through here, gathering the tribes as they advanced, and finally cutting in on us with a big force from the rear."

"They'll run against a stone wall hereabouts," said Kingozi with satisfaction.

"Lucky for us. I've only four companies—and these settlers. We are really only a reconnaissance."

"How did you happen to follow my route?"

"Ran against the messengers you sent back to get Doctor McCloud. They guided us. By the way, what is it? Must have been serious. You're not a man to run to panics. You look fit enough now."

"Eyes," explained Kingozi. His heart sank, for the failure of his messengers to go on after McCloud took away the last small hope of saving his eyesight.

"Fancy it will be all right," said Captain Walsh vaguely. He was thinking, quite properly, of ways and means and dispositions. "About this sultan, now; what do you advise——"

They rode forward slowly through the high, aromatic grasses, discussing earnestly every angle of policy to be assumed in regard to M'tela. At its close all the white men were called together and given instructions. Even the youngest and most flippant knew natives well enough to realize the value of the structure Kingozi had built, and to listen attentively.

These alternate marches and halts had permitted the foot troops to close up. Kingozi turned in his saddle to look at them. Fine, upstanding black men they were, marching straight and soldierly, neat in their uniforms of khaki, with the dull red tarboush, the blue leggings, the bare knees and feet. They were picked troops from the Sudan, these, fighting men by birth, whose chief tradition was that in case his colonel was killed no man must come back to his woman short of wiping out the last of the enemy. In spite of a long march they walked jauntily. Two mounted white men brought up the rear.

Now they entered the cool forest trail. The sound of distant drums became audible. Men straightened in their saddles. Captain Walsh gave crisp orders. They entered the cleared space before M'tela's palace with colours flying and snare drums tapping briskly.

The full force of M'tela's power seemed to have been gathered, gorgeous in the panoply of war. The forest threw back the roar of drums, of horns, of people chanting or shouting. Straight to the middle of the square marched the Sudanese, wheeled smartly into line. At a command they raised their rifles and fired a volley, the first gunfire ever heard in this ancient forest.

CHAPTER XXXIII

CURTAIN

The sun was setting. In a few minutes more the swift darkness would fall. After delivering the astonishing volley the troops wheeled and under Kingozi's guidance proceeded down the forest path to the great clearing. It was the close of a long, hard day, but under the scrutinizing eyes of these thousands of proud *shenzis* the Sudanese stepped forth jauntily. Camping places were designated. All was activity as the tents were raised.

But now rode in the two white men who had closed the rear of the column, not only of the fighting men, but of the burden bearers as well. They were covered with dust and apparently very glad to arrive. One of them rode directly to the group of officers and dismounted stiffly.

"McCloud!" cried Kingozi.

"The same," replied that efficient surgeon. "And now let's see the eyes. I have your scrawl." He stumped forward, looking keenly for what he wanted. "Sit here in this chair. Boy!" he bawled. "*Lete taa*—bring the lantern. And my case of knives. No, my lad, I'm not going to operate on you instanter, but I do want my reflector. Hold the light just here. Now, don't any of you move. Tip your head back a bit, that's a good chap." He went methodically forward with his examination as though he were at home in his white office. "H'm. How long this been going on? Five weeks, eh! Been blind? Oh—why didn't you use that pilocarpin I gave you—I see."

The officers and other white men stood about in a compact and silent group. A sudden grave realization of the situation had descended upon them, sobering their careless or laughing countenances. No one knew exactly what it was all about, but some had caught the word "blindness" and repeated it to others. Some one yelled *"kalele"* savagely at the chattering men. Almost a dead stillness fell on the clearing, so that in the falling twilight the tree hyraxes took heart and began to utter their demoniac screams. The darkness came down softly. Soon the group in the centre turned to silhouettes against the light of the two lanterns held head high on either side the patient.

Absorbedly Doctor McCloud proceeded. Kingozi sat quietly, turning his head to either side, raising or lowering his chin as he was requested to do so. At last McCloud straightened his back.

"It is glaucoma right enough," said he; "fairly advanced. The pilocarpin has been a palliative. An operation is called for—iridectomy."

He paused, wiping his mirror. Nobody dared ask the question that Kingozi himself at last propounded.

"Can you do it—have you the necessary instruments?"

"Fine spade scalpel, small tweezers, scissors—*and* a lot of experience. I've got all the former."

"And the latter?"

"I've done the operation before," said McCloud dryly.

"Will it restore my sight permanently."

"If successful the job will be permanent."

"What chance of success?"

"Fair—fair," rejoined McCloud with a touch of impatience. "How can I tell? But I'll just inform you of this, my lad, without the operation you're stone blind for the rest of your days, and it must be done now or not at all. So there's your Hobson's choice; and we'll get at it comfortably in the morning."

He turned away and stopped with a frank stare of astonishment. The other men followed his gaze, and also stared.

The Leopard Woman stood just within the circle of illumination. So intent was she on the examination and on Kingozi that she seemed utterly unconscious of the men standing over opposite. Her soft silk robe fell about her body in classic folds; the single jewel on its chain fillet blazed on her forehead; her hair fell in its braid to her hips, and her wide, gray-green eyes were fixed on the seated man. A more startlingly exotic figure for the wilds of Central Africa could not be imagined. The expressions on the faces of the newcomers were varied enough, to be

sure, but all had a common groundwork of fair imbe-
cility.

She seemed to be unaware of even their presence. When
McCloud had pronounced his opinion, she glided forward
and laid her hand on Kingozi's shoulder.

"I am glad—but I am afraid," she said softly. Kingozi
covered her hand with one of his own. His eyes twinkled
with quiet amusement as he looked about him at the stricken
faces of his friends. She whirled on the gaping McCloud.
"But you must have a care!" she cried at him vehemently.
"You must save his eyes. I wish it!"

McCloud, recovering himself, bowed.

"Madam," said he with a faint, amused irony. "It shall
be my pleasure to do my best in fulfilling your commands."

"It must be," she repeated; and turned to face the rest.
"He is a great man; he must be saved. All this is folly.
I have fought him to my best, for long, and I have used all
means—good and bad. He conquered me as one who—
what you call—subdues a child. And he is generous, and
brave, and when the darkness comes to him he does not sit
and weep. He is a great soul, and all things must be done!"

She was superb, her head thrown back. Captain Walsh
was the first to recover from the stunned condition in which
all found themselves. He bowed.

"Madam," said he, "in what you say we heartily concur.
We add our urgence to yours. You must forgive our stupidity to the surprise of your appearance. Even yet my

astonishment has not abated." He turned easily to Kingozi: "I hope you will afford me the pleasure of naming me to madam."

Kingozi arose to his feet.

"I do not know your name," he muttered to her.

"I am the Leopard Woman," she smiled back on him enigmatically.

Kingozi paused, embarrassed as to what to do. He could not use that name in an introduction to these men. She was looking at him mischievously.

"Captain Walsh—and gentlemen," said Kingozi suddenly, "I want the pleasure of presenting you to—my future wife!"

Her gasp of astonishment was lost in the chorus of congratulatory cries. It was all mysterious, profoundly astonishing. Much was to be explained. But for the moment each man was ready to believe the evidences of his own senses—that no matter how incongruous the fact of her presence might be, there she was, beautiful as the night. And every man facing her had seen the glory that shone from within when Kingozi had pronounced his introduction. Captain Walsh was speaking.

"This is an occasion," he said, "and the King's African Rifles cannot have it otherwise than that you become their guests. I see our camp is in preparation. We have nothing beyond the ordinary stores, but you must all dine with us." He paused, considering. "Say in an hour," he continued. "It must be early, for I do not doubt we must receive his royal highness this evening."

"You're right," said Kingozi, "and unless I miss my guess it will be an all-night job."

The travel-wearied men groaned.

"No help for it," said Captain Walsh cheerfully.

They pressed forward to shake the hands of this strange couple. The Leopard Woman carried herself with the ease and poise of one accustomed to receiving homage. She had drawn near Kingozi again, and managed to reach out and press his arm.

"Ye'll be married soon, I'm thinking," surmised Mc-Cloud.

"Depends," replied Kingozi, his brow darkening. "Part of it's up to you, you know," he added briefly. "A blind man is a poor man."

"We shall be married soon—now, if there is a priest among you!" cried the Leopard Woman vehemently. "As for poor man—pouf!" She turned to Walsh with an engaging smile. "And you, where you came, did you pass the people who live in the mountains back there, with a *sultani* who dressed in black——"

"I know," supplemented Captain Walsh, "very well."

"The *sultani* whose place has a fortified gate."

"Really? We did not get to his village; too much of a hurry."

The Leopard Woman shot a glance at Kingozi. He saw

the triumph in it, and understood. The ivory stockade was unknown to any but themselves; still remained there in all its wealth awaiting the first trader. And that trader should be himself!

"Poor, indeed!" she whispered to him.

At this moment a roar of astonishment came up to them from down the slope. All turned to see Winkleman, the forgotten Winkleman, standing at the door of his tent. He was in pajamas, and his thick hair was tousled about.

"But how I have slept!" he cried, "and the English, they have come! Well, well!" He came out, stretching his great arms lazily over his head. They stiffened in surprise as he caught sight of the Leopard Woman. For a second he stared; then dropped his arms with one of his big, gusty laughs.

"*Kolossal!*" he roared. "The Countess Miklos! I was wondering! So he has captured you, too, has he!"

With a simple and unembarrassed gesture she laid her arm across Kingozi's shoulders.

"But yes," she repeated softly. "He has captured me, too."

At the tiny fire burning before the tent reserved for the headmen of the camp sat Simba, Cazi Moto, and Mali-ya-bwana. The bone of the *saurian* lay before Simba, who was bragging.

"Great is the magic of this bone, which is mine. It

has brought us a long journey; it has won us the friendship of the great chief; it has revealed to us much riches in the teeth of *tembo,* the elephant, though that must not be spoken aside from us three; it has restored the light to *Bwana* Kingozi, our master; it has captured for us a great *bwana* and a rich safari; it has brought to us *Bwana* Bunduki* and many *bwanas* and *askaris;* it has brought to our master a woman for his own—though to be sure there are many women. Great is this magic; and it is mine. With it I shall be lucky always."

"Ā-ā-ā-ā!" agreed Cazi Moto and Mali-ya-bwana respectfully.

From the darkened mysterious forest the tree hyraxes, excited by the numerous fires and the voices of so large an encampment, were wailing and shrieking.

"The dead are restless to-night," said Simba, poking the fire.

---

*The Master of the Rifle—Captain Walsh.

THE END